BALL OR NOTHING

BY

GREG FIDGEON

Rock Solid Books
Leigh-on-Sea, Essex

Title: Ball Or Nothing.

First published in 2019

Address: Rock Solid Books, 75 Mountdale Gardens, Leigh on Sea, Essex, SS9 4AP.

ISBN: 978-1-9997938-1-4

Book design: Greg Fidgeon

Cover design: Greg Fidgeon

Editing: Greg Fidgeon

For press and publicity, please email greg@gregfidgeon.com

This one is for me.

CHAPTERS

1. KICKING OFF

THEY say when Man reaches his lowest ebb that his hard-wired survival instincts kick in. Preservation of life and all that. And that's what happened to me a few years back. Well, sort of. I mean, whoever said that was probably talking about that American lad who had to cut off his own arm with a penknife after getting it trapped while rock climbing. They even made a film about him. Or like when an old lady manages to find the strength of a WWE wrestler to lift a small family car that's accidentally parked itself on top of her beloved Westie.

Me? Well, I had an idea. And, to be honest, my life wasn't in mortal peril either. Yeah, sure, things were going pretty shit for me at that point in time, but I wasn't in any immediate danger of meeting my maker. I was just down on my luck.

So, in conclusion, you can probably keep all that survival instinct stuff and just say: 'Sometimes, when life covers you in shit, you can have an idea that'll dig you out of it.'

Not quite so heroic, is it?

Now, before we get on to my amazing idea, let me quickly tell you how I got into the position of needing it in the first place. We'll start way back so you get a fuller picture. I had really bad acne from the age of about 12 – my face looked like a stuffed crust margherita pizza that's been trodden on – which meant much of my secondary school life was as about as fun as a kick in the bollocks (which, incidentally, is what I got most days too).

'Pizza-face Price' was the rather unoriginal nickname I was given at school. It didn't help that our uniform was an ugly burgundy affair with a great daubing of gold on the badge, both of which clashed with my scarred, whitehead-clad face.

This was in the 1990s, so before your Facebooks, Twitters, Snapchats, Instagrams and all that. That was a blessing, I suppose. But it meant any actual socialising with people my own age was a complete no-no. They didn't want to be seen anywhere near me, and I was OK with that because most of them were complete bell-ends.

So I would go to school and try my best to hide away at the back of the class (or at the front if Kevin Morecambe had got there before me), keep my head down, find somewhere to keep a low profile at lunch times and go straight home after school. It was lonely, but it was OK.

My only real escape from the pressures of being an acne-covered schoolboy when all the other teenage lads were finding love – or mainly boob fondling and a clumsy quick hand job – was going to watch Southend United play. I loved football, but was terrible myself – another reason why I never joined in at school break times – and I never played for a team back then, just in the garden on my own at home.

But there was something magical about being in the stands at Roots Hall and watching my heroes play. From the outside, Southend have never been a great team. They never made it to the old First Division or the Premier League as it is now, but they are my team and they were the best on the planet in my mind. And to my grandad too. He used to take me to matches. Ah! Did I mention that I was orphaned at the age of six? I really should've marked that down as my lowest ebb, come to think of it. Anyway, we're here now. That can be a story for another time perhaps.

So my grandad and I loved going to watch the Blues from the West Stand at Roots Hall, especially when it was still a standing terraced stadium. I always went right down to the front and stood by the cracked wall just a few yards from the bright green pitch. It was up to my chest, so I could rest my arms and chin on it to watch. Grandad used to stand in the same place for every game; about halfway back, leaning against one of the stand's supporting pillars, puffing away on his pipe and chatting to mates around him. He always seemed to be an old man. He was probably in his 50s in those days, but his hair and moustache were already white and grey.

Later, once the ground was transformed into an all-seater, we got season tickets right near his pillar. Grandad liked the view from there, plus he could nip up the stairs to get his cup of tea and a pie from the kiosk at half-time quicker or make a sharp exit at the end of the game. They were really great times. All my worries disappeared on match day. Even if I saw someone in the stadium who bullied me at school, it was like a truce had been called for the day because we were both Shrimpers. (I should explain that 'Shrimpers' is one of Southend United's nicknames due to the area's maritime history. They're also called the Blues due to the fact their home strip is blue.)

But other than those outings to Roots Hall – and very occasionally an away game, usually down the road in London – I would just stay in at home when I wasn't at school. I never had any real friends. I had been an awkward child at primary school too because of losing my parents. And then, because of the acne and self-confidence issues, I wasn't brave enough to make new ones. So my teenage years, in particular, were quite lonely.

On the plus side, I filled my time learning everything there was to know about computers and computing. I liked to think of myself as a prodigy, although I was nowhere near the likes of Bill Gates or

Steve Jobs. That's obvious, I suppose, otherwise you would've heard of me long ago. But I got to grips with the basics of coding very early on and was able to set up my own business selling my expertise while still at school. Grandad let me use his image as the face of the company as companies weren't too keen on entrusting their IT solutions to a teenage boy with a face like a dropped lasagne.

As the years passed, I was also able to use this new-fangled thing called the World Wide Web to research and contact skin experts around the world to help cure my acne.

It took a while – and it could have just been nature taking its course, to be honest – but at the age of 17, I emerged from my bedroom fresh-faced and handsome and with a successful IT business and software consultancy firm under my wing. I became something of a novelty with the girls in the sixth form. I was like the frog that turned into a prince, but rather than a kiss that transformed me, it had been gels, creams and powders from the four corners of the globe.

My now dashing good looks – along with my new-found confidence, a smart little Mazda MX-5 and a fair wedge of cash in the bank – led me to start dating Julie Kingston. Wow! Julie Kingston.

She was traffic-stoppingly beautiful with long blonde hair, legs up to here and, well, let's just say everything was well sized and in the right place. She was perfection. And she was funny and smart too, and very caring and kind. I was in heaven.

But a quick word of warning chaps. Telling the woman of your dreams that she's fit enough to be a Page Three girl can lead to a pretty frosty first date. It's best to make sure you've spent the previous five years living as a hermit due to constant bullying and ugliness to use as an excuse. But even that only works after a couple of hours of pleading and apologies and the buying of flowers.

Fast-forward 20 or so years and the following had happened: I built up my company to such a level that another, much bigger operator came in and offered me a ridiculous amount of cash to sell up. So I retired from being a computer whizz in my mid-30s and opted for an easy life. We have a nice big house overlooking the Thames in Leigh on Sea, flash motors and a few holidays every year.

I say 'we' because the beautiful Julie and I continued dating and eventually got married on a beach in the Maldives. We also have a son, Tilson. He's named after my favourite Southend United player, Steve Tilson. He's just amazing and adorable in so many ways. My son, that is, not Steve. Although he is also amazing.

I got myself an executive box at Roots Hall for a while, but realised I preferred watching the games from my traditional spot in the West Stand. I still buy a season ticket for grandad too, although he's no longer with us. He died of cancer when I was in my mid-20s. I suppose that's another that should've been in there as a "lowest ebb" too. He was the greatest man I ever knew. A true gentleman and role model, who led by an example of hard work and effort. So I still get his ticket every year and let the seat go empty in his memory. However, it does get quite cramped in that stand now that I'm much bigger, so the extra space to spread out comes in handy.

All that sounds pretty dandy, doesn't it? Apart from grandad passing away, of course.

Well, sadly, things started to go a bit downhill for me and Julie. I guess she got a bit miffed that I retired to play golf and potter about the garden rather than get Bill Gates rich and buy her an island or something. I also put on quite a bit of timber around the midriff, if you know what I mean. Lucky I could afford the new, larger clothes really. I did have a gym membership, but never really liked fitness stuff. I suppose that was a hangover from years of disastrous PE lessons and being laughed at when I tried to play football.

And then, after a terrible spin of the investment dice, our retirement funds were severely depleted. That bloody financial crash. We still had the house, but we weren't able to maintain the old lifestyle as it was. Julie got a part-time job and I went back to work as a driving instructor.

Now, there's nothing wrong with that, of course. But I think Julie quite liked living the life of Riley. She was by no means snobby – her down-to-earth nature was one of the things I loved about her, and she came from a working-class family – but having a few quid in the bank did seem to bring out the best in her. And when there wasn't, well, we didn't see eye to eye as much.

I did try to return to my old area of expertise, but it seems people don't want you back in the computer genius game if you've been out for the best part of a decade. Things move on quite rapidly with technology. Rumours circulate too and jealousy looms.

All things told; Julie and I had to cut back on quite a lot. That caused more than a few rows and finger-pointing, and a bitterness and resentment grew. Very sad, really.

Tilson was much more understanding about the situation. He was in his teens now and I guess I made sure he didn't endure torrid and lonely teenage years like I did, so he went to things like Scouts and drama clubs and music lessons. Anything that helped him socially and to grow his group of friends. He was at a wonderful age where he was old enough to know what was going on around him, but young enough to be cute and express his thoughts rather than talk only through grunts. That would come in his later teenage years.

He had his mother's considerate side (not that she'd shown it recently). For example, for his 15th birthday I said I'd pay for him and five mates to go to Thorpe Park for the day, but he said: 'It costs loads Dad. How about just you, me and Mum go? Or we could go to a gig around here or something.'

He loves his music, see. When he's not out with his mates or at one of his clubs, he's somewhere with a guitar in his hand. I love it when I look out into the garden and see him with a bunch of friends sat on the trampoline and they're listening to him play and sing. Beautiful. I've been known to shed a tear at such scenes.

But he's not interested in football at all, which is a real kick in the plums. I'd like to have that time with him in the stands watching Southend United like I used to with grandad when I was growing up; sharing stories of the Blues and having a go at the players when they ballsed something up (which happens quite a lot, to be honest). I've taken him to games, obviously, and even let him sit in his great-grandad's seat. But he got bored really easily and I ended up spending most of the time trying to keep him occupied and happy with magazines and sweets rather than watching the match myself. I tend to leave him at home now.

I go to matches with my buddy Neil Jason instead. He started coming when grandad was still alive and we go to more away games now than we used to. It's great having someone to go with but – don't tell Neil – it's not quite the same as sitting with grandad.

Anyway, so now we're getting to the straw that broke the camel's back for Julie and me, and how I found myself in the position of needing the much-heralded 'idea'.

I had been giving driving lessons to a girl called Carly, who was the daughter of one of Julie's friends. She was in the sixth form at Tilson's school and was the object of his and many other teenage boys' unrequited affections. She was 17, traffic-stoppingly beautiful, long blonde hair, legs up to here and, well, you know the rest. Sounds familiar, right?

Well, telling Julie that Carly reminded me of a younger version of her wasn't taken as the whimsical reminiscing that I'd hoped. Instead, it was seen as me being 'proper paedo'. After that, my tutoring of Carly with her driving was already a bit awkward as the relationship between me and Julie teetered on the brink.

Back to the 'day of' and I had half an hour to kill before Carly's lesson. I decided to grab myself a coffee and whipped into a fast food drive through. I'd had a late night with Neil at quiz night down the pub (as a responsible driving instructor, I wasn't drinking) and needed something to perk me up a bit.

But my day – and my life – took a nosedive for the worse when the server at the hatch was more interested in talking to a mate behind her about something that had happened at a nightclub at the weekend than what she was doing with my drink.

The upshot of all this was that she let go of the coffee with her arm outstretched before I had a hold of it. The cup bounced on the open car window and fate decided that rather than fall innocently to the floor outside, it would remove the lid and pour the skin-peelingly hot liquid all over my lap. It was if this coffee were heated by lava. They must have special kettles that boil the water using nuclear fusion. I think they use the same technology to heat their apple slices. Anyway, the magma-drink soaked the crotch of my trousers and burned everything – and I mean everything – beneath.

Angry and embarrassed by the braying cackle and 'OMGs' from the server, I drove away quickly. I parked around the corner from Carly's house and looked down at the mess in my lap. I was wearing beige chinos and there was no hiding the stain from the coffee. Luckily, I knew I had a spare pair of trousers in the boot in my golf bag. So I wriggled out of my sopping wet and sticky chinos in the driver's seat of my car, carefully making sure I wasn't being over-looked by any of the houses. So far, so good. Then I realised there was another problem. My underpants were soaked through too and there was no way I could comfortably carry on wearing them. They had to come off too. It's quite a delicate operation trying to get your pants off in the front of a car without being seen – especially when you're a larger gentleman like me – but I had a good scout around before I attempted the manoeuvre and it was still all clear. In a flash, I was naked from the waist down. Just like Donald Duck on a normal day.

Now I just had to get covered up again as fast as possible. I poked my toes into the legs of the dry golf trousers in the footwell of the car and fed them through. What came next had to be execut-ed to precision and in milliseconds. I yanked them up over my thighs while simultaneously pushing my shoulders against the top of the seat and thrusting my midriff towards the roof of the car in order to get the waistband under my fat arse. But just as I did, the door opened and a traffic-stoppingly beautiful teenager with long blonde hair ducked her head in.

I froze.

I can only guess that Carly had seen my car pull up near her house and decided to come out for her lesson early. She paused, pulled her hair from her face and recoiled in horror as she realised my scorched-red cock and balls were a couple of centimetres from her face. The ear-splitting shriek she let out was enough to crack one of my wing mirrors. Either that did it or her dad and older brothers who arrived on the scene very soon after.

In the hour or so that followed, the aforementioned builder dad issued some threats that involved the many and varied tools of his trade, the police were called – possibly for my own safety – and I was led away in handcuffs.

Thankfully, there was CCTV footage at the fast food place to back my story up, along with the coffee-stained trousers and car seat. I was let go with a caution after an initial arrest for outraging public decency.

That was the best of it, however.

Julie, who already thought I held a Lolita-ish candle for Carly, was furious and kicked me out of the house that I had paid for. This was, apparently, the final straw. Even Tilson called me a sad old wanker. It was the first and only time he'd sworn at me and Julie didn't bat an eyelid to it. She just put her arm around his shoulder and guided him back inside the house while I stood on our driveway with a few possessions in a black bin bag.

And to top it all off, Paul from SafeDrive4Life stripped me of my instructor franchise due to bad publicity after the story somehow spread around on social media.

So that incident left me pretty much jobless, homeless and family-less. I found myself living in a dingy flat above the pub where I attend quiz night each week rent free in return for some heavy lifting, barrel changing, cleaning and maintenance, and doorman duties as required.

The only two things that I have in my life at this point are Southend United and my pal Neil. And he finds the whole thing fucking hilarious.

And that, dear reader, is why I needed saving.

2. THE IDEA

I KNEW who Neil was when we were at school but, as I have explained, I didn't really have any friends. He was never one of those who bullied me, but never stood up for me either. But then no one did, so I can't hold that against him. We became friends much later. We had seen each other out and about and while watching Southend United. We used to do that head flick thing that counts as a greeting when you see someone you recognise, but don't actually know.

Anyway, one day I happened to sit down next to him on the train to London. It turned out we'd more than likely been getting the same train to work each day for a couple of years, but never come across one another. We talked about football, of course, and after a while arranged to go for a drink. Then we started going to Southend games together. As I said earlier, he would come and sit with me and grandad as he used to go to games on his own.

We ended up getting into lots of scrapes together. I was there – literally there in the room in the next bed – when he popped his cherry with Sophie the Mouse (she had a squeaky voice and sticky-out teeth). He was there when I got chased by the Greek police after having one too many shots and puking on a restaurant owner in Hersonissos. I was there when he had to go to the STD clinic after that holiday due to putrid discharge. And, later, he was there as my best man when I married Julie. I returned the favour when he wed Katie. Although, I didn't see all that much of her after that day, to be honest. Or their kids. We never really went round for a couples' night or family BBQ. I think our nights out were his escape from the pressures of family life. Sad as it sounds, other than Julie, Neil was the only real friend I've ever had.

As well as going to the football, the nights out and the odd game of golf, Neil and I went to the Old Bell every Thursday for quiz night. It was like a tradition. We never missed it. We were pretty good too and won the £50 prize money quite a few times.

And now that I had lost my job as a driving instructor, I could drink and quiz again. Plus, it was so much easier to get home now that I lived upstairs. It was on one such quiz night that this whole ball of an idea began to slowly roll.

'Guess who I got a text from yesterday,' said Neil rather than just telling me.

'Question four,' said the quiz master. 'Who made his debut as James Bond in the Living Daylights?'

'Timothy Dalton,' said Neil, and I was confused.

'You got a text from Timothy Dalton? The actor?'

'No dick-splash. Keith Sykes. Timothy Dalton was in the Living Daylights.'

'Question five. Dalton also appeared in the movie Hot Fuzz alongside Simon Pegg, but what was the name of Pegg's character in that film?'

'What did he say?' I asked.

'He said, 'What was the name of Simon Pegg's character in Hot Fuzz?'.'

'Why would Keith Sykes text you that?'

'Text me what?' said Neil. 'Nicholas Angel.'

'Wait, stop. What did Keith say?'

'Was he a PC or sergeant?'

'Keith's in the police? Really?'

'Question six. What was the occupation of Pegg's character in the 2008 film How To Make Friends and Alienate People?'

'He's a journalist.'

'Keith's a journalist? I thought you said he was a copper?'

To cut a very long story a lot shorter, the connections round of the quiz had gone very well for us despite the confusion. It also turned out that a bloke Neil used to be good mates with at school was coming to visit. I remembered the guy, Keith Sykes, because he was a bit of an oddity.

For many years he was just another footie-loving teenager who hung around with Neil and a few other lads. But then one year he came back after the summer holidays and had gone Goth. He'd grown his hair long, dyed it black and stopped washing it. He still had to wear school uniform, but somehow managed to get a grey tinge to all his shirts and often wore black leather fingerless gloves and mascara. He also stopped talking to people. He would just glare at them until they got so uncomfortable that they moved away.

For a while, I selfishly hoped that his weirdness would take some of the bullying pressure off me, but it seemed those with a fondness for name-calling and wedgies were just too scared to go near him. If you had to put money on one kid coming into school with a gun, it was Keith.

This went on for about five or six months and then he just vanished off the radar. There were rumours at school that he had been sent to the nut house or he had murdered his family and fled. Others suggested he had been abducted, but his parents were relieved he was gone and so didn't call the police.

The latter conspiracy theory gathered some weight when Clive Wigmore saw Keith's aunt in the Co-op and she said she hadn't heard from him or the family for months.

But then Keith resurfaced a year or so later and the truth turned out to be quite mundane. His family had moved to Wales but he hadn't told anyone because he didn't speak any more due to his goth persona. But he was only back for a couple of weeks before disappearing again, one assumes back to Wales.

Many years later, using the power of social media, Neil made contact and found out Keith was performing as a hypnotist on the package holiday circuit around the Costa del Sol. Guess he learned to speak again, otherwise it would be a pretty dull show.

But the text Neil had received said Keith had now moved back to Leigh on Sea, which seemed weird timing as it was coming up to peak season in Spain.

'So I'm meeting him on Saturday night if you fancy it?' said Neil.

'Where are you meeting him?'

'Here.'

'Well, once I've finished alphabetising my DVD collection upstairs and washing what little hair I have left, I should be able to pop down for a pint.'

'You still have DVDs?'

Saturday came and before the grand reunion with the mysterious Mr Sykes, Neil and I went to watch Southend play in a friendly match against a local non-league side we really should have thrashed. We went 1-0 up, 2-1 down, pulled it back to 2-2 and could have nicked a winner if our supposed ex-Premier League striker knew what those funny white sticks at each end of the pitch were for. We lost in the end. 3-2. Last minute own goal. Standard.

When we got back to the Old Bell, Keith Sykes was already there standing at the bar with a three-quarters-drunk pint and another empty one by his side. He looked older than Neil and me despite being the same age and a lot more haggard. Maybe it was too many hours in the sun that made his skin leathery. Clearly, he was no longer a goth as they weren't particularly fond of the bright ball of fire in the sky, but Keith was still weird. He had now morphed into an ultra-loud uber-geezer and walked with a swagger that would put Liam Gallagher to shame – his legs spread as if he had King Kong's gonads dangling between them.

He also seemed to have lost all control of his volume and was permanently on heat. That meant that rather than reminiscing about old school times (which I was kind of glad about really, all things considered) he spent much of the evening shouting cringe-worthy chat-up lines straight from the 1980s towards the very few females in the pub.

As one woman walked past, he yelled: 'Your eyes are like spanners, my love. I look into them and my nuts tighten.' She shook her head in disgust as he broke out into a braying Cockney cackle that Sid James would be proud of.

Then he almost caused a fight when he walked over to a table where a husband and wife were enjoying a quiet drink and told the lady: 'Alright darlin'. Did you know that I'm a treasure hunter? And I'd love to have closer look at your chest.'

Unsurprisingly, none of his lines worked. Neither did hollering 'Oi, oi!' at a couple of young women who presumably walked into the pub by mistake on their way into town. Admittedly, he did score some points for imagination as he serenaded a woman in a red dress with the Chris De Burgh classic. But, in short, I stood there thinking Keith was a massive prick with no sense of decent behaviour or awareness of other people's feelings.

And he was so oblivious of his own twattishness and pomposity, that he had no shame in spouting snippets of life advice like he was the Prophet of Essex.

I'll give you an example. We were having a few beers and I was trying to be cordial; smiling at his attempted jokes rather than laughing. Neil then decided to regale Keith with the hilarious story about the demise of my marriage and the accidental flashing of my privates at a teenage girl. As my best friend then wandered off for a piss, Keith swaggered in close. He put a hand on my shoulder, bowed his head and placed a finger on his lips as if he was deep in thought. Then he lifted up his head to make some earnest eye contact before he spoke.

'We need such obstacles placed in our path for us to traverse my brother, otherwise our lives would be flat,' he said, quietening his voice for the first time in two hours.

'Thanks for that.'

'It's true geez. You know it. Now you must *hear* it and learn to move forward.' Jesus fucking Christ.

'Are you married?' I asked as he paused to sip his beer.

'Nah.'

'That's surprising as you seem really good with women.' My sarcasm was lost on him. 'Ever been married?'

'Nah mate. No chance.'

'Engaged?'

'Nope.'

'No kids either?'

'No geez,' he said with a nervous giggle. 'What's your point?'

By now, Neil had returned from the bogs and was wondering whether my line of questioning would end with a punchline or just a punch.

'Have you ever had a relationship that's lasted more than a year?'

'Nah.'

'So you've had no significant or meaningful relationship with someone of the opposite sex – or the same sex for that matter – in your entire adult life?'

A stern shake of the head followed. His back was up too. He shuffled from foot to foot as if psyching himself up for a row.

'So how on Earth can you suggest that being kicked out by my wife and having my son think I'm a sad old wanker should be seen as a fucking good thing?'

Keith paused for a second, reverted back to his prophet self and said: 'Listen son…' Son? He's only four fucking months older than me. '…while you were busy thrusting that under-used little pecker of yours into the face of teenage wank fodder, I have been out there observing.'

'Observing what? Me?'

But he wasn't done yet. 'Life…' he said, before raising a finger to his lips again. It was a warning sign that monumental amounts of bullshit were about to tumble from his mouth like an exploding sewage pipe. Here it comes. Brace yourselves. 'It is vitally important that you understand that the only person in your life that you cannot fool – no matter how hard you try – is yourself.'

I stood there, mouth open and brow furrowed, as I tried to work out what the flying fuck he was talking about. But Keith took my stunned silence as reverence for his words, clapped himself and offered a little bow. Then he turned to a woman walking past and said: 'Oi, love. If you promise they won't bite, will you let me stroke your puppies?' And with another blast of his creepy cackle, he swaggered through the door and into the warm summer evening to spark up a cigarette.

It was truly astounding that Keith had managed to sustain a job in the entertainment industry as a stage hypnotist for so long without getting beaten up by an audience member. Perhaps he had.

Performing as The Amazing Psycho, he toured hotels up and down the Costa del Sol getting lobster-red Brits tanked up on their all-inclusive holidays on stage night after night to make them do increasingly embarrassing things while under his spell, and all for everyone else's amusement. He was like a poor man's Paul McKenna. But he'd been doing it for years, so he couldn't have been all that bad, I suppose.

After he returned from puffing on his cigarette outside the pub, Keith explained that he had moved back to Britain because he wanted to help well-off housewives to – ironically – stop smoking, lose weight or overcome their fear of trying to pronounce the word 'quinoa' in public. He saw more money to be made in that than the holiday circuit, he said.

Despite him being a self-absorbed cockwomble and breaking off from his stories to hoot one-liners at the female clientele in the Old Bell, some of what he was saying was quite interesting. Against my better judgement, I now found myself hanging on his every word. I was hooked. And that idea – that one I mentioned at the very start of this story – was beginning to take embryonic shape in the back of my mind.

After bragging about the number of women who supposedly threw themselves at him every single night while doing the rounds, Keith started telling us about his favourite ever punter. This guy was, according to the master raconteur, about 24 stone if he was a pound. 'Not too dissimilar in size to you, big man,' the odious cretin added in my direction.

This guy was among a line-up of five people who Keith had hypnotised and instructed to dance like Michael Jackson. Due to his size, this bloke became the focus of attention and mirth.

After what seemed an hour of back-slapping and self-praise, Keith said: 'And so he does it; from one side of the stage to the other. A perfect Moonwalk. And the whole audience is on their feet applauding. It was fackin' magic.'

'Could he do it before?' I ask, 'any of it?'

'Is this another one of your sarky lines of questioning?' he said with a shake of his head and a sip of his pint.

'No, no. I'm interested. Could he do the Moonwalk before, do you know?'

'Pfft. I doubt it geez. It's probably the first time he's moved backwards without a warning signal like a fackin' dumper truck. Ha! Whoop, whoop! Warning, vehicle reversing.' He faded off when he realised I wasn't laughing with him.

'But no, I mean, he's probably seen Jacko do it a thousand times, ain't he. We all have. You see, the brain retains all of this stuff even if you don't know it has. In your unconscious. And then in the right situation – like when a genius like me hypnotises you – those memories can control your body into performing things you ain't ever done before. Like riding a bike. Just like riding a bike. It's all up there. Clever stuff.'

My mind was now racing and that embryo of an idea had grown and was nearly ready to start its journey towards the metaphorical birth canal.

'So, could this work on other things? Could you, say, get some-one who's never played golf before to hit a hole in one?'

'Nah, not that accurate. Too many variables. I mean, you'd be able to tell the difference between the fat bloke's Moonwalk and Jackson's one. But I could probably get someone who plays golf a bit to hit the ball better more often. If I had them for a while, I could do more, I suppose. Hey, that might be a decent earner. Cheers bud.'

For the first time in the night, Keith's geezer-ish voice was like music to my ears. Everything he was saying was falling perfectly into my plan. That embryo had grown, been born, learned to walk and was now in his mid-teens ready to share his post-acne face to the world.

'So Keith…'

'Yes mate, blimey, it's like being grilled by Jeremy Clarkson, or Paxman, some Jeremy. Yes Jezza, go on.'

'So, could you, in theory, hypnotise someone, anyone, and get them to follow your hypnotic suggestions, whatever, to the letter and train them how to play football? Like a professional, I mean? Get them to kick the ball, head the ball, run around and play like Ronaldo or Messi?'

Keith paused and began thinking. I could tell he was really thinking hard because his lips were pursed like a cat's arsehole and he was stroking his pencil-line goatee with one hand.

'It would take quite a bit of time I think, and research, of course. We'd probably have to start off small and build up and tweak things as we went along. But, in theory, yes it can probably be done. I could do that.'

Boom.

At that moment, despite his 'alright geez', his stupid swagger, his annoying fake laugh, his unwanted life lessons and his hideous approach to women, The Amazing Syko had just become my new business partner.

3. TESTING, TESTING

I T'S safe to say that not everyone was as keen on the idea as me and Keith. And by 'everyone', I mean Neil. He hated it. It wasn't so much that he didn't think it would work, he just seemed quite pissed off that we were taking it any further than drunken pub silliness. But despite his misgivings, he was sporting enough to stand in a goal in the middle of a field with a defensive wall made up of bar stools we'd borrowed from the Old Bell in front of him. He even nicked goalie gloves off his son for the day.

This was on the Thursday, so five days on from when I had the idea and those days in between had been pretty intense. Encouraged by the fact he was currently unemployed and I lived above a pub, Keith had come to my flat every day for hypno training. It meant I had to put up with him swaggering around the flat and asking crude questions about my sex life and the women I knew, but I needed his expertise and contending with his laddish bullshit was a price I was willing to pay.

Now, I must admit that my footballing highlights up until this point were limited to a mid-table finish in Division Five of the Southend Sunday League. As I said before, I was pretty shit at football and never really played during my school years. When I was older, I managed to sign on for a team because they were desperately short of numbers, plus I was happy to sort the water bottles, put out the corner flags and wash the kit more than anyone else in the team. I loved belting about the pitch during training. I would be out there in all weathers and I would always come off the astroturf pitch – well, it was more like a well-worn carpet laid across concrete – with a huge smile on my face. But when it came to game time at the weekend, I only usually got on for the last ten minutes and that was only if we had at least a three-goal cushion, which didn't happen that often.

I'm 42 now, so I play veterans' football. Although 'play' is a bit of a misleading term as it's still the same story as before. Water bottles, corner flags, wash the kit and last ten minutes playing. Still, it's nice to be involved though, right?

But now, if Keith pulls off his mind tricks and my idea actually works, the world of football could be my oyster. I could be a professional. Yeah, me. That would certainly surprise a few people. Plus I would be earning proper money – mega bucks – and I'd be able to convince Julie to take me back. I mean, all women love footballers, don't they?

We started off on that Sunday with The Amazing Syko going through some deep breathing exercises with me. I'm not entirely sure he had to be sat so close that I could smell the stale beer on his breath, but he insisted it was for the best. Then we did some visualisation, more relaxation techniques and then – boom – I was gone. While in the trance, Keith began programming my brain with just one thing, over and over – David Beckham's last-minute freekick against Greece in 2001 to send England through to the World Cup finals in Japan and Korea. He hypno-coached me through the stance, the run-up, how Becks places his feet, how he strikes the ball, the technique, the body shape, everything. Over and over and over.

When he brought me round, two hours had passed. It was a blink of the eye for me. I didn't feel any different, to be honest, and

I was a bit worried he'd got me to do all sorts of messed up stuff while in control of me. Even just making me Moonwalk across the kitchen would've been taking a liberty, but he insisted it was pure football. We had cheese and tomato sauce sandwiches and pinched a packet of crisps from the pub and then carried on for another few hours of training.

It wasn't quite Old Trafford and there certainly wasn't a capacity crowd cheering me on, but the park around the back of our old school was the closest thing we had at that point.

Despite his bad mood, Neil was primed in goal. Maybe he wanted to save my shot to prove the whole thing didn't work and that would be the end of it. Who knows? Keith brought a video camera along (I'd hate to think what he'd used it to film previously) and had set it up on a tripod. I placed the ball about 25 yards out, pretty much dead centre of the goal and had the stools lined up on the edge of the D. I pressed my left foot into the turf just ahead of my right like Sir David, and visualised over and over me booting the ball beyond the wall of stools and into the top corner of the goal, beyond Neil's reach.

'Ready when you are Becks,' Keith yelled from the camera with a thumb raised aloft. Deep breath in through the nose, filling my chest, and puffed out through the mouth. I was ready. This was it. I started my run-up, arced round slightly towards the ball, planted my left foot at its side and struck through with my right. But it dug into the mud three inches behind the ball. As my toes were bent backwards, a jolt of pain shot through my foot and up my leg. I staggered forward clumsily, desperately trying to maintain my balance, but it was like those guys who chase a rolling wheel of cheese down a really steep hill every year. The fall was inevitable. It took three steps, but I eventually went down and landed face-first in the hard mud. It hurt. I lifted my head from the ground just in time to see the football roll feebly into the legs of the bar stools. Beyond the makeshift wall, Neil was doubled over in hysterics.

'Well, at least we've made £250 from You've Been Framed today,' he spluttered with genuine tears rolling down his cheek.

'Er, right,' said Keith. 'Richie mate, that's not quite how Beckham did it. Shall we try again?'

I managed to kick the ball for take two, but it was miles wide. Take three even further. Take four hit the stools. Take five almost hit a dog, which then picked up the ball in its mouth and ran off. You could say take six was on target, but only if we had moved the target, which we hadn't.

By this point, Neil's hysterics had turned to boredom. He was sat down at the foot of one of the goalposts flicking through stuff on his phone. But the Amazing Syko was thinking again. I could tell because he was rubbing his chin.

'Come here a sec geez, let me try something. YEESSSSS, you fackin' beauty. We fackin' did it.'

Now, to me, Keith said that in one straight sentence, which wouldn't make any sense to a normal person. But it didn't go like that for him and Neil. After saying the word 'something', Keith used our trigger words to put me back in a trance. He got Neil to stand up and resume goalkeeping duties, while I was instructed to take the kick again but while in the trance.

I might not have believed it myself had it not been caught on camera. But there it was in full-colour glory. Watching it in slo-mo back at the flat on a bigger screen was even better. There I was, striding up to the ball confidently, just like Beckham, and curling a perfect right-footed shot towards the top corner. Neil's contorted face was a picture as he scrambled across the goal in a desperate, but futile, attempt to stop the shot. It flew into the top corner of the net. Well, it would've done had there been a net, but the council took them down weeks ago. Instead, it flew past the chipped white paintwork of the rusting, metal goal-frame and landed over near the kids' playground. The camera followed me as I even embarked on the same goal celebration as Becks did in that game; running off to an imaginary crowd with my arms outstretched, jumping and swinging an arm in joy-filled exuberance. But instead of Emile Heskey being the first to hug me in celebration, it was Keith with the camera in his hand. The video closed in on my face as he got nearer and I was back in the room.

'YEESSSSS, you fackin' beauty. We fackin' did it.'

Back at the Old Bell, the celebratory beers were flowing. Keith's swagger had grown even larger and he had taken to singing 'It's coming home' on repeat, but I cut him some slack.

'I told you bruv. I'm a fackin' genius…oi oi darling…I'm a wizard or somethin'.'

But Neil still wasn't on the same wavelength as us. As Keith and I stood nattering about football and taking our plan forward, he sat watching the golf on telly and shaking his head. He got the right hump when Keith went over and pretended his head was the FA Cup. Neil did have slightly bigger than average ears.

'Get off, you twat,' Neil said, pushing Keith away. 'So what you going to try next then, eh? Freddy Eastwood's freekick that beat Man United? What about that beauty Collymore scored in '93 against Huddersfield in the FA Cup? You're certain to be signed now. You'll win the Ballon d'Or. Piece of piss. More like the Barn Door.' He turned back to his beer with another shake of his head and mouthed the word 'twats'.

'Stop being a fackin' melt all your life,' Keith chipped in. 'We gotta fine tune it, ain't we? It'll take a few weeks, but we'll just keep filling fat boy's noggin with skills and goals and stuff of all the best footballers in the world, ever…'

My excitement levels were so high that I ignored the fat boy jibe and had to take over. '…and if I can score like Beckham or play like Messi or fucking Neymar, then I'll get a contract at Southend easy.

You'll be able to watch me from the stands. Megabucks footballer Richard Price at your service. 'Hello Julie, hello Tilson, here comes daddy'.' I even did a little bow.

Neil still wasn't impressed. 'Seriously?' He said it like a teenager asked to pick a dirty sock off the floor. Like it was the most depressing thing in life.

'Come on. You've seen what it can do and we've only scratched the surface,' I said. 'The sky's the limit.'

'And what if there ain't any freekicks? You're fucked.'

We tried to explain again that there was more to it – that, eventually, I'd be able to pass and shoot and tackle like the legends (hopefully) but Neil wasn't budging.

'I mean, that was a clever party trick. I'll give you that. But do you guys seriously think you can get Southend, or any club for that matter, do you seriously think you can get them to pay you shitloads of money for this? No chance. Not a chance.'

Keith took a step closer to Neil, put a hand on his shoulder and then raised the Finger of Truth to his lips before speaking. 'He who does not try will never discover his true capabilities.'

'Save your Socrates bollocks Sykesy. And no, I don't mean the Brazilian footballer. Listen Rich, you could play like Messi and Ronaldo rolled into one, but no club worth its salt is going to take an overweight 45-year-old with no footballing history and give them a long contract worth 50, 60, 70 grand a week. At least not without smelling a rat.'

'I'm 42. Same as you.'

'Not by the time you get in any reasonable sort of shape that a club would entertain giving you a trial you fat bastard.'

'Alright, there's no need for that. You're not exactly Kate fucking Moss are you?'

'Well if you two are the ugly sisters that makes me Cinderella. Wahey!' chipped in Keith with a swig of his beer.

'Rich, I love you buddy,' said Neil, 'but you're off your rocker here. And even if Southend get suckered in by this and offer you a wage that makes all this worthwhile – which they can't by the way – do you want to be known as the person who destroyed the club we love? Because you will get found out at some point and Southend would get huge fines and points deducted and who knows if we'd ever bounce back from that? And you'd be banned for life. Never be able to watch the Blues again unless they pop up on telly, which won't happen if you've got us relegated to the fucking Conference. Think about it. Both of you. And then go and get a proper fucking job. Speaking of which, I've got work tomorrow. I'm off.'

And with that, Neil downed the last of his pint and stomped out of the pub. He lifted his collar and hunched his shoulders up as he went out into the cool, dark evening. Then he dug his hands deep into his jacket pockets and walked off up the road.

Keith and I stood there in silence for a couple of minutes, just looking at the door Neil had just gone through.

Then a smile broke across his face as he said: 'I never liked having a proper job anyway.'

4. THE OTHER MAN

KEITH and I continued our training over the next week. He was able to tweak and refine parts of the process as we went. Despite appearing to be a brainless moron with very few social skills, Keith was actually very clever when it came to his hypnosis and knowledge of the mind. It was amazing really that he ever managed to complete any courses without being thrown out for his disgraceful conduct. But when he was in the zone, he was in the zone. He just sort of switched from chauvinistic wideboy to professional therapist. I guess that's how he managed to keep going on that Costa del Sol circuit for so long.

Most of our sessions took place in the flat, but we had to keep going over the park to practice the execution of whatever I'd learned. All the time, Keith was finding ways of speeding up the process and keeping me more conscious while in the trance. It would be good to remember at least some of the achievements I was going to make on the pitch.

But there was something that Neil had said that stayed in the front of my mind. I was in no condition to become a professional footballer, let alone a well-paid one. I could now replicate that Beckham freekick at will and had also perfected the Ossie Ardiles rainbow flick from Escape To Victory. I spent hours and hours effortlessly running all over the park, but as soon as Keith took me out of the trance it all caught up with me. I was fucked. I'd collapse on the floor in exhaustion and my face would turn a vicious purply-red. It'd take about half an hour to slow my breathing and heart rate down. Plus my back and knees would ache like a bastard. The first time we went full on, Keith had to nip back to the pub to get the trolley we use to wheel in the barrels so that he could get me home.

Some of that would improve with fitness and as I lost the flab around my midriff. Until then, the plan was to fake it till we make it.

But there was another point that Neil made that actually made sense. The money. Southend were never going to pay the sort of cash that I was hoping for. I mean, if you're going to gamble you might as well go big, right? I was thinking nearer one hundred grand a week than one grand. We were talking figures beyond my beloved Southend's capabilities.

So over a few drinks (I had a G&T as it's supposed to be healthier), Keith and I began to tweak our plan.

First, we needed to identify a club with money to burn and that we wouldn't mind ripping off. That was easy. London City United – a franchised, soulless club set up just to make money by shamelessly promoting itself to a global fanbase rather than the traditional path of a club serving the surrounding community and building itself up over decades and decades of hard work and dedication. LCU had billionaire investors, galactico players, was in the Premier League and going for the title. Boxes ticked.

'And you'll love this,' Keith said. 'My aunt knows a bloke who does some scouting for City United's youth set-up, or used to. She picked my uncle over him when they was kids, but he still holds a candle for her apparently. A bottle of whisky and the promise of dinner with Aunt Theresa and he could probably be persuaded to watch you play and see if you've got what it takes. And we know that you have.'

'Let's do it then. All systems go.'

I sat in Pizza Hut across the table from my handsome young son content that things were changing. At 15, Tilson was pretty much as tall as me and despite shovelling slice after slice of pizza into his gob like a starved Ninja Turtle, he was at least half my weight. He took a massive bite from a slice of Hawaiian deep pan and pulled a stupid face as the stringy cheese slowly fell from his mouth and slapped against his chin.

'Seriously dad, you're not having any pizza?' he asked with a mouth full of food. 'It's all you can eat and you love eating all you can eat pizza.'

I did. And my belly was close to declaring independence from the rest of me, climbing out and filling itself with BBQ chicken pizza and washing it down with full-fat bastard Coke. Instead, it gurgled at me in disgust.

'No, it's fine son. I'm trying to eat healthier so I'm going to stick with my salad.' It wasn't fine. I wanted a stuffed crust meatfeast. No, I wanted two of them laid one on top of the other to make a meatfeast pizza sandwich. I tried to think of something different.

'Do you fancy coming to watch your old man play football on Sunday Til? Should be a good game. The other team are top of the table I think.'

'Nah. No thanks. Not really into football and you never play anyway. It's boring just standing out there in a field doing nothing. I can't get wifi or anything on my phone and Mum says I have to wait till next month for more data. Although it might be worth coming now you've had a salad, you'll be amazing.'

I loved the cheekiness he was growing into. His jokes were funnier now he was a teenager, that's for sure. When he was about five he'd tell jokes like: 'Why did the horse go in the field? Because there were ants in the toilet.' Julie would smile and do one of those cute little nose laughs where you just push out a bit of air. I thought the joke was shit. But he was cleverer now and quicker with his wit. We giggled and I tried to reach over the table to tickle him but dipped my belly in the mayonnaise, which made him laugh even more.

'Think you need one more salad dad,' he added.

'Oi. Now don't take the mick. You should be encouraging me to get healthier.'

'I'm just kidding. It is really good. Mum will be impressed, and Matt especially.'

'Who?'

'Matt. Mum's boyfriend. He's a fitness instructor ain't he?'

'Er, it's "isn't" not "ain't". Sorry, who is he?'

'Dad, they've been together for ages,' he said with a face like he told me humans breathe the air. 'You know that.'

If you've ever been kicked in the bollocks, you will have experienced that horrible double-whammy of the searing pain between your legs and the hollowing sickness and nausea that fills your belly. This was kind of how I felt.

It was a mixture of heartbreak and anger crashing into one another and trying to get the upper hand before a barrage of uncontrollable emotion burst through my skull.

Tilson seemed to think I knew about my wife's new man and perhaps I should have. But I didn't. And it really stung. For all that had happened, I loved Julie completely. She was my 'one'. I'd known that since we'd started dating. We just seemed to fit – our likes and dislikes, our sense of humour, our taste in music and films. Obviously some of that changed over the years, but I had hoped that once I had some money rolling in again, I'd be able to woo her back with a bit of the old Richie Price charm. But it seemed I was too late for the party now. And she was already off in the corner having a snog during the slowies with some bloke who took advantage of her. Who the fuck was 'Matt'?

And if having that initial toe-punt in the bollocks wasn't enough, it now seemed there was a whole line of people waiting to give me a second boot. Sadly, Tilson was next in line.

'He's actually really cool, dad. He's way younger than you and works at the gym, so he's got loads of muscles and that. And he plays guitar and sings, so we've been having jamming sessions and he's helped me write a song. Cool, yeah?'

What little appetite I'd had for my salad was now long gone. I wasn't due to take Tilson back for another hour or so, but I thought it best to have a word with my darling wife sooner rather than later.

The drive to the house was a real white-knuckle ride. I wasn't speeding – a hangover from my driving instructor days meant I stuck rigidly to the rules of the road – but my hands were clenched tightly around the steering wheel. I turned into our road, pulled up outside the house and was off towards the front door before Tilson had even unbuckled his seatbelt.

The house was a grand, modern affair. It was rendered in white and grey with a large driveway at the front with a willow tree and water feature off to one side. It was our perfect family home with four bedrooms, a study, a games room and a pool, along with views over the Thames Estuary. After Julie and Tilson and Southend United, this house was my greatest love. I had paid the mortgage off before things went tits up both in the financial world and between me and Julie, which was a bonus. And I couldn't wait to get back into it and call it home again. Although, what happened next rubbed off a bit of its shine.

'Oh, ah, hi, hello, um, you must be Richard.' The door had been opened by a man in his mid-20s, wearing nothing but a loose pair of shorts that displayed the size and direction to which their owner was dressed. He was taller than me and was stood up on the step, so my eyeline was pretty much at his nipple-level. His body was straight from the cover of Men's Health. Six-pack – check. Defined pecs – check. Bulging biceps – check. Dark tousled hair – check. Overly-white teeth – check. Horrific spray tan – check.

I looked up at his face and saw a perfectly chiselled jawline with a glittering of stubble and a smile designed for a toothpaste advert.

His name was Matt Curbishley, although he marketed himself online as 'Turbo Curbo' and was a 'body transformation guru'. I did not like him one bit.

My fist was already clenched and I had considered going straight in with a classic thump to the face, but I had never thrown a punch before and it seemed highly likely that I would shatter my fingers on contact with his chin and he would then proceed to beat the shit out of me.

That said, I wasn't about to be cowed by this physical specimen either. I decided to use my words as my weapon.

'Yes, you posing pouch prick. I'm Richard. Thanks for opening the door to *my* fucking house where *my* wife and son live. Now, where is she?'

'Whoa, whoa! There's no need for the aggression, OK pal? Chill. Jules is just, er, finishing up in the shower.'

'Oh, been having a work-out have you?'

'Something like that,' he said with a glint in his eye and it took a second for my rage-addled brain to click. I had genuinely been asking if they had been doing an exercise routine. So much for beating him with brains. And Jules? Her name is fucking Julie. She hates Jules. Always has.

I went to push past, but he put a hand on my chest and held me off with ease. 'It's OK, I'll call her, let's not make a scene,' he said and then yelled out, 'Jules, Richard's here with Tilson.'

At that moment, my darling son unknowingly gave my already battered heart another wicked slap.

'Hey Matt, how's it going?' he said in a voice so polite it was like he was addressing Santa Claus himself. 'Got time for a jam this afternoon?'

'Yeah, should be fine mate. No worries.'

Fuck! I hated this guy more than Colchester United and decided to go full Roy McDonough on him.

I went in like a rugby prop in a scrum, spearing my shoulder into his midriff with my arms around his waist as I tried to force him back and knock him off his feet. He barely budged. Well, not because of my strength anyway. He took a couple of steps back as he tried to shake me off. Admittedly he made no aggressive moves, but the movement left me flat on my belly with my hands on his ankles. I gripped them and tried to pull them from under him, but the manoeuvre was a pathetic failure. He just stood there and as I looked up I caught sight of not-so-mini Turbo Curbo giving me a taunting wink from inside his shorts. For a second I thought about punching him in the bell-end, but a voice snapped me back.

'Dad, what are you doing?' said Tilson, stood looking terrified at the bottom of the stairs.

And before I could respond, another voice piped up. 'Yes Rich, what the hell are you doing exactly?'

Julie was stood next to our son with a large white towel wrapped around her body and another like a turban on her head. Water from her shower glistened on her shoulder. My goodness, she was beautiful. Although, to be honest, I did prefer her without her jaw clenched in anger and hatred in her eyes.

By this point I knew that the dive at Matt had been a foolish move, but I wasn't about to back down and refused to either let go of her lover's ankles or get off the floor for a full five minutes. Julie should have told me she was seeing someone else and that he was coming to the house in just a pair of shorts. I wasn't in the wrong here. Stubbornness was a trait I had inherited somewhere along the way. You needed this foolhardy resilience to be a Southend fan.

Anyway, to cut a long story a bit shorter, I told the Armani pants model that it would be best for everyone if he got dressed and fucked the fuck off. Tilson got the hump for ruining his guitar jam session and stomped up the stairs to his room, calling me an 'idiot' on the way. There had been a word beginning with 'f' bursting to come out I'm sure, but he held it in – unlike his mother, who launched into an X-rated tirade and told me in no uncertain terms it was her house, that we had split up some time ago and she would see whomsoever she wants whenever she wants.

I told her he was far too young for her, but she hit back saying that she thought I was the one who liked them young. I thought that was a bit of a low blow and – hurt – I *may* have called her a slag. It wasn't my proudest moment and I regretted it as soon as the word came out of my mouth. But the damage had been done. At least now I knew that 'smoothing things over' was completely off the table – and not just because that muscle-bound, chiselled-jaw, roid-popping twunt was banging my wife on it.

I got in the car and sat there for 20 minutes trying to think of what to do next. There was no chance I was going to apologise to Julie, although I did intend to text Tilson later to say sorry. I looked up at his room and saw him looking out. I waved weakly, but he walked away. I'd fucked things up even more than they had been.

There was only one way I was going to fix this and it involved Keith Sykes whispering sweet footballing nothings into my ear. Being under the trance seemed like the perfect escape.

5. SIX WEEKS ON

THINGS had picked up quite nicely, even if I do say so myself. Not with Julie and Tilson though. My wife is still knobbing the Adonis from the gym and my son needed some persuasion before understanding that I'm not a complete loon. I told him that I love him and his mother very much, and I was trying to protect them but went about it the wrong way

'But you got beaten up without him having to hit you, dad,' he pointed out. It was pretty much true, but I explained that it was more about being prepared to fight for what you want than the actual winning. He didn't seem so convinced.

So, although all that was a mess, I had been making great progress with Keith and our plan for footballing brilliance. Against my better judgement, I allowed him to move into the flat with me so that we could work as and when it suited. It was only a one-bedroomed place so he slept in the living room, which also doubled as our hypnotism laboratory. Keith still hadn't been able to perfect the dodgy toilet flush mechanism, so it wasn't the most pleasant of atmospheres. But the worst thing was putting up with the life lessons every 30 minutes. Being in the trance was a blessing. He had so much terrible advice about how to win back Julie to the extreme of saying I should let her 'peg' me to let her get rid of her anger. If you don't know what that is, google it – but only in incognito mode and not in a Costa Coffee like I did. Keith also said he might know someone who would 'off' Matt. This was another of his offers that I declined.

These were the sorts of mind-numbing conversations that now filled my waking hours and I couldn't even escape to the pub downstairs because a) I was trying to stay off the booze at that time and b) Keith was usually in there when he wasn't taunting me.

But, I must admit, the training had been going well. For hours on end each day, The Amazing Syko will put me in a trance and fill my mind with the beautiful game. Videos and clips of brilliance from all the greats – Pele, Maradona, Zidane, fat Ronaldo, thin Ronaldo, Messi, Cruyff, Beckenbauer, Best, Maldini, Gascoigne, Charlton, Muller, Crouch.

I ingested tricks, flicks, goals, tackles, headers, when to run, when not to run, how to run – everything needed to transform a 42-year-old chubster into the world's greatest footballer. And after all that, we'd head to the park to try everything out. Everything was working, but we now needed to test it out in a match situation.

I mentioned to my manager at Leigh Ramblers veterans that I had a couple of mates coming to watch on this particular Sunday morning and asked if I could start the game so they get to see me play. Those 'mates' were Keith and a guy called Graham Malcolm – Aunt Theresa's old love interest and some-time football scout.

Things didn't start off too smoothly as, despite my pleas, Dave the manager still made me a substitute for the game. Graham wasn't too bothered as he got his bottle of whisky and wrinkly date either way, but I was royally pissed off.

To make matters worse, the Rams went 1-0 down early on, 2-0 down by half-time and conceded a third shortly after the restart. They were sinking faster than my chance of getting a game.

However, fate was on my side that morning and it came in the shape of our man-mountain centre-back, Karl. Now Karl was genuinely a lovely bloke. He listened to opera, went to the theatre, volunteered to help the homeless and rescued stray dogs. But once he stepped over that white line on a Sunday morning, he became a proper nasty cunt.

In this game, he was being riled up by the opposition's nippy young forward, who made a few comments about Karl's weight and pace after scoring their second goal. When he scored the third, he said something about Karl's missus and the red mist didn't so much descend but smother every element of his being with a dark, crimson hatred.

Normally in football, the forward(s) take the kick-off. In park football, it's almost routine that the ball is tapped back to a mid-fielder to try and launch an attack. But Karl, our central defender, strode up from the back and demanded the ball be passed directly to him. No one was about to argue with a man who had steam coming out his ears.

The ref blew the whistle to restart the game, and our forward did as he was told and rolled the ball back to Karl, who amid shouts of 'Don't just hoof it Karl', just hoofed the ball as hard as he could towards the far corner of the pitch. Every player, spectator and match official to a man, woman and dog watched as the ball sailed high into the air, over the heads of all the opposition players and bounced off the pitch for throw-in deep in the other team's half.

But as the ball had come down from orbit, there had been an almighty yelp.

Everyone turned back to see Karl gently whistling to himself as he jogged back towards his own area and the opposition's nippy striker prostrate on the turf, clutching his face in agony. Karl had diverted everyone's attention and decked the mouthy little shit.

A huge melee ensued as players from both sides piled in. There were threats, pushing, shoving and shouting all over the place.

Karl's face was a picture of innocence. Then the ref held up a red card to send Karl off, but our man wasn't done yet.

'What you doin' ref?'

'Sending you off son.'

'What for?'

'What for? Don't make me laugh. You just punched that No9 to the floor.'

'No I didn't.' The denial was beautifully blunt. 'Did you see me hit him ref? Did you actually see me do it with your own eyes? Or are you going off what the opposition are saying? You can't send me off for something you didn't see on the say-so of the other team otherwise I'll say six of their players hit me and you'd have to send them off too.'

And the ref knew Karl was right. He hadn't seen it and, therefore, couldn't send him off. The other team went ballistic. The ref could sense it was about to kick off again – the fighting, not the game – and walked over to the side of the pitch to speak to Dave, our manager. He asked him to substitute Karl or he'd be forced to abandon the match for the safety of the players. Reluctantly, Dave withdrew Karl from play and called over his only sub – me.

'Stop cuddling your boyfriend and get on there, will you. And don't make it any fucking worse than it already is,' the manager said with the hump.

But I wasn't cuddling my boyfriend; I was being put into a trance by Keith. And then I was on the pitch.

The game restarted with a throw-in to the other team. The ball got knocked around for a bit and then back to their keeper, who booted it upfield. I brought the ball under control instantly on the halfway line – an astonishing feat in itself – before pulling out another Beckham treat from my library. Manchester United versus Wimbledon, August 17, 1996. I swiped across the ball with my right foot and it sailed high into the air just like Karl's hoof 15 minutes earlier, but mine was headed only to one place – over the back-pedalling keeper's head and into the back of the net. 3-1.

For the first time in my footballing career, I was mobbed by my teammates.

'You jammy fucker,' Karl yelled from the sidelines. 'Take that you cunts!'

The opposition kicked off, played it back, hoofed it forward and I got the ball again in the middle of my own half. Maradona for Argentina versus England in the 1986 World Cup quarter-final in Mexico. Not the handball, the other one. I began running with the ball at my feet, evaded two challenges and shoulder-barged one of their players away from a third. Then I accelerated – yes, me accelerating – which saw me glide past the next defender like he wasn't there. They tried to chase me down, but I was too fast and the ball was still glued to my feet. The central defender came across to try and block me but I skipped past him too and into the area, went around the on-rushing keeper and slid the ball in the back of the net. 3-2.

You can see where this is going, can't you? I'll save you the blow-by-blow account, but we ended up winning the game 7-3. I scored five goals – my first goals ever – and set up the other two. I hadn't been at the bottom of a bundle pile-up since school when my tormentors had put me there as a punishment for being spotty. But that day, my teammates did it out of sheer joy and astonishment. They had never seen a game like it. They had never seen anything like it from me – how was I even capable? Even some of the opposition players came over to congratulate me despite all that had happened in the game.

And then Keith came over and took me out of the trance. In a second, all that running and movement and effort caught up with me and I collapsed on the floor in a sweaty mess.

When I came round, I saw the wrinkly, greying face of Graham Malcolm looking down at me.

'I don't know what I just saw, young man, or what you hope to achieve – and I don't think I want to – but you brought a smile to this old boy's face. I'll do what I can to get you a trial at City United. I still know a few good eggs there. The rest is down to you.'

6. THE TRIAL

I DECLINED Graham's invitation for him to share the juicy details of his whisky-fuelled date with Keith's Aunt Theresa – his use of the word 'juicy' being a key factor in that decision – but he had also rung with some exciting news. He'd called in a few favours and someone at London City United had agreed to give me a trial. It would be a match and mainly feature youth players and a couple of reserve teamers. I had a week to prepare.

Then, a few days before, things escalated somewhat. At first I thought the call from London City United was to cancel, but instead they told me the game was now 'behind closed doors' as they were using it to boost Brazilian striker Horatio Emmett's return to fitness. Emmett had cost the best part of £80million and was seen as the man to fire in the goals to propel LCU to success. But he had picked up an injury pre-season that was taking a while to shake off. Of course, the club didn't want any details of the match or Emmett's fitness being leaked, so I was sent very formal and legal-looking non-disclosure forms to read, sign and return. Long and the short of it was that if I breathed a word to anyone, they'd sue me for all I had. Which wasn't actually that threatening when you consider I had little for them to take. But I signed anyway.

And when it came to matchday, they had bolstered the teams considerably to make sure Emmett got a proper test. It was now fringe first-teamers, reserves and the odd smattering of kids. Pretty much every player taking part was an international worth millions, or was at least earning more in a week than most of us do in a year. If I'm honest, just being invited along to this game was a lot further than I thought my idea would get us.

The match was taking place at Scott Park, the stadium of the old Blenheim United side that City United's billionaire American owner Buck Schulz had bought, pillaged and bastardised to create his central London 'soccer' franchise giant. The old ground on the outskirts of the city now hosted reserve and women's team fixtures. The first team played in a 100,000-capacity monstrosity right in the heart of the capital.

Scott Park, though, was a traditional English football stadium not too dissimilar from Southend's Roots Hall, which helped to ease my nerves a little. I had thought of dropping the whole thing in case I ballsed it up and made a right show of myself, but Keith assured me everything would be fine once he'd worked his magic and I was on the pitch.

But I was still unsettled as we approached the security guard on the gate.

'Sorry lads, no admittance to fans today I'm afraid. It's a behind-closed-doors game.'

'Yeah we know,' said Keith. 'My man here is playing. He's the reason it's top secret.'

'Alright, yeah, nice one. Jog on now,' said the guard.

'No, it's true,' I piped up. 'I've got a trial.'

The guard, who was not too much different in size and age to me, began to giggle. Ripples shot across his strained hi-viz jacket as his man boobs wobbled in merriment. You'd have thought he'd just been told the funniest joke in history. It took him a couple of minutes for him to compose himself. 'Mate, you make fat Ronaldo look thin. I've got as much chance of getting a game as you. Now, go on, fuck off lads.'

Keith's patience was shredding at a pace. 'Awight you silly fat prick, have a look at this,' he said and pushed the non-disclosure agreement into his flabby chest. The guard's smirk dropped and he walked away talking into his radio. He returned a couple of minutes later, apologised for his mistake and directed us across the car park towards the players' entrance.

'Silly fat wanker,' he muttered under his breath as he resumed his position at the gate.

A blue wooden door that had more paint peeled off than still on served as the entrance to the bowels of the stadium that housed the changing rooms. It seemed the club's fortunes hadn't extended to paying for a pot of Dulux and a decent brush over here. There was no handle on the outside of the door. I assumed that was to stop the fans getting in at the players, but it was possible that it just fell off due to poor maintenance. I knocked and waited.

Thirty seconds or so later, a shiny head with a huge smile poked around the corner. It was another hi-viz. 'Yes?'

'I'm, er, here for the match. Richie Price.'

With the door still barely open, he looked down at his clipboard and began running his finger down the list of names. It stopped and he slid it across before bursting into a booming laugh.

'It's got "fat old bloke" written next to your name in brackets here, look.' He showed me and it did. 'They got that pretty much spot on, no offence. Awesome. Don't know how you wangled this my man, but please come through.' He was genial enough and he held the door open for me to enter before directing Keith round to the stand where he took up a spot near the dug-out.

Despite it being a pretty warm night, the corridor that led to the changing rooms had a chill to it. There was no sunlight and the strip lighting across the ceiling did little to add any brightness or warmth to the place. My stomach flipped with nerves. Although footballer Richie didn't experience nerves, the real one did and it wasn't pleasant.

I stayed there alone as I listened to the hubbub of players chatting while they got into their kits and the coaches as they dished out their instructions. There was a funny smell in the air – a mix of the staleness of the old stadium, the players' expensive cologne, sweat and treatment oils.

I lifted my hand and it was shaking. I felt a gulp bounce down to my chest where my heart was pounding ten to the dozen. It was not too late to walk out.

A hand landed on my shoulder with a thump and I nearly pissed myself in sheer fright. A young Eastern European lad in a club tracksuit smiled and apologised as he squeezed past me in the narrow corridor, doing his best to avoid belly-to-belly contact, before ducking into the changing room. As the door hung open, I saw the other players inside for the first time. Every single one of them was a perfect specimen – ripped full of muscle, athletic and at peak physical fitness. Not too dissimilar to that twat Turbo Curbo. 'Weapons' was the term Tilson used to describe blokes like this. I was more of a spud gun.

Then I saw Horatio Emmett right there opposite me. We made eye contact for a second before he looked away and carried on talking. Fuck. An actual Premier League player right there. And that was Danny Diegbe next to him. He'll be an England star one day. Maybe in time for the World Cup. And Carlos Menezes. Jesus, he's a beast. He should be playing in defence for the first team more regularly. Then the face of Mike Cusick, one of the coaches, appeared in the doorway and looked me up and down.

'Right, fat boy,' he said loudly. 'Stop staring at all the pretty boys will you and get changed. I think you're going to need plenty of warming up son.'

I walked into the centre of the changing room trying as best I could to hide behind the kit bag I was holding. It felt like everyone stopped what they were doing and fixed their eyes on me. That was because they really did. I half-expected someone to say, 'You're not from round these parts are ya stranger,' like I'd walked into a saloon in the Wild West. Instead, the younger lads nudged each other and I could tell they were making jokes. It was like being at school again. The more experienced players just looked on in disbelief. 'What the fuck is that supposed to be?' bellowed one voice off to my left. I'm not sure who said it, but the voice was English so that would narrow it down.

But then Coach Cusick intervened, told everyone to shut up and concentrate on their own game, before directing me to a vacant seat to get changed.

I pulled my mud-clad Puma Kings out of my kit bag and dropped them to the floor next to my Sondico shinpads, trying not to make eye contact with anyone. I started to get changed into the red, white and blue of London City United's kit laid out for me, but faced the wall as I did to hide my physique. It wasn't pretty. Unsurprisingly, the shirt designed for those with the body of male models didn't quite make it all the way over my belly and it poked out the bottom. And the shorts were so tight that I may as well have just spray-painted them on. There was a real danger that any swift movement could see them tear.

Fortunately, I was told I would be starting the game as a substitute (I was used to that) and it meant I could put on a tracksuit and a large coat to cover me up and keep warm.

'We really need to give the proper players a run out more than anything to get them match fit as soon as possible,' Coach Cusick told me. 'We'll try and get you on for the last ten minutes or something, but I can't promise anything.'

Boy did that sound familiar.

None of the players spoke to me directly during the warm-up. You'd think they'd be curious as to why I was there, but nothing. It was like being the class freak again. I was back at school feeling like an outsider as the bullies and posers shared their in-jokes and played football. I copied what everyone else did as we jogged and stretched, but did my best to hide – which was quite tough considering I was twice as wide as all the others. It was a relief once the whistle was blown to get the game underway and I was able to find the furthest seat back on the bench and hunker down, out of sight and mind of those around me.

As the match went on, the shouts from the players and coaches echoed around the decaying old stadium and memories of the old days as a kid on the standing terraces at Roots Hall with Grandad came flooding back. It was a romance of the game of which a club like London City United could never be a part. The history. That connection with the fans. Yeah, they had this old ground for now, but there were plans to knock this down and rebuild it too – with shops and flats included in the new development, of course.

As the second half cracked on and with no one really taking any notice of me being there, I went for a jog down the touchline to have a nose around the stand at the far end. I stopped by the corner flag and pretended to do some stretches as I fell into a daydream about Southend United.

I remembered Grandad telling me about the time the Blues played the great Liverpool team of the 1970s in the FA Cup in '79. He'd found the matchday programme while tidying some stuff up in the loft. He and my dad went to the game, he said. He didn't talk about my dad much because his and mum's death upset him so much. I would've been a toddler at the time. Liverpool had Ray Clemence in goal; Phil Neal, Emlyn Hughes, Phil Thompson and Alan Hansen in defence; Graeme Souness, Jimmy Case, Terry McDermott and Ray Kennedy in midfield; David Fairclough and the legend Kenny Dalglish up front. The great Bob Paisley was in the dugout. The game was in early January and Grandad said everyone was worried it would be called off because it snowed heavily during the afternoon. 'I had to wear a pair of your grandmother's tights under my trousers to try and keep warm,' he told me. 'First and last time, I tell you.' But the match went ahead after they brushed the lines clear of snow and brought out the old orange ball. You don't see those much anymore. The game ended 0-0 in front of more than 30,000 at Roots Hall – that's more than double what you can get in there now – but Liverpool won the replay 3-0 a week later at Anfield and valiant Southend were out.

'Hey, hey, hey! You! Big guy! What you doing over there? You meant to be there?' A voice pulled me out of my reverie and back to the game at hand. At first, I thought it might be Keith, but I turned to see a much older man who looked vaguely familiar and carried with him an air of authority.

'Huh?'

'What are you doing by the pitch? No fans allowed today. You better get outta there before security comes over,' he added with a genuine hint of concern in his voice.

'Oh, no. I mean, I'm a sub. In the game. I'm here for a trial. They said I might get on for the last ten minutes or so.'

'You're going to be playing?'

'Yeah.'

'You?'

'Yeah.'

'Well, what the fuck are you doing staring at an empty stand for an age?'

'Ah, well.' I didn't really know what to say, so just told the truth. 'I was reminiscing. The old ground, being so close to the pitch, standing terraces and all that. Brings back some nice memories, you know?' It lightened the guy's mood.

'Yeah, I know,' he said with a smile and a nod. 'I used to watch Fulham back when I was a kid. My dad would take me. It's where I got my love of soccer from. We lived that side of London when we were in the UK, so it was easy to get to. I couldn't wait to move here once I grew up, mainly for the soccer. But the game's so different now.'

You may have guessed from how he said 'Full ham' and 'soccer', but I should explain that the guy I was speaking to was American. I said his face was familiar, but I couldn't place it initially. It was all very clear now. The chap was probably in his early 60s, but looked at least a decade younger with a healthy tan. His hair was thick, conditioned and perfectly coiffured, as was his large moustache. He wore smart cream chinos with a blue blazer, the watch on his wrist was the size of a dinner plate and he oozed wealth. It was Buck Schulz, London City United's owner.

'I'm surprised to see you here. I didn't think billionaire football club owners actually liked or came to watch football. Especially not a game like this.'

'Huh! Some do, some don't. I'm a soccer fan first, billionaire second. But I don't see the point of investing heavily financially into something if you're not going to invest heavily with your heart and mind too. You gotta be willing to go balls deep, you know?' I nodded. 'It's a business, don't get me wrong, I don't wanna lose money on this sonofabitch. But I'll put money in to make sure it works. I'm involved. I watch every game I can, I speak to the tea lady, I speak to the fans. I am a fan for Christ's sake.'

Bugger. This was slightly tarnishing my image of Buck Schulz and his London City United club as a soulless corporate entity driven solely by money.

'So, what's your story? Not exactly your average player, are you?' he said with a wave of his hand directing my attention to my body, as if he thought I hadn't noticed I was over 40 and overweight.

'I, er, had confidence issues when I was younger, so I never wanted to play much in front of other people. But I've had some, er, counselling and therapy now and I want to give it a shot while I can still run...just.'

'Well I'll be. That's frickin' great. But how can you give it a shot if you're on the damned bench?' He looked at me for a while and I wasn't sure if he actually wanted me to answer or not. As I finally opened my mouth to reply, he turned and strode towards the dugout to speak to the coaches previously engrossed on matters on the field. I could see Buck jabbing a finger in my direction and Coach Cusick looking mightily pissed off. He shook his head in dismay, but did what he was told. For once, I approved in owner interference in footballing matters.

'Fat boy, you're on,' shouted Cusick and the dozen or so heads allowed in the stands to watch the game turned in my direction in puzzlement, along with the other players on the benches.

My heart lurched so far forward in my chest that it nearly tripped over the left-back. I nodded to Buck and slowly jogged back to the dugout, stopping at Keith on the way for him to put me into my trance.

'I'm his therapist. It's just a quick pep talk,' Keith told Buck as he and Coach Cusick looked over, wondering why I looked like I'd just dozed off on some random bloke's shoulder.

'Riiiight. Well, OK buddy. Just get him out there and add some fun to this game because so far it's been as dull as horseshit and a complete waste of my frickin' night.'

No pressure then.

For the first five minutes I was on the pitch, I barely got a touch of the ball. It seems the London City United players didn't fancy giving the new boy a chance and so never passed to me. You could understand it I suppose. If they keep knocking it to me and I lost possession, it looks bad on them, and they're all trying to impress the coaches too for a place in the first team. I glimpsed over at the stand and made eye contact with Buck, who had the look of a disappointed parent on his face. It was as if he had gone into bat for me and I'd screwed him over, but Keith and I both knew I would only need one chance and I'd be away.

Then it came.

The ball was played into me on the halfway line as the only man unmarked. An opposition player moved in but I flicked the ball with the outside of my left boot before spinning to the right to leave the guy bamboozled like Dennis Bergkamp's beautiful pirouette goal for Arsenal against Newcastle in 2002. I then nutmegged the next player and whipped in the perfect cross for Horatio Emmett to score at the far post.

'Greayt stoof,' he yelled in his broken English, before adding 'you forking melt.' That bit took me by surprise, but he followed it up with a high ten and a hug, so I took it I was still in his good books. I was in Buck's too, as he gave me a knowing nod and thumbs up when I looked across. But there was more to come.

Emmett and I began linking up brilliantly and more of the other players began thawing towards me too. There were neat one-twos and crosses, and rather than just copying the goals and tricks of the legends of football I was now integrating them into my own game. Emmett got another two goals and called me both a 'mug' and a 'forking slag' in the process, which was utterly bizarre. Then I took the ball round two defenders, sold a dummy to a third to create just enough space to dink the ball up over the keeper's head and into the back of the net for 4-0.

There were more backslaps and high fives. 'Where did you come from?' said one player in astonishment. 'That was incredible.'

Buck Schulz looked happy too. He was deep in conversation with Coach Cusick as the game ended and we all walked off the pitch. Keith pulled me to one side and brought me out of la-la land just as the billionaire broke off and approached us.

'Now that, I did enjoy,' he said shaking both our hands. 'That was some of the best soccer I've seen in a very long time. My boy Horatio there may have scored the goals, which he should considering he cost me over a hundred million dollars, but you were the architect. I like you. I like your story and where you've come from.

Mike over there don't show it, but he agrees with me that you're one hell of a player. Those weren't kids you were destroying out there; those are internationals. I think we can sort out a contract with us if you want it. I want to see you in our squad. I'll sort out a meeting with our chief executive for early next week, but I want you to shake hands with me now that you won't start whoring yourself round to Man United or Chelsea or Spurs in the meantime. How about it, partner?'

I nearly tore his tanned Texan arm out of its socket.

7. DEAL – OR NO DEAL

'OH god sake, what do you want?' It wasn't how my wife used to greet me, but such fruity pleasantries had become commonplace in our relationship. If you could still call it one. I may have brought it on myself, but seeing as I needed access to the house I didn't rise to it. Instead, I just gave her the cute smile that always used to melt her heart.

'Stop doing that stupid goofy grin; it makes you look like a fucking moron. What do you want?' We were still standing at the front door and she hadn't shown any signs yet of letting me in. I couldn't tell her the real reason I was there of course. I had received the call from London City United to arrange an appointment for me to go and discuss my contract with the chief executive. Keith and I had done some reading up on things like image rights and bonuses so it looked like I knew a little about what I was talking about, because I wasn't really able to get myself an agent who'd be clued up on all that stuff. But I was running out of time and thought the least I could do was look proper smart and at least make this management guy think I knew what I was talking about.

'I've got a job interview. Just needed a couple of bits from the house. Is that alright? Is, er, matey boy in?'

She said he wasn't and seemed OK with me entering off the back of the job interview excuse. 'Come in. I was just making some coffee, do you want one?' Wow! That stopped me in my tracks. It was the most civil she'd been to me in months. It felt nice, so of course I agreed to a coffee. It was great being back in the house without clinging to her lover's ankles.

We made small talk and she told me about how Tilson was doing at school. He's such a clever lad. I told Julie the interview was at London City United.

'Not as a player I hope.' Julie was never one for going to matches but she knew a bit about football. Enough for that comment to sting a little.

'Oh, I reckon I could show them a thing or two,' I replied. She smiled enough to create those beautiful little dimples in her cheeks. Our eyes met for a definite moment and my heart started racing as it had done 20-odd years ago. Then she shook it off.

'Ah, so when's the big interview?' she said, taking a sip of her coffee.

'Today. At 3.30,' I said and glanced across at the cooker clock. 'Fuck, I've got to get moving.'

'What did you come here for?'

'My suits. The wedding one.' As far as I could recall, I only had two suits. A snazzy electric blue number for weddings and parties, and a sombre black one for funerals and more serious occasions. I hadn't worn either for a while.

'That horrid blue thing? I know you're meant to dazzle the person interviewing you, but it should be with your personality rather than the brightness of your suit. Anyway, I thought the jacket of that got torn up at Max and Clem's wedding.'

Flashback. Champagne at the table, beer on the dance floor, shots at the bar, more beer, more shots, a failed attempt to steal a golf buggy and a six-man tug-o-war using my suit jacket as the rope. Rip. Bollocks, she was right.

'The black one then.'

'No Rich, the trousers split.'

Jesus, yes. Not the best look at a crematorium, especially when you're wearing SpongeBob Squarepants boxers underneath.

'Fuck it,' I said.

'I think Matt might have a suit upstairs, let me go and have a look. You could borrow that.' My darkening mood dropped off a cliff in a nanosecond.

'He's leaving clothes here? Already?'

'Just one or two bits.'

'A suit is two bits. Who leaves a suit at his...?' I couldn't bring myself to say the word 'girlfriend' and I think she saw the hurt that caused. I was deflated.

'Do you want to try it at least? Just in case.'

'Julie love, he's a 14st, ripped-to-fuck fucking Adonis. We're not in the same league. None of his clothes are ever going to fit me.' And with that, I felt whatever little grip I had left on my marriage loosen even further and edge closer towards falling into the gaping abyss below that would see it snatched away forever.

London City United's Grand Postal/MegaMobiles Arena stadium was a behemoth. Situated in the City less than a mile from Tower Bridge, it looked as though a gargantuan spaceship had landed in among the skyscrapers and office blocks of the capital. It made absolutely no effort to blend in with its surroundings. So much so, that it was covered in a special cladding that allowed it to change colour and flicked between the red, white and blue of the club's colours – and those of the Stars and Stripes. Buck Schulz would diplomatically say it also represented the colours of the Union Jack, but no one really believed him.

This was a truly modern stadium. It had a hotel, bars, restaurants, shops and its own Tube station underneath. It was what it was meant to be – a spectacle and tourist attraction right in the heart of London. Where better to site yourself to attract that global audience? It was so far removed from Roots Hall or even the old Scott Park ground where I had my trial that it was bordering on grotesque. Equally as grotesque was the reflection I saw in the glass doors that led to the club's offices within.

With no other option, I had chosen to combine the two surviving suit halves I had at the house. To make matters worse, they had been in a black bin bag in the loft for god knows how long. I was now wearing neon blue trousers with more creases than Gordon Ramsay's forehead and an equally crumpled black blazer that had faded to a turgid dark green. Both stank of damp and dust. And I was running late. What a way to make an impression.

Helen, the chief exec's PA, inquired as to whether I'd had a rough night and offered me the use of the men's room if I needed to sort myself out. She looked puzzled when I emerged a few minutes later looking no different from when I went in.

Such was the size of the stadium that we needed to take the lift to get to the floor we needed and we walked out onto a plush landing with the walls decorated with pictures of players from the club's history. They were all in colour and HD-quality because that history had only amounted to eight or nine years, although they had achieved much in terms of silverware in that time.

I was shown into the office of Sean Clark, the club's chief exec, who also seemed to be in high definition. His shirt was as white as a Daz advert and pressed to perfection. It accentuated the orange glow of his face and was framed by the tidiest beard I have ever seen. There wasn't a single hair out of place. I assumed he would be groomed similarly all over. Then he caught me staring at his glistening white teeth and I realised I hadn't yet shaken the hand he'd extended a minute or so earlier.

'Thanks Helen,' he said. 'So, Richard, welcome to LCU.' It took me a second to work out the abbreviation of the club. I finally shook his hand and we took our seats as Helen re-entered with a cup of tea for me and a coffee for the luminous yuppie sat opposite. He gave me a moment as I scanned his impressive office. He obviously liked using it to amplify his power – it was certainly making up for something. He sat behind a huge glass desk engraved with the club's badge and behind him was a vast window that looked out into the stadium and the brilliant green of the pitch beyond. It was magnificent. One wall was covered in shelves filled with books and files, and on the other was a mural of the City United players from two seasons ago as they lifted the Premier League trophy. There had been little to smile about since. Four managers, a huge turnover of players, a failure to qualify for the Champions League at the end of last season and a mid-table position so far this time around. I didn't say it out loud, but it seemed like desperate times called for desperate measures. The ball was firmly in my court.

'I've seen the video from the game the other night, your trial as it were,' said Clark. 'I have to say I was more than a little surprised. Not sure I would've offered you a contract off the back of that one performance, but Mr Schulz seems to like you and the man gave his word.' He said those final words as though he was less than impressed with his boss.

'Yeah, he seems a nice guy, Mr Schulz. For an American billionaire football club owner that is.' My slight attempt at humour was met with a stony face.

'You've not played professionally before, have you?'

It took me a second to realise he wanted an answer. 'Er no, nope.'

'OK, good. Well, let me explain how this works as it can be tricky to get your head around all the different parts and details yeah?' I nodded in agreement and he continued. 'At LCU, all our deals are done using our agent friend Mr Mario Gonzales over there…'

I turned to where Clark had indicated and jumped in my seat when I saw a pot-bellied Hispanic guy with a bushy moustache sat in the corner of the room with a huge cigar in his mouth. Only now could I smell it, and him.

'Where the fuck did he come from?'

It turned out that he came from the dark and seedy underbelly of football that often gets dismissed, ignored or brushed under a very expensive carpet paid for with cash delivered in a plain brown envelope. You see, there was something of a scam going on at LCU. Sean Clark had been in football for decades and he would've been earning a decent wedge in his job at one of the biggest clubs in world football. But no matter how far up the ladder he climbed, he would never get as much as the players. In comparison, his yearly salary was a pittance and a source of great jealousy. So he brought in Mario Gonzales, through whom nearly all of the club transfers and contract negotiations went. Sean would agree massively inflated salaries and bonuses for the players, who would then pay an inflated percentage to their new agent, who in turn would pay it into a company whose secretary and fellow director just happened to be Clark's long-term girlfriend, who spent most of her days shopping, lunching and getting spray tans. It was all a big con so that Clark could bleed money out of the club – or Buck Schulz to be precise – and line his already tidy pockets. The players were forced to accept Gonzales as their agent or they wouldn't be able to sign for the club. You couldn't blame them really. He would tell them they would get X number of thousands per week after the deductions and he and Clark would do the maths and sort out the formalities. That's what you paid an agent to do anyway, and they were still getting huge amounts a week for kicking around an inflated pig's gut, so they weren't really that bothered.

And that was the scam Clark was trying to pull with me, despite the relatively shit deal on the table.

'You're an unknown quantity, Richard. You're clearly not your average footballer. This is a huge risk for LCU just signing you, both in terms of reputation and finance. But I think we are being very generous with the deal Mr Gonzales has negotiated on your behalf. It's all ready to sign. It's just a deal until the end of this season with an option for two more years, with us, of course, holding the option. Your salary will be a flat £3,000 per week. Mario's fee is 35 per cent off the gross. You just need to sign here, here and here. Don't worry about the rest of it, just formalities, and we can get the ball rolling.'

Clark held out a London City United-branded pen for me to sign the papers on his desk. I leaned forward and took it, but my brain was still trying to run through the numbers. £3k a week is £12k a month, which is £156k a year, but Mario takes 35 per cent, which leaves me just over £100k before tax, but less than £40k after tax because I've got to pay tax on the full amount, and then I have to split what's left 50-50 with Keith, so it's less than £20k a year. So I'll actually be taking home about £375 a week. I dropped the pen.

'It's not enough,' I told Clark. He slumped back in his soft leather chair with a grimace on his face and smoothed down his beard. Not that a hair was out of place. It was still immaculate. Then he stared at me as if he were looking into my soul and didn't break eye contact for a couple of minutes until I relented and dropped my gaze. He took that as a signal of victory.

'Get offered three grand a week to play football often do you? Let me be blunt Rich, you are fat and you're old and you're a complete joke. Everyone thinks so. A gimmick. I really don't want to go anywhere near you or this deal, but our glorious and eccentric owner has insisted I must. It's pathetic. I think you remind him of his dead son or something or a cattle he had back on the ranch as a kid. You'll make the news for a couple of weeks and then you'll fade away. These two extra years will disappear – they're only really on this contract to make you feel good, they'll never happen – and then you'll go back to your sad little life doing whatever you do now. Working in a pub, isn't it? We're basically giving you a few thousand pounds for absolutely nothing. You'll get your moment in the spotlight, get to pretend to be a footballer for a bit and hang around with the real players – hey, you might even get your knob sucked by some over-inflated bimbo at a nightclub, Horatio Emmett will show you where's best – and at the end of it all, we all go our own separate ways. All you need to do is agree to give Mario a slice of the pie and everyone's happy. Sign here, and perhaps then you'll be able to afford a proper fucking suit.'

The journey home seemed to take an age. It was as though someone had smeared the tracks with treacle and the wheels of the train just kept spinning, but the carriage going nowhere. It reminded me of a holiday we once took in the Welsh countryside when Tilson was about four or five. We tried to walk through a muddy field as a shortcut back from the only shop for miles around, but our boots kept getting stuck. Then a herd of cows – about seven or eight of them – began to traipse their way over towards us. We were trespassers in their field. We tried to speed up, but just couldn't because of the mud. In the end, I had to lift Tilson up onto my shoulders – the runny mud and cow shit dripping from his wellies onto my jacket in the process – and then I attempted a fast sort of waddle with my legs flailing out from side to side rather than front to back in the hope I could move across the ground quicker. Being much lighter than me, Julie had got across the field much quicker and managed to climb up over the stile to the safety of the road before turning to take a picture of me and Tilson. I had a pained and panicked expression on my face because I knew the cows were really closing in by that point, but Tilson was chuckling his little heart out on my shoulders like he'd been told the world's funniest joke. My god, I love that photo.

I had taken the train out of LCU's stadium to Tower Hill, walked round to Fenchurch Street, got the overground back to Leigh-on-Sea and walked back from there to the pub. Other than my family, mud and cows, I thought about the contract on the way home. Yeah, £375 a week isn't to be sniffed at. I'm fully aware that's a lot of money for some people. But I was hoping for thousands. Tens of thousands, in fact. This was meant to be a get-rich-quick scheme, but two of those words would no longer apply. A 'get scheme' just doesn't have the same ring to it. It even doesn't make sense.

Keith must have seen me coming up the road from the kitchen of the flat as he opened the door just as I got there with my keys in hand. Honestly, I could really have done without him at that point. All that swaggering and laddishness. But I needed someone to punch, so he could've filled a role.

'Geez,' he said, hands out offering up that one word – not even a full word – as both a greeting and a question. I puffed my cheeks out and shook my head.

'It's not good mate. They made a proper offer and all that, but it was nothing like what we talked about. Nowhere near. I said no.'

'Yeah, yeah, I know all that,' he replied bluntly. How did he know?

'How do you know?' I asked.

'Because Buck fackin' Schulz is upstairs in the living room having a cuppa in your World's Greatest Dad mug.' Shit.

When Sean Clark demanded I sign his stinking contract and insulted the two halves of my suit, I only had one response. It was two words long. I hated that side of what football had become – a corporate juggernaut driven by cash-hungry loons and where the fans and the actual game itself were almost an unwanted by-product. It was all money and business. And where there is money, there is greed and corruption. Before, I had thought Buck Schulz would be the embodiment of that evil soul. He was, after all, a mega-rich out-sider. But having spoken to him at the trial, I knew he wasn't that at all. No, the real Devil at play here was Clark – a sneaky, slimy little cockwomble who had weaselled his way into the sport I loved and was destroying it from the inside out. Did I want a contract at

London City United? You bet I did. But did I want his offer of a cheap and nasty deal that cut a big chunk out for his scumbag mate? Did I fuck. And I told him so.

'I'd rather trot out for Southend United for nothing than to sign that worthless piece of shit,' I'd said, and then marched out of his office. And just to rub it in, I kept his branded pen.

It seemed that during that epic journey home and my stroll down memory lane to happier family times, Mr Schulz had called the club to see when he'd be able to unveil his rather unconventional new signing to the Press and was rather upset to hear that I'd stormed out without signing.

He was now perched on the sofa drinking tea out of an oversized mug that championed my abilities as a father. Tilson had bought it for me, of course, and I didn't let anyone else use it. I'd given Keith a short shrift a few days earlier when I caught him brewing up in it. I mean, he isn't the World's Best at anything, let alone being a dad. And I would've given Buck Schulz the same treatment, but he was telling me in quite industrial terms about his disappointment that I hadn't signed on the dotted line despite me having shaken hands with him on a deal after my trial.

'I judge a man by the word he gives and you've gone back on yours already,' he scowled with a shake of the head and slammed the cup down with too much force for my liking.

The version of events to which he was privy was not quite how I remember it. Clark had clearly been good at making up stories. He told Schulz that I'd demanded £85,000 a week after tax plus bonuses and image rights and a £2million signing on fee, all on a five-year contract. And when Clark suggested we negotiate, I flipped like a toddler told he can't have any more sweets and stormed off – stealing company property in the process.

'What company property?' I asked.

'You stole the man's pen.'

Well, at least one part of Clark's story was true. But then I told Buck my side of things, Mario Gonzales and all.

'No way. Mario has been involved with our club business for many years now and helped us to bring in some of the most talented football players available in the world. We wouldn't have won the Premier League if it wasn't for his input and contacts. If there was anything untoward going on at my club, I'd know about it,' the American said, firmly. He stopped just short of accusing me of 'fake news'.

'Buck, they're all getting paid – Gonzales, Clark, the players – so who's going to rock the applecart by telling you? It does none of them any favours.'

'I'm sorry Richie, but I just don't believe it. I can't believe it. This is my club, my business. Yes, there are other investors and board members but it's my baby, the whole thing. I know what goes on; it's my job to do so. I trust Sean to do a good job and he's doing it – OK, so last season and this haven't been too great, but other than that he's doing great. And I trust Mario to help him to bring the best players to LCU. You coulda been a part of that, but I guess not. I guess this is where we part ways. It's a real shame, it's killing me, but…' he didn't finish the end of that sentence. He just thanked Keith for the tea, took a glance around the flat and then said he might 'see us around'.

Keith saw Schulz down the stairs and out the door. I saw his shoulders drop once he'd closed it and he trudged his way back upstairs. We sat quietly at the kitchen table for a few minutes. The silence was excruciating. Our plan was in tatters. The only other club I could get a trial at now was Southend United, but I knew I didn't have the stomach for that. As my buddy Neil had pointed out, I didn't want to take advantage of the club I loved and risk ruining them. Plus they didn't have the money I wanted either.

Keith broke the silence. 'You facked it right up, didn't you?'

'Don't start. It wasn't worth it,' I said. 'All that for less than £400 a week? Yeah, it was money, but fuck all in the scheme of things. It wasn't worth the risk.'

We sat in silence again and my mind drifted to another disappointing thought. After weeks of salads and exercise and running and lifting things and virtual sobriety to get into something of a reasonable shape, I had nothing to show for it. Regardless of what those personal trainers say, I didn't feel better. There was only one thing for it.

'Beer?' I asked. An olive branch I wasn't all that bothered about extending.

'Yeah. Yeah, I want a beer. But not with you. I'm going into town.'

And with that, Keith grabbed his coat and was down and out the door. Seconds after, I picked up my phone off the table and slid it into my neon blue suit trousers and went downstairs to the pub.

'Pint of whatever's ale of the day and a bag of nuts please love.' I must've said that line at least a dozen times that evening.

8. AGENT EX

NOW, you may think that I'd been pretty lucky on this adventure up until this point. I'd not only had this idea to be hypnotised into becoming a Premier League footballer, but managed to find a hypnotist willing and able to do it and then get a trial match with London City United, who then offered me a contract to become a professional footballer. Me. Over 40 and overweight. And that's not to mention the fact that the actual hypno-football trick worked in the first place. With luck like that, I really should've bought myself a EuroMillions ticket.

But fate was about to roll the dice one more time with it landing firmly in our favour.

It was a Sunday morning and I must admit the Saturday night had ended in a blur. I know there was beer, shots, karaoke and kebabs, but I wasn't entirely sure where they were consumed and in what order. I had been on a downer ever since Buck Schulz left the flat earlier in the week. Keith was still technically my flatmate, but we saw less and less of one another as the days passed, which was fine by me because I'd had just about enough of the bloke. He was really getting on my wick. I had decided that it would soon be time for him to sling his hook because there wasn't any point in putting up with him if our football dreams were in ruins. But in this instance, I didn't even feel like opening my eyes.

I was woken on this Sunday morning by the sound and waft of a broadsheet newspaper as it was dropped on the cold tiled floor next to me. I lifted my head and bumped it on the loo. A flashback told me I'd been sick and slept in the bathroom for convenience purposes. As I looked around it seemed like a bad choice. The dirt around the skirting boards and pipes made me gag. Luckily, I'd already sicked up everything in my body, although my throat now seemed to be trying to detach my brain and sling that out too. God, I had a headache. I finally turned to see Keith stood in the doorway. Surprisingly, he looked fresh-faced and ready to challenge the day. He pointed to the paper, told me to have a look and quickly left the room. It was only then that I realised I was starkers. It was the only time I ever felt sorry for Keith.

I pulled a towel for the bath and wrapped it around myself, groaning all the while like a beached whale calling for its mate. I propped myself up against the side of the bath – looking not too dissimilar to a beached whale myself – and finally picked up the paper. Right there on the front page was a picture featuring the familiar face of Mario Gonzales and the headline: 'Super-agent in contract bung shame.'

The article spoke of an undercover investigation in which Gonzales had been filmed boasting to a bunch of Asian 'businessmen' interested in third-party ownership of footballers in England about how he was able to extract funds from Premier League clubs by negotiating inflated contracts for players and then taking a huge slice off the top. They had been in a strip club where the booze had been flowing and he couldn't help himself but boast. Gonzales was quoted as telling them: 'I get my money and usually send some back to those at the clubs who help the deal go through – chairmen, chief execs, secretaries, and so on. The players are getting paid their money and the clubs earn it back by signing top-quality players whose names help to sell millions in kits and merchandise to fans. It's a win-win-win-win-win.'

Keith reappeared in the bathroom doorway when he heard my yelp of joy, but quickly ducked back out again when he saw that I was now stood up and the towel had dropped to the floor. 'For fuck's sake geez, put your pecker away. You'dve thought you'd learn your lesson by now flashing that thing around. I ain't one of your driving students.'

'Shut up and give me a cuddle,' I replied and chased after him.

It wasn't all perfect. The article didn't mention Sean Clark or really insinuate the investigators knew how deeply Gonzales's fingers were stuck into the London City United pie. But it did mean the agent's involvement in football was off the table for some time – possibly forever – and especially at LCU. Buck Schulz would see to that. It also meant that eight players at LCU were suspended while the club, the FA and the players' union carried out their investigations and reviews into their transfers. That left the squad quite a bit short of eligible, quality players and with the transfer window well and truly closed some time earlier, they could only sign free agents to plug the gap. And because I had never signed for a professional football club before in my life, I was technically one of those free agents. I just had to wait for the phone to ring.

It was more than a week before I got the call from Buck Schulz. During the intervening time, there had been a lot of focus on the administration and ownership of LCU and the pressure was mounting. They had also lost two more matches in the Premier League. On the playing side, they were desperate for reinforcements. But the club as a whole was in desperate need of some positive news to distract the media.

I sheepishly tried to hide the packet of pork scratchings as one of the world's richest men sat opposite me at the Old Bell and tried to persuade me to become a professional footballer. Then I realised that hiding the pack behind the half-drunk pint of ale and two empties in front of me was a lost cause. He was never after me for my physique anyway.

'Listen,' he said moving his chair in a few inches and awkwardly clattering his knees into mine under the table. 'I know you tried to warn me about this and I didn't listen. I'm sorry. OK? I hold my hands up.' He did actually hold his hands up.

'But you've still got Clark at your club Buck. He was as involved as anyone.'

'There's no evidence of that. And if they had any proof, those reporters woulda printed it. He may have been a poor negotiator when it comes to contracts, I admit, but there's nothing to suggest he was in on it. Nothing. But I am going to be more involved in things, for the time being at least, when it comes to the contract side of things. Huh! As if I didn't have enough to do already. But I have seen what you can do on a soccer pitch Richie and I really think you could make a difference to the team and the club at this time. It's a great news story and we could really do with some good news right now. We need you Richie. Please consider it. Not for Sean Clark, but for me. Whadya say?'

I tried to play it cool but then knocked my remaining pork scratchings on the floor and nearly lost the rest of my pint when I bent over to pick them up. It'd be my job to hoover them up in the morning anyway. I regained my composure and told Buck I'd consider it. 'But you have to make it worth my while. None of that cheap-arse nonsense I was offered before.'

'Of course. But don't rip the shit outta it. I didn't get where I am today by throwing my money at every kid with a nice story. Come by again tomorrow and we'll have a new offer for you to discuss. Hopefully you'll stay in the room long enough to sign it this time.'

Buck rose from his seat, told the barmaid to pour me 'one more beer and one only' and chucked a £50 note on the counter. 'You can keep the change doll,' he said with a wink and left the pub.

The smile on my face couldn't have been wider. The football deal was back on and I got a free pint. I loathed the fact I would still have to deal with someone like Sean Clark – the guy should've been exposed and dumped out of football for life along with Gonzales. But at least I would get to enjoy seeing his face as I'm offered a much better contract that he wouldn't be able to get his grubby little mitts on. Perhaps I wouldn't have to pick the pork scratchings up tomorrow after all.

I didn't even bother with a suit this time as I went back to LCU. I was just in jeans, t-shirt and trainers. Keith came with me this time too, but insisted on sitting downstairs near the receptionist rather than coming into Clark's office to discuss the deal. He clearly fancied his chances with the young lady behind the desk. Having seen and heard the fallout from his chat-up lines numerous times over the past few weeks, I was worried he would get us kicked out of the club – or worse – before I'd had the chance to put pen to paper. But my attention was now on Clark, who had been told by Buck to apologise for the last time I was in his office and was now being made to read out the details of the new offer.

'The offer on the table is a basic wage of £45,000 per week plus a £5,000 appearance bonus, £5,000 goal bonus, £2,500 bonus for any assists, and a £7,500 win bonus. You will also go into the club bonus pool too. The initial contract is until the end of the season, but if you make ten appearances it will automatically trigger a two-year extension. Under the terms of the extension, your basic wage will rise to £55,000 per week in the first of those extra years and £65,000 per week in the second. In addition to this, we are offering a signing on fee of £550,000 to be paid in four equal instalments between now and the end of the season.'

There was a stirring in my underpants usually reserved for Julie or a quick five minutes in incognito mode when the house was empty. Having it while in a room with two men was certainly a first.

'I would offer you a pen to sign the contract, but someone stole mine,' Clark added.

'Stop being a smartass,' Schulz said pulling one from inside his blazer. 'You should really be having a medical before we let you sign this, but I'm sure as fuck you wouldn't pass so let's not bother.'

Clark muttered something about him thinking transfers were being done properly now, but Schulz ignored him and added: 'Just do what you did in that practice game a few weeks back and we won't have a problem, OK?'

He looked at both of us for approval. It was more than OK with me. And that was that. At the age of 42 and having never played football at any sort of decent level before in my life, all 20-odd stone of me signed on for a Premier League football club.

9. FAMILY MATTERS

I PUFFED out my cheeks and switched off the engine of my car, glancing over at the beautiful property I called home for so many years. Not anymore though. At least, not at the moment. I tried to swallow but everything became clogged up in my throat. I looked down and saw my hands were trembling. A shiver shot down my spine and made my elbows tingle. *Why did this feel so hard when negotiating the contract was so easy?*

I looked back up at the front of the house again and saw the blinds twitch in Tilson's bedroom. If I had X-ray vision, I would've seen him chuck his PlayStation controller on his bed, scuttle out of his room and across the landing at speed, pounding down the stairs and running to the door as he shouted: 'Muuuuuum. Dad's here.' I watched the front door as he opened it and waved at me like a loon while pulling a silly face. *This is it. You have to do this.*

Julie had been expecting me this time. I rang her in advance and said there was something important that I needed to tell her and Tilson. She asked if I had a new girlfriend. I told her there were several. All of Girls Aloud and the Pussycat Dolls. But I stumbled over the 'cat' and 'Dolls' of the latter and what came out sounded really pervy, so I tried to swallow the phone and hoped it all went away. Instead, she pulled me back from the hole in the ground I was hoping would eat me up by asking if I wanted to stay for dinner. I agreed and then realised it was her test of how serious the thing was I needed to tell her – whether I needed to make a quick getaway or not.

I said yes to dinner. The huge leap I was taking with Keith was a desperate attempt to win back the love of my life and be closer to my son again – to reunite our family – and taking the next step of that journey while sat at the table in our house and eating a meal together seemed like the perfect way to do it.

'Can I get you a beer, Rich?' I hadn't thought for a second that Julie's boyfriend would be there too. But there he was, parading around the living room dressed like a hipster in skinny jeans and an oversized and ripped t-shirt that exposed one of his nipples. His smile dazzled against his perfect face as he offered the beer like he'd been told to be on his best behaviour. I didn't answer.

'Richie,' Julie bellowed from the kitchen, an apron around her waist and tea towel slung over her shoulder. 'Matt just asked if you want a beer. Be polite and answer him please.'

I'd been told. 'No thanks. I'm cutting down.'

'Looks like it,' he said in a bitchy whisper. I looked towards Tilson and then at the kitchen, but it was clear that only I could hear him. I was about to reply with something less subtle when Tilson asked if he could sit next to me at the table. The conversation was stilted and tough-going. Julie – as she did so magnificently at every party or event we went to – did everything she could to include everyone in the conversation. 'Oh, that's interesting don't you think Matt?', 'Really? I think Tilson covered that at school recently didn't you darling?', 'Richie, you've got gravy on your top.' But there was no way I was talking to Matt. He was an intruder in our home, our lives, that dinner and the conversation I intended to have. But it was clear that Julie was setting out her new stall and the pretty boy had his orders to stay put and be polite. So I had to share my big news with him there too.

There's a team of people at London City United dedicated to helping the players' lives run as smoothly as possible when needed. Usually, it's when players move to England from abroad and need to find somewhere to live, schools for their kids or even just to know where the nearest Tesco is.

In the meetings I had with them, they tried to prepare me for the increased media interest in me and my life and suggested I have a sit-down with my family to tell them what was likely to happen. Julie and Tilson were the only family I had now.

Quite rightly, the officials at the club thought I would be of special interest to the Press due to my unique circumstances and physical attributes.

I would also become a special case to the Press because – unbeknown to me at that time – my old friend in the chief exec's office at London City United had now made it his new life's mission to destroy me and my reputation. He hated the fact I had even got a contract with the club let alone one that far outweighed his salary. He was so angry that he now crunched his Extra Strong Mints rather than sucking them.

Sean Clark had already begun leaking information about my signing and current residence to a journalist at the Daily Citizen, a national tabloid newspaper that loved a bit of scandal, sleaze and gossip. I wasn't party to the conversation of course, but I heard later that within minutes of me leaving his office Clark had got on the blower to tell Jim Neale all about me.

He told his lapdog to dig and sling as much dirt as possible my way and even suggested I had been the last player brought to the club by dodgy Mario Gonzales.

So it was a good job that I told Julie and Tilson to prepare themselves for the shit-storm that may be brewing and coming our way. Matt? Well, I couldn't give a flying fuck about the muscle-bound prick so long as it didn't bounce back onto my wife and son. He couldn't contain his laughter at my new profession though.

Tilson, it must be said, seemed completely bemused at the prospect of his dad signing for London City United. At first, he thought I was straight out fibbing and when I promised I would never do that to him he just said: 'But you're really rubbish at football Dad. You don't even get picked for your team in the park.' That set Matt off again until Julie gave him a look. That look.

Tilson went up to his room after dinner to play on his PlayStation again. While Turbo Curbo put his bulging muscles to good use and loaded the dishwasher, my wife told me in no uncertain terms that if I hurt Tilson with my idiotic caper then she would cut off my bollocks and kick them around Roots fucking Hall like she was Alan fucking Shearer. She always used Shearer in her football analogies because she used to fancy him when he was still playing.

'I don't want to be dragged into this nonsense either, really,' she added. 'But if Tilson comes home from school having been picked on because of you or we have to force our way through paparazzi photographers to get to the shops or whatever then we'll have some serious fucking words, alright?'

'Is that a "good luck" then?'

But I got the picture. And so did the photographer who'd been sent to tail me by Jim Neale.

I never saw him parked out the front across the road from the house as I left and neither did Julie. But there we were the next morning on the front page of the Daily Citizen. Me walking away from the house while taking a bite out of a slice of leftover apple pie, while Julie was stood in the doorway in the background with her arms crossed and a face like a disappointed estranged wife – which is exactly what she was, to be honest.

OBESE-CITY UNITED

Prem crisis club sign unknown 23st bloater - aged 42

CRISIS-hit London City United are trying to quell their desperate player shortage by signing a 23-stone unknown who lives above a pub.

Richard Price, 42, who recently split from wife Julie, has never played professionally, with his footballing highlight winning Clubman of the Year for park side Leigh Ramblers Vets.

A former teammate told The Citizen: 'It's an absolute joke. He's s**t.'

Full story - Pages Four and Five, and SportCitizen

Across the double-page spread inside the paper were exaggerated tales from my non-existent footballing career, more quotes from some people I had considered mates taking the piss out of my ability to play – 'We used to say he had a head like a Toblerone because you never knew which direction the ball would come off. But if it were a Toblerone he'd probably try to eat it' – and alleged details of my private life. In the sports section they tore into the club for signing me and laid bare all of its failings, hinting at a connection between me and Mario Gonzales but not going as far as saying it outright. Thankfully for the preservation of my testicles, the paper had not mentioned Tilson by name and just referred to me as a 'dad-of-one'. They called Julie a 'pretty blonde', which I guess she could take as a compliment. They also hadn't got hold of details of the incident that ended my driving instructor career, but it was surely only a matter of time.

All this nonsense had started even before my signing had been announced by London City United. The club had arranged a press conference for the Monday afternoon so they could control the flow of information and everything else, but Sean Clark had given his dog the scent and he had delivered by the Sunday morning. The cat was not so much out the bag, but now walking round with a 15ft luminous green placard announcing its arrival.

My phone was going off all day. I checked and responded the first few times, but then I just put it to one side as it buzzed more than a nympho's vibrator. Text messages, phone calls, Facebook notifications, emails. People I hadn't spoken to in decades were trying to get in touch to either congratulate me or take the piss. Usually the latter. Memories of the endless bullying at school came flooding back. Some of these messages were from those people, getting their chance again after all these years. Outside the flat was a gathering of around ten or 15 journalists and photographers waiting to get a word from me or a photo. I didn't want to give them either, and the club had told me not to speak to them.

Keith was nowhere to be seen. We had a lot of work to do before I went into the club for the press conference and started training with the team, but he'd gone AWOL. I sneaked downstairs to see if he was in the pub and was met by an enormous roar of cheering. Keith had invited a load of people in for a celebratory drink or two or eight. It was only 10.30am. Now they clamoured for me rather than the booze my business partner had been supplying them, presumably funded by his slice of the signing on fee. They wanted selfies, hugs, autographs, tickets, kit, all sorts. I must admit, although I was frosty at first, I did start to warm to it a little. But they were relentless and it soon became a draining and repetitive experience. It was the same conversation over and over, and the same sycophantic plaudits. One guy I was certain I'd never clapped eyes on in my life told me: 'I always knew you'd make it someday.'

As I looked away for a second, I noticed for the first time that there was a line of photographers on ladders up against the window. They were all snapping away; bagging pictures of LCU's latest signing getting back-slapped and glad-handed by a bunch of drunken strangers in a pub before midday. I needed to get out of there. Not just at that moment, but in general. I couldn't live in a pub anymore and I couldn't live with Keith anymore. Yeah, he was vital to the success of the plan but the guy was a time bomb. He was destructive and being near a pub 24/7 was not helping.

Job number two for the day would be finding somewhere new to live as soon as possible. Job number one was the press conference.

I don't know if you've ever seen or been to a press conference where a new player is unveiled, but it's a bit like feeding time at the zoo. It was being held at the stadium and, first off, I had to pose in about a thousand different photos while holding up a club shirt or scarf. Some in the club's PR department wanted to do one of those 'announce' videos where it's like a glorified version of the mystery sportsman round on A Question of Sport until they reveal the new signing right at the end. But seeing as everyone knew who I was already, they scrubbed that plan. Plus Buck Schulz had decreed I was an old school footballer so we'd do things the old school way. There were pictures taken from the front, back, both sides, from beneath and above. One photographer asked if the manager – an Italian by the name of Franco Capece – would be posing with his new signing, but he was cut off swiftly. It was only at that point that I realised I hadn't yet met or spoken to the manager – or gaffer as I was sure I would have to call him. Buck said we'd do that later and just get the photos done and dusted for now.

Next, the club's PR and media folks gave me a little grooming before I was brought out onto a stage in front of the gathered journalists from newspapers, magazines, TV, radio, websites and blogs.

I recognised one of the presenters from Sky Sports News and gave him a thumbs up before realising I didn't actually know him. Having already had an informal introduction via the front page of the Daily Citizen (and several pages inside), there were a few more interested parties here than would normally attend such a function.

It started off pretty tame...

'How does it feel to join such a big club at your age?' Generic response of being delighted to be here and doing all I can to help the team succeed in the remainder of the season.

'How do you think you will fit into the team?' Diplomatic reply, saying that my job is to do my best on the training ground each day, work hard, impress the manager and let him make the decisions about who fits into his team.

There were then questions about my past, my lack of experience, and so on. I repeated the same line that I'd given to Buck Schulz in the stand at my trial match about anxiety and a lack of confidence holding me back, but that the counselling I had got from Keith helped me to overcome that and I was now ready to seize the opportunity.

Then came a barrage about my weight and whether I thought I was a bad role model for kids. It all seemed to go on for ages and LCU's media guy seemed happy for that to happen. He'd probably been told by Sean Clark to let the sharks inside the cage for as long as possible. The journalists just kept asking the same questions but in slightly different wording just so they got the chance to hear their own voice. Would I go on a strict diet? How much would I have to lose before I could play for the first team? How much do I normally eat on a day-to-day basis? Have I got clearance from a medical professional to play? Did I have diabetes? Was I worried about having a heart attack during a match? Had the club put any additional safety precautions in place? (I would have to check the latter).

Then, in an instant, it shifted up a few gears.

'Why did you split up with your wife?' Shit. Even the press officer tried to step in and wave that one away, but the guy carried on.

'Can you explain the police caution you got for flashing at a teenage girl?'

'I did not...' The press officer – a guy called Gary – cut me off, said the question was out of order and would not be answered.

The grubby guy wouldn't back down. He told Gary it was a valid question and of interest to the fans; they would want to know what sort of person their club had signed. Gary, to be fair, held firm. He said there was no arrest, no offence and that reporting otherwise would be followed by legal action from the club for defamation. We probably wouldn't have a leg to stand on seeing as I did, technically, flash at a teenage girl.

'So, what does your son make of all this?' continued the hack like a dog with a bone.

'That's enough Jim, alright. Let's not get personal. Let's keep families out of this. Now if there are no more questions about football for Richie then we'll call an end to this for today. Thank you all for coming.'

And with that, Gary was ushering me up from my chair towards the exit and telling me not to worry about 'that guy'.

Then a voice said: 'You're a fat fucking joke mate.' It wasn't shouted or even said in my direction as such, but it was aimed at me. Obviously. And it rankled.

'Listen pal,' I said turning back to the pack with my blood boiling. Gary the press officer was trying to pull me back and telling me to say nothing, but this hack was a horrible little shit with arrogance and a sense of entitlement. I wanted my say and for him to hear it. 'I appreciate the fact that one day, long ago, you wanted to be a footballer and it never worked out for you. You probably weren't good enough, like hundreds of thousands of other blokes across the world. Good for you that you sought to stay involved by writing about the sport you love, except you don't love it any more, do you? That's why you're so full of anger and bitterness towards it now and won't let it go. If you can't have it, no one can. That's why you hammer England whenever they have an off game – OK, so I grant you they have a few of those – but it's why you hammer the players constantly and look for fault in everything even if the players and the coaches and the managers are trying their best. But let me lay a few facts down in front of you pal. People at this football club – professional, experienced football people at a championship-winning football club, not just journalists, football people – they watched me play and decided that I have something that will add to this very talented squad. That I was worth a punt. I'll take their opinion over yours any day, you sad little man. And you ask about my weight and about being a role model? Well, no, I don't want to look like this. Of course I want to be in better shape. Who doesn't? I'd fucking love to be all buff like Thor or Matt fucking Curbish-ley...' (OK, so I didn't mean for his name to slip out and that would come back to bite me on my rather fat arse, but I was on a roll and blinded by anger). '...and I'm trying to shift the weight. I am. But yes, I am a positive role model for people who are over-weight, the chubbies of the world, and those who have been held back or pushed down by bullies like you. I'm carrying a torch for them to follow, right? Because if you put your mind to something and have the support of the people around you, your loved ones, then you can achieve your dreams – even if that dream is to be a professional footballer player. Got it?'

Part of me had expected the journalists in the room to break out into rapturous applause and cheering, but Gary finally ushered me away with half of them in stunned silence and the rest giggling in pity. Video clips of the confrontation were on the news that even-ing and went viral across social media. I thought I'd blown it again until I got a text from Tilson. 'Lol dad. Well done. Proud x.'

10. FIRST DAY

I DIDN'T sleep much that night as I thought about the press conference, but it had put a new level of resolve in me. I was doing this to win Julie back and to show Tilson I was someone to be proud of, but now it was also to prove the bullies wrong. I would see this through.

By 6.30am, I was up and dressed and ready for my first day of training as a professional footballer. I didn't have to be at the training ground until 10am and a lackey from the club would be coming to pick me and Keith up so we wouldn't be late or get lost. The same guy had come to the flat the night before – I hadn't been able to get out of the pub into more appropriate accommodation yet – with bags full of stuff from the club. Outfits and that. There were training kits, tracksuits, trainers, football boots, shinpads, club gloves, club hats, club snood, club thermals. And there wasn't just one set of each, there were three or four. Our living room looked like we'd just robbed the London City United Megastore of all its merchandise. The lackey also measured me up for a few club suits and shirts that I'd have to wear to some games. The lad was only about 23 but carried himself like a 58-year-old financial adviser on his third marriage and having undergone a humour replacement operation. What it had been replaced with I was yet to find out.

'Have you got any club toenail clippers?' I joked. But not even a hint of a smirk. He just said he'd bring some in the morning when he picked me up.

'For the rest of the week, the club will send me in a car to collect you and take you to the training ground and to any matches you are involved in to ensure that you get to the right place at the right time, or earlier. After that, it will be your responsibility to get to the training ground or the designated collection point or arrival point for any matches you are involved in. Failure to do so will likely result in a club fine, do you understand?'

'Yes Dad.' Fuck's sake.

As part of my contract negotiations with the club, I had insisted that my 'therapist' Keith be allowed to attend training and matches with me unquestioned by the club's management team, who I had still yet to meet it must be said.

'If that's what gets you ticking on the pitch, no problem,' Buck Schulz had said as his chief exec looked on disapprovingly. This therapist would be another one for Sean Clark's journalist hound Jim Neale to get his claws in to.

I was good and ready to go, but the problem I had was that Keith had continued his celebrations throughout much of the weekend and into last night. How the guy still had a liver left was beyond me. He hadn't got to bed until after 1am and when the lackey honked his horn outside the flat to indicate it was time to go to training, Keith was heaving his guts up into the toilet bowl wearing only his grey and stained undercrackers. With a lot of agonising effort, we managed to get him fully clothed and down into the car in 20 minutes. But then he insisted that we stop at a McDonald's on the way to pick him up three sausage and egg McMuffins, three hash browns and very large, very black coffee.

'Geez, I don't have to run around, do I? That's you. And you don't want me chucking up everywhere at the training ground, do ya? I won't do no harm. Just whizz through the drive-thru. It'll only take a second. Go on Michael, swing in there son.' The lackey's name was Martin.

And no harm? Guess which one of us got snapped by paparazzi sat in the front of a car going through the drive-thru at McDonald's? I'll give you a clue: it wasn't Keith as he was too busy being sick in a bin on the other side of the car park. The guy was becoming more of a liberty the further this went on. He was threatening to bring the whole thing crashing down before it got going.

I was in a dark mood for the rest of the journey, although Keith's wellbeing did actually take a turn for the better once the McMuffins were down his neck and the coffee drunk. My mood also improved once we reached the training ground. My word. It was a world away from anything I'd seen before. To be fair, I had only seen Southend United's training ground before, which wasn't much more than a few pitches in front of a big clubhouse. We used to get a sandwich from the Waitrose round the corner and then go and watch the players train. I'd even been to a few birthday parties in that club-house. But you couldn't do that here. This was something else. You couldn't even get past the gates unless you were part of the club, and now we were. As we drove through the security barriers, the hairs on my arms stood to attention as a tingle of excitement shot through my body. Honestly, it was magnificent.

The roads inside were jet black and immaculately smooth. All the grass, flowers, trees and shrubs that lined the road were manicured to perfection. London City United probably spent more on that than Southend did on maintaining their whole training club for a season. But the fauna wasn't what got me excited though. What did were the acres of the greenest grass known to man out in front of me that made up the training pitches. They shone brilliantly. I could see the racks of metal men lined up to act as a wall to protect the goals behind them. I could see a group of players – youth teamers I guessed – jogging around on the far side of the field, and others sprinting in and out of cones and going through drills in front of dozens of barking coaches. It was a football paradise.

It all slowly disappeared from view as we pulled up in front of the gargantuan main building – a space-age-looking construction with an enormous glass front offering a glimpse into an atrium decorated with giant portraits of players in action, trophies and a display fountain.

As we started to get out of the car, we were greeted by a man in a club suit who I recognised immediately. Well, his wheelchair was a bit of a giveaway. Jamie Andrews had come through the ranks at London City United all the way to the first team and had represented England at various levels up to Under 21s. He was primed for the top. But then he was hit by a drunk driver while out with some friends and lost the use of his legs. The legend went that he had pushed one of his pals to safety in the knowledge that the car would hit him full-on. They say that if he hadn't done that, he wouldn't have been hit. The club had paid for his medical care and rehabilitation, and then offered him a job. They didn't have a job in mind at the time, but that later turned into him becoming manager of the training ground complex. Jamie greeted me with a warm handshake, reaching out to also grip my forearm with his left hand as he did.

'Hi there Richie, welcome to London City United. Great to have you here. I'm Jamie. And you must be Keith. I'm glad you're not the one training today mate cos you look like shit. Don't worry, there's plenty of coffee inside.' His smile was genuine and friendly and it didn't drop from his face for the next hour as he gave us a quick tour of the facilities inside the main building. Gyms, physio rooms, massage rooms, changing rooms, restaurant, smaller restaurant, coffee shop, sleeping area, counselling area – you name it, it was here. There were even study rooms for players learning new languages or wanting to gain qualifications. And all the staff in the building seemed just as welcoming as Jamie had.

This was also the first time I got to meet some of my new teammates in person as they arrived for training. These were world famous footballers I had only seen on the telly before and they were now strolling past me as casual as anything. Well, they were just at work I suppose. To be honest, most of them were shorter than I expected but all looked solid, if you know what I mean. You could tell they were athletes. They all had a smile for Jamie – I think everyone agreed that he was a lovely guy – but not so much for me. Really much less welcoming. It seems that footballers can be quite insecure and any new arrival is greeted, initially at least, with extreme caution. Competitiveness ran in their blood with everything. You may not be after their position, but you may earn more than them, drive a nicer car than them, have a prettier wife or girlfriend than them, or even have the squad number they want. The caution and wariness they show are amplified extraordinarily when the new arrival is an inexperienced, overweight 42-year-old whose temperament was already under scrutiny.

In fact, only two players stopped to talk to me (although it's possible the others thought I was a competition winner on a visit). The first was Horatio Emmett, my Brazilian buddy from the trial match. He told me he was delighted I'd signed, that he was looking forward to scoring from more of my crosses and that I was 'filth'. I just thanked him.

The second was the club captain, Adam Bush. I would like to tell you that he gave me an equally warm greeting, but that would be a lie. Bush was a 6ft 4in man mountain of muscle. He had signed for the club in his early 20s for £30million when £30million was a lot of money. He had become an icon in the red, white and blue stripes of London City United and was also the captain of England. But more importantly, he was one of the strongest driving forces at the club. He had the ear of the owner, chairman and the chief executive. He had the power to make or break managers or players at LCU – and he hadn't taken a particular shine to me.

'I don't know whose cock you sucked to get here or how many times you did it, but you're already a fucking embarrassment to this club and yourself and I will do all in my power to ensure you never pull on the shirt and leave this club without playing one second of football.'

I didn't respond.

'That's what I thought. Pathetic,' he said, and strode off towards the changing rooms.

I walked back to where Keith and Jamie were talking and puffed out my cheeks.

'Intense that guy. He always like that?'

'Ah, Adam's great,' said Jamie. 'He just likes to win at everything. If you play well and help the team then you'll get along fine, I promise. Fuck it up and he'll kill you. Probably actual like.'

'Ha. Right, OK then,' I said as the butterflies began to whip up a fervour in my stomach as I realised what was coming next. 'I suppose I had better go in there and win over the rest of my teammates at training with my dazzling personality and silky skills then.'

I started to turn, but Jamie halted me. 'Oh no. You're not training with the first team yet,' he said with a laugh and pointing at my stomach. 'Sean said we've got to get a few of those spare tyres off you first before you get near first team training. You've been allocated your very own personal trainer to sort you out a fitness regime for the next few weeks, where is…?' He started looking around him and then spotted his target coming out of a doorway in conversation. 'Ah, you'll be with Harley over there.'

A tall and extremely well-built young man bounded over to where we stood. 'Here he is,' added Jamie. 'Richie Price meet Harley Wells, Harley meet our new signing Richie Price.'

Harley Wells took one look at me and his face dropped. 'Fucking hell. What the fuck are you doing here?'

11. OH HARLEY

I T'S safe to say that Harley Wells wasn't entirely pleased to see me, but a glare from Jamie was enough to chide him and make him more cordial towards me, at least for now.

You see, as you may have guessed, Harley and I had actually met before and that first encounter left him with the wrong impression of me – and him in handcuffs being carted off to the nick in the back of a police car.

Let me explain what happened. Back then Julie and I were still together, but the strain on our finances was beginning to tell and it meant that we had to sell her beloved Mercedes C-Class and get something a bit smaller, cheaper and more economical. She was upset about it, but it was needs must at that time.

Julie sorted out the sale online through eBay or something and the guy had come down to view the car while I was out with one of my driving students (this time keeping my privates private). During his conversation with Julie, he mentioned how tricky it was getting to ours on the bus and train especially when he had to leave his wife at home with a newborn and two other children. My wife has always been a compassionate soul, except when it comes to me, and she told the guy that I would be more than happy to run the car up to him. It was no bother, apparently. I think it was her way of getting revenge for selling her car and said as much, but that just led to another argument.

I know it sounds incredibly snobby, but the guy – Ahmed – lived on a housing estate in East London. I've seen the TV shows and documentaries and they're never portrayed as the nicest of places, are they? It's all gangs of youths, drug dealers and junkies in grotty stairwells and people arguing. I wasn't looking forward to the hand-over anyway, but Julie had sold me a right pup by arranging it at night time. 'Well you can't go during the day because you've got driving students, haven't you?' She had a point I suppose.

It was about an hour's drive from home and I found the estate with no problem. Ahmed was waiting for me by a row of garages with a wide smile and a warm handshake.

'Lovely, lovely. I'm going to park it in the garage straight away if you don't mind,' he said. 'It's best not to leave cars out around here, if you know what I mean.' Christ, even the locals are worried.

I had to go up to Ahmed's flat to sign the documents and get the cheque. He was a funny guy and his wife Saanvi made me a cup of tea and told me to take a couple of chocolate Hobnobs, so I couldn't grumble really.

Ahmed had already transferred a large chunk of the cash over to our joint account as a deposit and a show of faith that he wasn't a timewaster. And when he said he would just pop to the other room to get the rest of it, I assumed he would come back with a cheque that I'd fold into my wallet and be swiftly on my toes to the train station around the corner to get home.

But as I dunked my third Hobnob into my tea and made small talk with Saanvi about the joys of parenthood and tried to remember Tilson when he was as small as their new one, Ahmed returned with a brown envelope packed full of cash. Ten and a half thousand pounds in £50s and £20s. I protested, but he said that was the only way he could do it. A couple of minutes later, those Hobnobs in the warmth of his lounge were just a sweet memory. I was walking down a dark and piss-stinking stairwell just like those people in films who get stabbed or mugged or both and left for dead. I had the most extreme sense of paranoia I'd ever experienced. Every pair of eyes was most definitely pointed in my direction and each knew exactly what was tucked in the inside pocket of my coat despite the fact it was zipped up to my chin and buttoned down too. They were surely all just biding their time before they pounced. A pack of lionesses circling a dumb antelope just before dinner time or some other terrifying David Attenborough shit in the wild. I was sweating buckets both through the stress and the warmth of a winter coat on a warm autumn night, and I was trembling uncontrollably. But there was no way I was undoing the coat and allowing them easier access to the wads of cash hidden inside. I heard footsteps coming from further up in the stairwell, so I sped up and race-walked out across the courtyard towards the main road. When I got 20 yards from the stairs, I braved a glance to see who was behind me. Nothing. I must've imagined it. Then a tall, athletic-looking figure emerged from the darkness and began striding in my direction. I hadn't imagined it. The man had his hood up so I couldn't see his face, but he was coming right for me. Fuck. He was coming to get me. This was all a scam, I knew it. Shitting bollocking fuck. Ahmed was in on it too, I bet, so he can get a half-price Mercedes. Fucking Hobnobs.

I turned a corner and the train station came into view. Its glowing lights welcoming me like a warm hug from a cuddly aunt. Not that I had an aunt. The station had security guards and cameras and people bustling around, so I knew I would be safe there. I looked back and couldn't see the scoundrel following me anymore. I sped up even more, while keeping my head down to avoid eye contact with anyone. They'd be able to tell from one look in my eyes that I had £10.5k in my pocket.

Then BAM! A man, a very large and solid man, blocked my path and we collided. I bounced back in a daze, but he barely budged an inch. I looked up and saw a young man, about 6ft 4ins tall and built like an ox. He had his hood up so I couldn't see his face that well, but I recognised the top and him from moments earlier – it was the guy from the estate. He had carried on following me and now he'd caught me. Now, for certain, he was going to knife me in the stomach and steal my money. I would be left bleeding at the roadside as I cried out the name of my wife and son. I didn't want to die.

To be honest, what actually happened next was a bit of a blur. What I can say for sure is that 15 minutes later I was sat in a security office at the station, still alive, nursing a steaming hot cup of sugary tea while speaking to a police officer. I had not been stabbed, but the cash was gone from my pocket. The good news for me was that the culprit had been apprehended at the scene and was now en route to a local police station for processing.

That was until they checked the CCTV.

They made me watch it too. Six times.

It showed an overweight man, around 5ft 10ins tall, who was wearing a large coat and walking quickly with his head down. The figure (i.e. me) walked past the entrance of the station, then realised that he had done so by mistake and performed an about turn without looking up and walked straight into a bloke coming the other way – aka Harley Wells. As the two men collided, the younger guy stepped back and held his hands up in apology but the older bloke, for some reason, unzipped his coat, reached inside, pulled out an envelope full of cash and threw it at the younger man before running off hysterically while shouting something that even without sound looks like: 'Just take it, don't hurt me.'

Harley was then seen on camera picking up the envelope from the floor and standing bemused like he was on some hidden camera show. A minute later his smile disappeared as two security guards bundled him to the ground having been alerted to a 'mugging'.

As fate has a habit of being a bit of a dick, a trip to the cells – however short – meant promising non-league footballer Harley missed a cup game he was meant to play in and that his team lost without him. The finger of blame for that was pointed at him and then by him at me. Hence the not-so-polite welcome.

I did say sorry though.

Right now, Harley was being put in his place by training ground manager Jamie – he even did that in a friendly manner – and I was told I would be embarking on a dedicated fitness and nutrition programme for at least a fortnight before I could even consider kicking a ball. So it turned out that Keith, who was still nursing a mammoth hangover boosted only by the sight of some of the LCU women's team arriving for training, could've stayed at home after all.

Now, if they ever decide to make a film out of my story, which I'm sure they will at some stage, then this is the bit when the montage will kick in because the next fortnight or so was pretty dull and repetitive.

The montage will flick between Harley Wells joyously torturing me to near-death with treadmills, sit-ups, weights, running, cycling, salads and skipping. You might even see me run to the top of some steps and jump around like a champion. You'll also see Keith and me using our new-found wealth to move out of the flat above the Old Bell pub and me moving into a plush apartment block just a stone's throw from Tower Bridge and London City United's stadium. You'll see me going to test drive an Aston Martin and then realising it's not really the right car for a man of my girth as my belly folds over the bottom of the steering wheel. I wore that car like a coat. Instead, I get myself one of those BMW X5s which are much more forgiving. As we head to December, you'll see the Christmas trees going up and me training in the snow with plumes of steam rising from my body and bright red face in the cold as first-teamers point and laugh. You'll see me buying a top-notch electric guitar and amp for Tilson and the magnificent smile on his face when he opens it up on Christmas morning. He also gets tickets to a heavy metal concert and you'll see me cowering in the corner at that gig as Tilson and hundreds of other youngsters throw themselves into one another in front of a wall of noise. You'll see me delivering Julie a replacement Mercedes C-Class with a pack of Hobnobs on the passenger seat as a peace offering. I also give her the cockapoo puppy she'd always been on at me about getting. I didn't care for dogs too much, but I didn't live at the house anymore so I wouldn't have to pick up its shit in the pissing rain. You'll also see me getting into a row with Six-Pack Matt when I found out he's moving into *my* house and then Julie kicking me out again. You won't hear it because it's a montage, but you'll see Julie mouthing the words 'fucking wanker' while making the well-known wobbly wrist gesture. All class that girl. You'll see Keith pissed out of his skull in some nightclub with a couple of my teammates while surrounded by a ton of fake women with fake tans, fake tits and fake teeth drinking lots of very real and very expensive champagne as they welcome in the New Year. And then you'll see me stood on the balcony of my new apartment at the same time with a cup of green fucking tea in hand watching the fireworks over London. Sober and alone.

And as the montage comes to an end and the 80s power ballad playing over the top fades away to nothing, you'll come to notice one thing – that no matter how hard you work in the gym or how well you eat, it takes longer than a couple of weeks to get a 20-plus stone man into any reasonable shape. Still, at least Harley had warmed to me now. Another ally in the London City United camp. I was getting there, slowly but surely.

12. IN THE SQUAD

'RICHIE! Rich mate,' Harley shouted excitedly as I sat on the rowing machine, drained. 'You need to get changed quick mate, the gaffer wants you out for a training match in 10 minutes.'

The gaffer. By that, he meant the Head Coach or 'manager' in old money. Franco Capece was a no-nonsense former Italy international who spent his playing career at some of Europe's elite clubs. Now he was doing the same as a manager. The reason you haven't heard me mention him yet is because football clubs don't work in the same way as they used to or how you might think. Well, not this one anyway. Managers don't have all the say on signings anymore and Capece certainly had nothing to do with mine. I had seen him about the training ground over the last couple of weeks of course, but I was yet to speak to him. It seems that unless you're involved then and there with the first team, you're not worthy of his attention. The players only really become relevant when he needs to call upon them. Like now.

The club's form hadn't been that good anyway this season, but the loss of those players suspended in the aftermath of the Mario Gonzales scandal had deepened the crisis. And even though the transfer window was now open again, the club was barred from paying cash-money for any players until the full investigation into Gonzales's antics was complete.

London City United had a must-win match against Liverpool in the league coming up, but before that was an FA Cup third round game against Carlisle to play. It meant that Capece had decided to field a weakened team in the cup match and allow his overworked star players a bit of a rest before the trip to Anfield. A defeat in that game could cost him his job. I was being considered for a place in the squad against Carlisle off the back of Coach Cusick's recommendation and Capece wanted to have a look at me play personally before making a decision. This was my chance to impress. And the excitement gave me renewed energy.

I walked out of the changing rooms into the cool January air and then trotted across the lush green grass out towards the crowd of players gathered by one of the pitches. As I approached the group, I could see them whispering to one another like a bunch of gossiping teenage girls on the playground. Then I saw Franco Capece look across at me, shake his head and then gesture something very Italian to one of his assistants. It was all in the hands.

A small guy in a club tracksuit broke away and walked towards me with a broad grin while holding out a luminous bib for me to wear. At least there was one welcoming face around the place.

'Here you go. Good luck getting that on fatty,' the grinning little prick said.

Keith had still been coming to training as he kept up his watchful eye on the LCU women's team but had now dashed out to the training pitch after Harley told him what was going on. This was it. We stood on the side and he whispered the trigger words to put me under and passed on some instructions. Our brief conflab had brought about more looks of derision from the players and staff, but now was my chance to show these doubters what I could do.

It was an 11-a-side game on a full pitch. Horatio Emmett was on my side for the first bit and he gave me a little salute as I took up my position wide on the right. At least I had one ally – but then he threw me right in at the deep end by kicking the ball to me from the off. I was closed down in seconds as the ball got stuck between my feet, but I regained control and rainbow flicked it over the on-rushing opposition player and then knocked a simple pass infield. We were off.

Club captain Adam Bush was watching from the side and his opinion of me hadn't changed since day one. He was barking out as many instructions to the players as the manager or coaches, but no one told him to stop. 'Close him quicker. Sharp tackles. Get up his arse. On him, ON HIM! Don't let him do that to you. For fuck's sake, how did that fat wanker get past you? Fucking hell, don't let him shoot. Don't let him...shit. Fucking useless.'

One thing that I learned quite quickly in this practice match was that although footballers don't like new players arriving who could threaten their chances of regular first-team football, they don't mind players who play in other positions coming in and being excellent. So I was quickly winning favour with much of the squad as I played neat, creative and clever football. I more than held my own, did my job brilliantly, and they respected that despite what I looked like.

Bush still wasn't a fan. He was going to be rested for the Liverpool game and had been told he was done for the day, but he insisted on coming on during the practice game just so he could try to hack me down and make sure I didn't get near the first team.

'I'm going to end you, you fat fucking prick,' he growled in my ear as he marked me at a corner. Seconds later, the ball broke loose in the box. As Bush closed in and jumped two-footed in a bid to snap my legs, I kangaroo-hopped into the air with the ball held between my feet like the Mexican Cuauhtémoc Blanco. As I landed, I back-heeled the ball sharply against the back of Bush's head so that it lifted into the air and then I volleyed it into the top corner of the net. The ball that is, not Bush's head. And that was my hat-trick. I'd also set up two goals for Horatio and won a lot of nods and conversation from those on the touchline.

As my teammates back-slapped me for a job well done on the walk back to the changing rooms, the grinning little assistant came jogging over to tell me the manager wanted to see me in his office as soon as I was showered. I would be in the squad for the Carlisle cup game. I was going to make my professional football debut. It was all going to plan.

Keith grabbed me and kissed my forehead before working his magic. 'That was fackin' awesome bruv. Bootiful. We're gonna be fackin' stars. My brain and your twinkle toes will make us millions. Now gahn av a wash. You fackin' stink.' We looked up and saw Harley Wells stood within earshot looking straight at us. He looked like he wanted to say something, but didn't utter a word. After a second, he turned and headed inside.

A few miles away, tabloid hack Jim Neale was sat in the Wetherspoon's pub in the departure lounge at Stansted Airport nursing his second pint as he waited for a flight to the Costa del Sol. He had the scent of blood in his nostrils. It may have been Quavers too as he'd picked his nose right after eating his packet of crisps. But there was definitely blood.

13. THE DEBUT

ADAM Bush was a sly fucker. It seemed that his love for the manager was diminishing to the level of love he had for me. He wanted him out of the club ASAP too at that point. He felt Franco Capece wasn't the man to lead London City United back to glory and he was incensed that he would even consider me for a place in the first team. He believed I would bring humiliation and mockery, and if that were to happen then he wanted to be in control of it. So he leaked a 'story' to his own friends in the media to allow him to play puppet master. He told them that the club's owner Buck Schulz had zero confidence in Capece, whose days were surely numbered, and was now picking the team himself. An 'insider' at the club said that I had become Schulz's pet project and novelty act and that was the reason I was in the squad for the cup game against Carlisle. Bush sought to undermine all three of us for his own ends.

Panicked, and keen to show that he was still in charge of first-team affairs, Capece only named me as a substitute despite my remarkable performance in training and suggestions from some of the other players and coaches that I should start. But a side-effect of Bush's story in the papers was that it whipped up added pressure on the already underperforming players, some of whom really didn't fancy the 600-mile round trip to Carlisle on a freezing cold Saturday afternoon in early January. This must've been what it felt like for the Southend and Liverpool players when they met at Roots Hall in '79 like Grandad had told me about.

With just over an hour gone, we – ha! I'm already calling us 'we' and I'm meant to be a Southend fan. Let's do that again. With just over an hour gone, London City United were being held at 1-1 by the League Two side and Capece decided it was time for a change. But it wasn't going to be me he put on. Two promising youth teamers who looked like they'd rather stay in their warm sub suits got stripped off and went on – and did nothing. They froze, literally and metaphorically. The LCU players were nervous, the few travelling fans started to get on their backs and Carlisle sensed the opportunity to become the proverbial banana skin. With 75 minutes on the clock, the home side hit the bar as the LCU defence seemed to melt away. It was time for divine intervention and in football the fans are God.

While most of the City United supporters loved having the 50-60-70 million pound players in their line-up, their overall response to me – an unknown freebie – had been positive. Especially since that rant from my press conference went viral. I was one of *them*. A normal. I cared, really cared. They loved that and it turned out they already had a song for me.

To the tune of Bad Manners' Lip Up Fatty – you can see where this is going – they started singing: 'We want fatty, ah we want fatty, fatty Richie.'

I can't say it was the most flattering of songs to hear about yourself but it was, as they say, music to my ears.

'We want fatty, ah we want fatty, fatty Richie.'

Now, I don't know at that point whether they wanted me because they thought I had the footballing ability that would turn the game around or whether they just wanted some entertainment after what was, in reality, a pretty dull match. Either way, they carried on singing. The spectators at Carlisle's Brunton Park are much closer to the pitch than they are at LCU's monolithic Grand Postal/MegaMobiles Arena and Franco Capece turned to look at the away supporters as the song really took hold. He made eye contact with one fan, who took his chance to shout: 'Give him a go Franco. He can't be any worse than the shit you've got out there now.'

He turned back to the pitch without a flicker of emotion on his face, but he did seem to be thinking. After a few moments of contemplation – his side still drawing 1-1 and threatening to be the victim of an FA Cup giant-killing – he sighed heavily, turned to the bench, looked at me and flicked his head. This was it. I was going on.

PRICE FIXER

TUBBY newboy Richie Price came off the bench to save London City United's FA Cup blushes yesterday as his 10-minute debut hattrick sunk plucky Carlisle.

The Premier League crisis club struggled with the wintry conditions and the opposition at Brunton Park and were on the ropes as the home side hit the bar with 15 minutes to go and the score at 1-1.

But under-pressure boss Franco Capece threw on Price for his professional football debut at the age of 42 – and he showed why the former Premier League champions have taken a chance on an overweight nobody.

Price scored with his first touch – a 30-yard rocket akin to Ronnie Radford's FA Cup classic for Hereford in 1972 – before bagging a second five minutes later with a neat finish after a jinking run past two defenders.

The obese rookie, snapped a few weeks ago at a McDonald's drive-thru on his way to training, sealed his quick-fire treble with a diving header in the last minute. Manager Capece said: 'It was a great debut from Richie. We have been watching him closely in training, and he's been working hard, and today he took his chance.'

Asked if the rotund forward will feature in the crucial clash against Liverpool in mid-week, the Italian said it was 'too early to say.'

I was walking on air as I came off that pitch. The way Keith had continually tweaked the hypnosis since the early days meant I was a lot more present for a lot of it and it stayed in the memory banks afterwards, which improved my enjoyment of the process no end. The City United fans were facing a God-awful journey home and could've been excused for making an early exit before the game had ended. But a group of them had waited behind and were chanting my name. I walked over to them mouthing 'thank you' and applauding them above my head as is the norm for a footballer. They appreciated the gesture and returned the applause. Then it dawned on me. I was actually a footballer. If it all ended then, I'd done it.

As I made my way to the tunnel, Keith stopped me quickly and took me out of the trance – fuck, I was knackered. I may have fallen down if it hadn't been for of my teammates coming up behind and grabbing me in celebration of my efforts. The cheers and back-slaps continued in the changing rooms, including from the manager.

'From my heart, thank you for your performance today,' he said with one hand on his chest and the other on my shoulder while looking me directly in the eye. In that instant, the tiredness drifted away and I felt like a million dollars. I may have even blushed, but it was hard to tell with my cheeks already being so bright red. That was the legendary man-management skills everyone raved about. If Franco Capece had asked me at that moment to go and rob a bank for him, I'd be pulling my football sock off my leg and back on over my head. Luckily, he didn't.

Then I got an overly-strong hug from Harry Jacobs, a short Scottish international with a heart of gold and a terrifying stare. He had a way of talking that always made it seem like he was threatening you, even if he was being kind. He spoke in questions and I wasn't sure of the consequences if I gave the wrong answer. If he offered to buy you a pint, he'd say the last word through gritted teeth and as if he were tensing every muscle in his body. 'Ay, yoo wan a *PINT*?'

But we weren't in the pub right now so he just threatened me about the game we'd just won. 'Ho son, whit a hattrick. Where'd yoo pull tha oot frum?' His eyes bored through my skull and into my soul and for a split-second I almost caved in to the pressure and told him the truth. But I pulled it together and said it was something I'd been saving for a rainy day. 'But it's fookin' snowin' no?'

He didn't quite get my rainy day metaphor and, technically, he was right. It was snowing, so I gave him a 'Yup' and began to pull my shirt over my head to break eye contact.

The sense of relief in the dressing room was palpable. There were more handshakes and platitudes and a few of the lads were working out if the plane would get us back from Carlisle to London in time for them to hit the town seeing as it was Saturday night. They extended the invite to me too, but I just wanted to rest and sleep. I checked my social media on the plane and I had made headlines across the world it seemed. Video clips of my goals were racking up hundreds of thousands of likes and shares and views. All the congratulations gave me a warm glow, but that may have been the spray the physio put on my hamstrings before we left.

But you and I know that I didn't get into all this for the acclaim of strangers, and the greatest feeling came the next day when I got a phone call from my son, Tilson.

'Dad, dad, I watched the clips on Snapchat and you were really brilliant. I can't believe you're an actual footballer. That first goal when you whacked it from miles out was amazing. And I can't believe you jumped that high to head the ball for the third one. My mates are so jealous. Some are being mean, but most of them are texting me all the time saying how great it is. Oh, can you get Adam Bush's autograph for my friend Chris, or a signed shirt...'

He spoke without pause for about half an hour solid. I'm not sure I answered any of his questions. Not because I didn't want to, but because he didn't give me a chance before he excitedly moved on to the next thing. I couldn't get a word in edgeways, but I was too emotional. I could hear it in his voice – pride. I bathed in it. For once – perhaps for the first time – he was proud of his dad. Since he'd been old enough to know what's what, I'd just been a driving instructor who used to have money and lost it and then flashed at a teenage girl he fancied. Now I was a role model. I wanted to run to his house, scoop him up and squeeze him like I used to when he wasn't nearly 6ft and sprouting his first chin hairs. Maybe I'd get a hug off his mum too. And a kiss. I wondered what she thought of it all. Had I impressed her? Had I given her the tingle I always got when I saw her? I don't know. But right now, the love from Tilson was enough. And besides, I had a visitor sat in my living room.

Perched on my pristine white leather sofa was Harley Wells, swigging from a bottle of mineral water. He was a handsome guy. He was wearing a smart pair of dark grey jeans, a black Armani turtleneck and a burgundy blazer. You'd easily get confused as to which of us was the professional footballer. It was certainly not an outfit I could get away with, but I decided then and there that I needed to up my game in the fashion stakes.

I finished the call with Tilson, put the phone on the side and entered the living room wearing my Avengers pyjama bottoms, crumpled white T-shirt with a ketchup stain on the belly and my comedy hamburger slippers.

Harley's eyes had been scouring the living room for something of interest while he was waiting for me to get off the phone, but seeing as the apartment was new to me there was very little of my 'stuff' in the place. My outfit snapped him out of his daze.

'Sorry about that, but it was my son, you know.' He didn't respond for a while. He looked as though he had something serious on his mind but didn't know how to say it. Perhaps he was just stunned into silence by my slippers. But it was the same face he'd pulled at the training ground a few days ago. He stood and walked away from the sofa to the full height window that looked out over the River Thames. Then he turned, ready to start.

'I know you're up to something, man. I don't know exactly what it is, but you're up to something.' We stared at each other for a few moments. I was pretty sure he didn't have the faintest clue what was going on, but didn't want to give anything away. I stayed silent. 'I've seen you and Keith at the training ground, talking and so on, away from everyone else.'

'Keith's my counse...'

'Bullshit. I've spent a little time around Keith but I know he ain't no counsellor. The guy's a menace. And I worked hard for years to be a footballer; I had pace and skill and I was good, real good, but I didn't make it. I gave it till I was 25 and then concentrated on this full time. Fitness. People don't just become a Premier League footballer at 50, you know...'

'I'm 42!'

'Whatever man. It just doesn't happen. It's some voodoo shit or mind control you two have got going. I don't know what it is or how it works, but I do know that at London City United I am the one stood closest to you and I don't want to be right there when it all goes off. You ain't knocking me down a second time Richie.' His face was solemn and despondent. Part of me wanted to confide in him. Flesh out on the bones of what he knew already. He had, after all, been my closest ally at the club over the last few weeks. He had shown me the ropes, introduced me to the people I needed to be introduced to and shared with me some of the warnings of life as a footballer. He may not be a pro himself, but he'd observed enough during his time at LCU. But I barely trusted Keith with our secret, let alone someone else.

I denied everything and when he didn't look completely convinced, I volleyed the ball back into his side of the court saying that if he was really, truly that worried then he should ask his bosses if he could be moved off the 'make the fat boy slim' project. There would be no hard feelings from my part, I was thankful for all he'd done and would like to keep working with him, but I would under-stand. He didn't give an answer one way or the other, but as he left my apartment we shook hands and shared a bro hug – a coming together of shoulders while the hands are still clasped. With a smile and a wave, he headed to the lift.

With that possible crisis averted, my meteoric rise to football super-stardom at London City United continued in the league game against Liverpool. With the first-team regulars, Adam Bush includ-ed, back in the starting XI, I was on the bench again. But after a lacklustre start to the game, I was introduced at half-time to spice things up a bit and got a raucous reception from the LCU fans in the away end – although they were immediately drowned out by the vociferous home support. Anfield was a majestic place for all involved on matchday.

Now, however good you are at football – and I was now pretty fucking good – it is impossible to be a one-man team. It's not like when you're playing Fifa on the PlayStation and you set the opposition's standard to amateur and then spank them 10-0 every game. I was coming up against elite footballers coached by some of the best managers in the world. Lionel Messi and Cristiano Ronaldo might score tons of goals every season, but to do that they need their very skilled teammates to be on form too. They need to defend, cancel out the opposition and create the chances so that Messi and Ronaldo can do what they do extraordinarily well. I tell you this not as any sort of excuse, but just as an explanation in advance that you're not going to hear me say that we won every game from now until the end of the season really easily with me scoring a hattrick or more in each. You've been watching football long enough to know that's not how the game works. It is a team sport and sometimes the individual cogs don't click into place and the thing doesn't work properly. Yes, those teams can be boosted by exceptional individuals, but the individuals cannot be consistently exceptional without the support of the team.

In terms of LCU's game against Liverpool, I only scored one – albeit an overhead kick like Wayne Rooney's athletic effort for Manchester United against Manchester City in 2011. Some joke that the whole of Liverpool shook as I hit the ground and that the outline of my arse remains indented in the turf of the penalty box in front of the Kop to this day. But that goal and an assist for my Scottish buddy Harry Jacobs was enough to secure a 2-1 victory. We then drew against Spurs in our next match – my first at LCU's Grand Postal/MegaMobiles Arena – and beat Newcastle in the game after. I started and scored in both. Even Adam Bush couldn't deny the positive impact I was having on the team's fortunes. Life on the pitch was going beautifully.

14. FUN AND GAMES

THERE was a week between the Spurs and Newcastle matches, and on the Wednesday night I was invited to a squad team-building party at Adam Bush's house. Well, I say invited. What actually happened was that Harley was invited and he asked me after training that day if I was coming along too. When I said I didn't know anything about it, he called Bush over in the gym to make sure it was OK for me to come along too.

Needless to say, our club captain didn't look too happy but he said: 'Yeah, it's for the whole squad 'spose. Just make sure you leave some of the buffet for the other guests, yeah?'

Now Bush may have been a brutal and effective centre-back – an aggressive bastion of manliness in a sport becoming overrun by snowflakes who roll around on the floor at the faintest of touches and spend as much time in front of the mirror ahead of a game as they do on the training pitch – but none of that was reflected in his home or its decoration. You had to assume that this theatrical palace was his girlfriend's influence. She'd been an actress after all.

Hidden behind grand wooden gates, the gothic castle looked as though it had been lifted from the clutches of a Disney villain. Grey gargoyles loomed over the heavy oak door, surrounded by dark green ivy that threatened to strangle entry to the mansion. Impressive and proper fucking spooky in equal measures. And the entrance hall was larger than my entire house – not the apartment I'm in now, but the one where Julie and Tilson live with the absbomination. It was decorated in black and gold and in front of a huge double staircase was a fountain with a sculpture of an adult and child (not too dissimilar to the one in the middle of Basildon high street) that spewed out glittering water. A smattering of coins littered the bottom, but goodness knows what Bush had been wishing for as he seemed to have pretty much everything in life. I suggested to Harley that he may want a new personality, but may have said it too loud. Bush was standing by the doorway to a room labelled as The Den. As we walked down a set of marble steps towards him, he greeted Harley with a warm handshake, a smile and one of those bro hugs. But as he released, he put his hands into his pockets so he couldn't shake mine. The smile from his face dropped too. 'We'll be checking your pockets on the way out. Don't want none of my stuff going missing, do I?' He stood in front of me to block my path and stared straight into my eyes. I had been in the sort of situation many times before at school, of course, but I hadn't got any better at dealing with it in the intervening years. I know that you're meant to keep staring back at the starer to prove your mettle, but I looked down at my feet and shuffled them about.

'Ah, look at you two,' Harley said in a mocking voice as he tried to break the tension. 'Play nicely and you'll soon become the best of friends.'

Bush relented, stood aside and allowed us into The Den. From its name, I was expecting a smallish room with a few sofas and maybe a telly with all us players squeezed in snuggly. But I should have known better. It was at least 100 metres long and 60 or 70 wide. There was a bar at one end and a dance floor at the other. In between were indeed all sorts of sofas and chairs, but also numerous giant TV screens, games consoles, pool and snooker tables, a dart board, arcade and fruit machines, a putting green, roulette and cards tables, and the walls were decorated with trophies and the shirts of famous footballers he'd swapped with during his career. There was also an almighty sound system that boomed out RnB songs that boasted of parties, sex, booties and booze. This, I assumed, was the one room in the house he had been allowed to decorate. His man cave. The name, it turned out, came from the fact he had grown up in a family of Millwall fans. I should've guessed.

It seemed that every player from the squad was here, some with their wives or girlfriends and others with someone else's wife or girlfriend or a girlfriend that their wife didn't know about. There were loads of other people too – male and female – that I did not recognise. I guessed these were mates of Bush or his missus.

As Harley and I sauntered through to find a spot to perch, we were handed a glass of champagne by a smiling waiter dressed all in black. I had by now accepted some fashion advice from my personal trainer and was wearing a smart pair of jeans and a navy blue jumper. My frame, it must be said, was becoming slimmer by the week as the pounds dropped off under Harley's instructions and fitness regime. It gave me a bit more confidence. I'd also learned the difference between aftershave, eau de toilette and cologne. Turns out they are not all the same and it's all to do with the perfume content. Who knew?

My new threads and smell must have been working because we'd only had our drinks in hand for a couple of minutes when we were approached by two young and very attractive women. Well, young to me, not Harley. And I say 'we' were approached, but it turned out they were actually making a beeline for him.

'Excuse me, are you Harley Wells?' asked the woman on the left. She was tall, curvy and beautiful and I immediately recognised her as our host Adam Bush's long-term girlfriend. Her black dress clung to her body and she had a perfect, bright white smile with a hint of deviousness in the corners. Harley, of course, answered in the positive because he was Harley Wells. He may have said yes even if he wasn't because he knew who she was too. After all, as well as attending matches and being papped alongside our glorious captain as they wined and dined and partied in London, she also had fitness DVDs and calendars out and regularly appeared in just her swimsuit or underwear in the tabloid newspapers under the name Shima.

As Harley stood nodding gormlessly, his eyes lost to her cleavage, she added: 'We used to go to school together.'

Harley looked stunned. 'Really? I don't...' he paused for a moment, stepping back as if seeing her from a slightly different angle would jog his memory. It didn't. 'Nah, I'm really sorry, I don't know, I don't remember a Shima at school. Secondary or primary?'

'Shima's not my real name. It's Ayesha.'

That name didn't so much as ring a bell with Harley, but set off a cacophony akin to every campanologist in Europe practising in his head all at the same time. Ding!

'Ayesha Khan? No way.'

And that was pretty much all I saw of Harley or Ayesha for the rest of the evening. They swiftly found a seat and spoke animatedly and at length about the good old days, barely breaking eye contact for several hours. The two of them had been friends as small children. Close friends. They had lived a few doors away on the same housing estate that I first bumped into Harley on. They were as thick as thieves by all accounts, playing together at each other's houses and while they were at school. They only began to grow apart when Harley's love of football took hold as he got to seven or eight. No time to speak to girls on the playground when there's a football to be kicked. No time to go to a girl's house to play when there's a park around the corner where all the boys are having a kickabout. And then Ayesha's family moved away. Not too far, but far enough that they didn't see each other on a daily basis anymore. They then went to different secondary schools and that was that.

The contact was lost. A once joyous, youthful friendship gradually faded and became consigned to memory for 20 years or so.

We know all about Harley's career trajectory from what I told you earlier and now he knew that his old friend Ayesha had grown up to become the sensational Shima. He knew about her too – a supposed actress who seemed to make a living out of being pretty and famous, although he didn't put it to her in such terms. Which was a good job, because they were getting on like a house on fire.

But that kind of left me in a funny situation though. Although it was in her house, Ayesha had been at the party with a friend who had – like me – seemingly been ditched for the night. I mean, I could have walked off and spoken to some of the lads – and I eventually did for a bit – but I couldn't just leave her then and there on her Jack Jones. That would be rude. But it had been a very long time since I had exchanged small talk with a woman I didn't know, especially one as pretty as the girl next to me now. She was probably in her mid-20s and only a little shorter than me. She had bobbed blonde hair and I could see she was wearing very little makeup compared to some of the other women in the room who were so caked in it that their faces started to arrive in the room a full three minutes before the rest of them. And while they were glammed and sparkled to the max, this lady wore a pair of faded black ripped jeans, Converse trainers and a Metallica T-shirt. She was effortlessly cool is what I'm trying to say, I suppose.

'Hello,' I said to her with my hand outstretched, ready to be shaken. 'I'm Richie.'

She shook my hand and with a wry smile told me in a Mancunian accent that her name is Mollie. That's when my brain got confused. I've never been good at 'chat'. Do I ask her about Coronation Street? Although just because she's Northern, it doesn't mean she watches it. Maybe then I should go the other way and ask about EastEnders? But maybe she doesn't like telly soaps at all. I know, I can ask her about the band on her T-shirt. She wouldn't wear that if she didn't like them, would she? Although it might be like the Ramones top that every third person seems to have despite not having any of their albums. Plus I know my son Tilson likes Metallica, but I don't know anything about them so the conversation would be short. Perhaps I should ask what she does for a living or does that sound judgemental? She might be unemployed and or just been sacked or something. That could be why she's not dressed up like the other girls, because she can't afford it right now. But then surely Shima or Ayesha or whatever she's called would lend her friend a dress.

Two silent minutes after we'd shaken hands, I finally asked: 'So, do people call you Moll?'

'Not many, no.'

'Oh, I just thought your friends might shorten Mollie as a term of affection.' It was going terribly.

'Well, Mollie is a tricky name to get your mouth around. What do your friends shorten Richie to?'

Due to the nerves and brain fuzz, I didn't quite detect the sarcasm or the fact she was really calling me a Dick. I actually replied, seriously. 'Oh, well, er, some people call me Rich. How do you know my name?'

'Er, you introduced yourself a couple of minutes ago. And I read the papers.'

'Ah yes, sorry, of course. So, er, what do you do for a living?' It seemed safer ground now to go with that question.

'I'm an actress.'

'Oh wow. Cool. Anything I might've seen you in.'

'I was in Spunk-Loving Sluts 3. I was dressed as a nurse. Well, at the start.'

My jaw fell so far that it was almost open enough to ram my foot into it. I didn't know what to say or where to look. My cheeks were so bright I looked like the Ready Brek guy. I was stupefied. There was another long silence as my brain raced through a gazillion options until I noticed a wicked smile spread across her face.

'You're pulling my leg aren't you?'

'Yes, I'm pulling your leg, Dick.' Blimey. I had never been so relieved. 'I have done a bit of television, but I mainly do musical theatre.'

'Oh, I fucking hate musicals,' I said without thought. Mollie erupted into contagious laughter that caused a few of the other partygoers nearby to turn and giggle themselves in a sort of 'I'll have what they're having' way.

Mollie turned out to be an absolute hoot. So much fun and easy to talk to. Well, after the initial nerves got out the way. Over the next hour or so we spoke about everything from my theory that Bugsy Malone and Blues Brothers are the only acceptable musicals to her love of Guinness and then to the state of my marriage before we got to what a man of my age should be wearing and, more importantly, shouldn't be wearing. I needed to get rid of my Crocs apparently. I did check that she was OK with hanging around and talking to me rather than going off to speak to any of the handsomer, younger and richer men milling about the room, but she declined.

'I like you, you're funny. You make me laugh. Plus, I don't really like footballers. They're all self-absorbed prima donnas.'

'Oi, I'm a footballer.' And we creased up again. OK, so that doesn't sound that funny when I say it back, so it may have been the booze. But the two of us had a great time.

We people-watched the others in the room and made snide comments about his suit or her makeup, that guy's dancing and so on. At one point we fixed on one of the players – a short, but extremely skilful Italian called Luca Tartaglia – as he spoke to a dolled-up girl across the other side of the room and we improvised the conversation. Mollie took on the role of Luca as she did a pretty good Italian accent, and I played the tart. Then I thrashed her at pool, because I had a bit of talent with the cue, before she wiped the floor with me on Fifa on one of the consoles.

'Right, I need to go for a piss,' I told her, because I'm polite like that. I stood and wobbled a bit. I hadn't drunk very much that night but because I'd hardly had any at all for a good few weeks it was having a rather large impact. 'Whoopsy.'

It was getting late, pushing near midnight, but the gaffer had given us the day off training tomorrow to let us fully enjoy the team-building night. He knew it was important for us to let our hair down, but had warned us not to go silly. The two toilets down in The Den were currently in use so I asked Ayesha if there was another as I really was quite busting. She directed me out into the entrance hall, up the stairs, along a corridor, or was it two lots of stairs before the corridor? I couldn't remember, but she had asked me to take my shoes off in the hall because the carpet upstairs was white and they wanted to keep that way. Fair enough, I suppose. And then she was back buried in her joyful conversation with Harley.

The first floor in Adam Bush's house was beautifully decorated, which I again took to be Ayesha's touch. It was like something out of one of those home magazines Julie used to buy and I'd flick through while sitting on the loo. Well, it's boring when you leave your phone downstairs, isn't it?

There were some wonderful pieces of art on the walls of Bush's place that I probably didn't have the eye to appreciate fully, but it grabbed my attention as I passed on my way to the bog. There was also an impressive library or study that was filled with actual books. I didn't even know Adam could read. I had expected him just to have lots of pictures of himself and rooms filled with gadgets and garish clothing.

My bladder tensed and I returned to my mission of finding the toilet, but I wasn't sure if I was going the right way. I had gone up two flights of stairs, but surely they would have a loo on each level. I tried a door handle, it opened effortlessly and I walked straight in to see two men stood kissing passionately. One of the men was Alexis Colombo, a defence coach from London City United. I hadn't seen him downstairs and there were no other coaches at the party. Nice guy Alexis. Not sure where he's from in the world, but he spoke with an accent. He was always telling players to 'work back harder'. It was almost a catchphrase.

Oh, and the bloke he was snogging the face off was our man-mountain club captain, Adam Bush.

15. TRIPLE THREAT

I WOKE up the following morning with a head like a cement mixer and the quick realisation that I wasn't in my own home. I pulled back the blanket that lay over me, covering the clothes I'd worn the night before, and sat up on the sofa. Then things started making sense.

After coming down from the bathroom at Adam Bush's party and looking for where Mollie had gone, my teammate Harry Jacobs said that I looked like I needed a good whisky. Well, he more threatened it with an ice-cold stare that had made grown men cry. I managed to hold it together, but panicked after telling him I didn't like whisky. Being a Scot and the owner of a whisky bar in London, he took offence and replied: 'Naw, youse just haven't tasted the reet one, have ye?' I caved and said he was probably right, which led to him strong-arming me out of the party and into a taxi along with a couple of other players to the aforementioned whisky bar. Then he made me taste at least a dozen whiskies before we found one that I thought was alright. It wasn't, but it was gone 2am and I realised he would've had me there till dawn if I didn't say I liked something.

As it was, we ended up having a few more and a couple of beers before heading back to his house to watch a film. I don't know what film it was because I passed out drunk as soon as I sat on the sofa. I quickly checked in the mirror to make sure the lads hadn't drawn a fake moustache or a massive cock and balls on my face while I was asleep. They hadn't.

Slowly, the others woke and gathered in the living room. Harry, myself, Horatio Emmett and our goalkeeper Paulo Antoine. Harry's fridge contained very little food so we decided to go out for some breakfast, during which I made my second mistake of telling the others I wasn't really into fashion and clothes. Just a T-shirt and jeans will do me.

'Yoo wha?' Harry said.

'No my friend, you must change this,' added Paulo.

'Forking turn it in, you plum,' chipped in Horatio. You may remember that my Brazilian pal had previously called me a 'mug', a 'melt' and a 'fucking slag'. It turned out that after moving to London he attempted to get a better knowledge of the language and the English game by watching movies about football here, but could only find hooligan films. So he picked up certain nuances of English from The Firm, Green Street, The Football Factory, ID, and countless straight-to-DVD fight fests that feature more in the way of creative insults than actual football. He'd now been left with a sort of hooligan Tourette's that meant nearly every sentence ended with an offensive barb.

Anyway, none of my trio of friends were happy about my lack of interest in haute couture and said if I didn't go shopping with them then they'd tell Harley and Franco Capece how much I'd drunk the night before as well as the eggs, sausages, bacon, beans, fried tomatoes, mushrooms and fried bread sat before me now to ease my hangover nausea.

Julie had always gone out and bought clothes for me because the high street and scouring through countless rails wasn't my thing. She was as excited as a seagull with a stolen chip. Pair of Levi's here, a nice shirt there and socks and pants from Primark and I was sorted for six months. But the shops the lads had taken us to were nothing like Southend town centre. We went to Harrods, Harvey Nicks, Selfridges and Matches. These places were proper swanky. And the clothes? Well, they looked like a regular shirt or pair of trousers you'd find in H&M or Next, but they had an extra digit or two on the price tag.

I'd told them over breakfast about my clothes-buying habits and Julie and then gone into more detail than intended about the state of my marriage, my wife's new man and how he trumped me in the music, looks, and fashion stakes. They decided that I dressed much older than my years and some simple choices in threads could sort that out.

Harry Jacobs pointed out a pair of black skinny jeans he thought would suit me. I thought we'd need a ton of Vaseline and a team of engineers to get them on and over my arse. They cost £435! The jeans, that is, not the engineers. Then he picked up a pair of socks – one pair – that were £85. And there was a bag I thought Tilson might like for school, but I looked at the tag and it was £635. Just for a backpack.

'Youse have git the money noo pal, ye may a-swell spennit, no?' Harry threatened. He was right, I did have the money, but it seemed an obscene amount to spend on clothes when only a few weeks earlier I was scraping by in a dingy flat above a pub. I'd splashed out on a nice apartment, a flashy motor and some bits for Tilson and Julie, but this was too indulgent from me.

'Nah, I'm fine with what I've got lads, seriously, this isn't my thing.'

'Wella, why don'ta you go and get us all a coffee then?' said Paulo. 'Let us look in peace.'

'Yeah, we've av clothes to try on, ya dozy twat,' added Horatio.

An assistant in the shop did offer to get the drinks, but I took my leave and nipped to the Costa Coffee across the road, returning with a cardboard tray holding lattes and cafe mochas to find all three of my new friends grinning like morons and holding out bags towards me. They'd clubbed together and bought the clothes I'd tried on and they refused to take them back. Paulo Antoine, who like all goalkeepers was a couple of pork pies short of a picnic, ate the receipt in front of me to show we were past the point of return. 'Ye one of oos noo,' Harry said. It would have been the most genteel thing he'd said to me had he not been squeezing my shoulder to the point of breaking the bones underneath.

I left the shop wearing the black skinny jeans (they were ripped too, which I never really got the idea of. Why buy ripped clothes, especially when they cost 400-odd quid?), a white Prada T-shirt that at least came in a pack of three for its £160 price tag, and a £1,500 army-type Valentino coat. I also had a pair of £540 Gucci trainers to top it off.

All the gear and no idea was how I would describe my new look, but Julie had a much more fitting analogy when I drove over to the house to drop the backpack off to Tilson.

'Fuck me,' she said with a hand over her mouth to stifle her giggles. 'It looks like a boyband has sicked up over you.' I smiled.

'The jeans *are* pretty tight,' I said.

'Tight? I can see which way Simon is looking.' My cheeks lit up like Blackpool illuminations. It had been a long time since she'd used the pet name for that part of my anatomy. It got the moniker after a particular frisky game of Simon Says some years and many bottles of wine ago.

'OK, they're very tight,' I said, trying to bring things back to the present day. 'And I think I added another rip across the arse when I tried to squeeze into the car.' She smiled the dimples smile.

Julie did invite me in, but I could hear Matt in the background so thought it best I didn't. For someone who worked as a personal trainer, he didn't seem to be at the gym very often. I avoided saying as such to Julie as it was nice to have her smiling at me for once.

Then Tilson came bounding to the door and gave me a massive hug. He was an affectionate teenager, I'll give him that.

'What do you think of your dad's new clothes?' Julie asked him with a smirk.

'Yeah, really cool. Are those Gucci trainers?'

'Yes son. Yes they are,' I replied with a 'that told you' nod to my wife and I handed him the bag. 'This is for you. It's Balenciaga and it cost a lot of money, so don't let your fountain pen leak in it if you use it for school.'

'What's a fountain pen?' Teenagers. They've never had it so easy. Tilson withdrew into the house to show the bag to the Protein Shake Kid in the living room and I started to say my goodbyes.

'Hey, not so fast. Where's my present?' asked Julie, which left me a little confused. Not by the question, but by the fact she seemed to be flirting with me while her new boyfriend was quite possibly within earshot. It was the first time in a long time she had been this friendly to me. I didn't know if she was teasing me or encouraging me, but there was nothing I could do about it either way.

'Next time,' I said, eventually. 'Plus I got you the car and that thing.' The dog was standing at her side looking on expectantly. It probably wanted something too. A Dolce & Gabbana collar maybe or Givenchy bags to have its shit collected in down the park. 'Next time,' I repeated, and left.

It was gone eight by the time I got back to my apartment. I pulled up at seven, but it took a while for me to be able to get out the car with the skinny jeans on. They seemed to have got progressively tighter throughout the afternoon like some sort of medieval hipster torture garment. I'd already undone the top couple of buttons on the drive back up the A13 towards London. I wasn't even able to fit my keys, phone or wallet in like more normal jeans. At least now I knew why the kids started wearing those man bags.

I came crashing through the front door, dropped the bags on the sofa and set about getting those things off my legs. However, the usual technique of removing trousers by putting a hand on either hip and pushing down didn't work. They only budged about an inch. I tried one side at a time and got a little more joy, but then it sprung up again as I let go to start on the other. I was starting to panic a little. I wiggled, jiggled, pushed and pulled, but no joy. For a second, only a second, I tried to figure out if there was a way of pulling them up over my head to get out. I was stuck. I decided to google 'how to get out of skinny jeans when you're stuck' but my phone was completely dead. I'd been out since the evening before, after all. I plugged it in to charge and then got a breakthrough. Not from the phone, but when I lunged across to find the charger down by the sofa I heard a tear. There actually was a split in the arse cheeks now. I repeatedly lunged around the living room, as big a stride as I could take. There were more, smaller rips and I could feel a loosening around my bum and thighs, but the side-effect was a tightening around my calves that felt like all the circulation was being cut off.

My phone, now with 1% battery, buzzed. There was a message from an unknown number. The unknown sender had said they had come to my house today but I was missing. Missing? I was shopping. I flicked it away and then got back to the matter at hand. I'd had an idea, and we all know how good my ideas are. I waddled to the kitchen, grabbed a bottle of olive oil and poured it liberally down the front of my jeans. Due to the tightness, most of it pooled around my testicles. It wasn't the worst feeling I'd ever experienced, but not much help in getting the jeans off so I started to pour more through the various deliberate rips in the denim and around the rim at the top.

My phone buzzed again with the unknown sender this time telling me not to ignore them. I wasn't ignoring them. In the words of Freddie Mercury, I was trying to break free.

With teeth gritted and my hands red from the strain and covered in oil, I pushed down on the jeans again, wiggling as I did. There were a couple of slips but then, boom, the jeans shot down to my knees. I'd never been so pleased to see my pasty, chubby thighs.

Buzz. 'Reply will you, FFS!' I still wasn't sure who the messages were from and although it seemed important, my number one priority was getting out of the jeans. I was hot and flustered, so took my top off. I took hold of the denim again and pulled. Millimetre by millimetre they came down my calves, but they were still not coming off in a hurry. My left foot was starting to go numb. Fuck. Fuckety fuck. I tried to put my right foot on the jeans and pull my left foot up and out, but I lost balance and fell to the floor, clattering into the stools against the breakfast bar and pulling a load of stuff from the side as I went.

It was then – lying on the floor half-naked, with my trousers round my ankles, covered in olive oil and with a length of kitchen paper that had unrolled at my side – that the security guard from downstairs popped his head round the door to check I was OK. There had been reports of a struggle and shouting from the neighbours. He'd used the master key.

My phone buzzed again and things became crystal clear. 'I don't know what you think you saw last night, but if you mention a word of it to anyone I will ruin you.' The message added that the sender – Adam Bush – knew people, 'nasty people'. So did I. Julie could be a right cunt at times.

But I put that to one side as I explained to Colin the security guard, who was looming in the foyer with a puzzled expression, that I was a prisoner of my trousers and needed help. It would be like the Great Escape. He could be Big X or Hilts or Ives. He'd never seen it.

'We pour some oil on my ankles, I hold onto the breakfast bar and you give them a good yank off,' I explained.

'Why don't you just cut them off with scissors?'

'Because they cost 400-odd quid. They're designer.' It sounded pathetic and Colin's reply that they hadn't been designed very well sealed it. It was a struggle just to get the blade under the seam at the bottom of the jeans, but after a couple of snips the blood was rushing back to my feet. Hilts and the boys were out of the tunnel and into the woods. Although it didn't turn out so great for them in the end, did it? But my legs were now buzzing more than my phone. I still had to decide what my reply to Bush would be but, now alone after Colin had returned downstairs, I took a moment to recover on the cold tiled floor of the kitchen. The heavy night before, the hours walking around shops, the drive to Essex and back, and the epic struggle to get free of my jeans had taken their toll. I fell into a deep sleep.

16. CLIQUES

ADAM Bush had come up through the youth ranks at West Ham before his big money move across the capital to London City United. He was always the biggest, strongest and loudest kid in his year group. I had assumed that was what made him stand out to the coaches as a lad, but I later learned that he was an avid student of the game. Bobby Moore was his dad's hero and he'd watched footage of the great England captain many times after deciding that he too would be a world-class defender. Franco Baresi, Paolo Maldini, Tony Adams, Franz Beckenbauer, Jaap Stam, Alan Hansen and Matthias Sammer were among the greats he studied, as well as the likes of Nesta, Puyol, Thuram, Desailly, Terry and Ferdinand. But it wasn't just their technique and ability on the ball he looked at, he also wanted to see how they communicated, how they carried themselves on and off the pitch and how they established themselves as leaders and captains.

Bush carried that attitude into the West Ham first team and then to England before Buck Schulz dug into his sizeable wallet and pulled out 30million notes in return for his services for his new London City United project. It was a snip really. And Bush quickly spread his roots through the club so that he effectively had a say on the running of the place. Schulz, the board and chief exec would often seek his advice on footballing matters (although not always follow it, clearly, else they wouldn't have signed me). He was a talisman. An icon of the club that the fans adored and a leader followed by devout members of the squad. However, there were some at LCU on both the playing and coaching staff that thought he wielded too much power. And some, like me, just thought he was a cock.

That meant there were definite cliques within the squad that could affect performances, especially when things weren't going well. It seemed that walking in on Bush kissing a man and then not replying to his texts had exacerbated the situation. I hadn't uttered a word to anyone and didn't intend to, but I wasn't about to tell him that. He'd not been at all welcoming and so I saw it as an opportunity to ensure he didn't hold all the cards.

I had, in effect, created my own little clique with Horatio Emmett, Harry Jacobs and Paolo Antoine being my buddies, Bush had his close group and then there were those in between. It led to a bitter atmosphere in training for the rest of that week which then spilt over into the game against Newcastle. Not good considering that mid-week party was supposed to be a team-building event.

The match itself was in the next round of the FA Cup and we found ourselves 1-0 down at half-time. It all kicked off at the break when Bush came storming into the changing room and fronted up to Harry for giving the ball away for the goal. Harry was never one to back down from a fight. To be fair, he had lost possession in the midfield and gone to ground easily to appeal for a freekick rather than chasing back. But he knew full well of his own mistake and didn't need to be bawled out in front of the whole team.

'Aye, ah lost tha baw, but he still hud ta get pass yoo tae score, eh? Did tha pretty easy, no?' he said thrusting his chest towards Bush, although the mismatch in size meant it looked like an eight-year-old arguing with his grown-up brother. Bush shoved him away and then there were more pushes and shoves and angry voices as the rest of the team joined in. A few had clenched fists, but no punches were thrown. We were all too pretty for that. I did my best to pull Harry away and calm a few others down, but the melee only stopped when the manager Franco Capece let rip.

While he was an overly-aggressive player, Capece was seen as a calmer and more considered coach. He was a clever man-manager and master tactician not given to angry rants. But not today. He was so furious that his face went beetroot and he kept slipping into his native Italian. We all still understood what he was saying. We were playing as individuals and individuals cannot win a team game. We needed to forget about fighting each other and channel that fight towards the opposition. Kick the ball, not his head. Work together and we would win. Now calm and heading out for the second half, Capece pulled me to one side and said: 'I need something special from you today. I'm counting on you.'

We were almost as bad in the second half as we were in the first. Passes went astray, tackles were missed and there were lots of snide comments and bickering among the players. Then we got a lucky route back into the game when we were awarded a penalty. I had collected the ball wide on the right, jinked past the defender and got into the box ready to cross when I was brought down by what the commentators called an 'agricultural' challenge. That phrase always seemed a bit unfair to farmers as I'd never had one of them two-footing me from behind or seen one elbowing a field of wheat in the head as it lay on the ground. But still, agricultural it was and Horatio Emmett easily tucked away from the spot to make it 1-1. It was far from what we deserved for our performance. Then, with two minutes to go until full time, I scored a winner straight out the scrapbook of Newcastle's own hero, Alan Shearer – albeit from his Blackburn days in the early 90s.

I played a neat give-and-go with Harry Jacobs and found myself running into the opposition half with two back-pedalling defenders in front of me and Horatio off to the right calling for the ball. As the keeper came off his line towards the edge of the six-yard box, I scooped the ball up and over his head and watched it drop into the back of the net to make it 2-1. I even did Shearer's one-handed salute celebration, inadvertently in front of the Geordie supporters. That earned me a yellow card and a fine from the FA for inciting the crowd.

The dressing room was subdued after the final whistle. We had won, but the victory only papered over the cracks of the splits in the camp. But the biggest shock for me was to come the following morning in the Sunday newspapers. They had the match report and suggestions of a changing room bust-up in the sports sections, but on the front of the Sunday Citizen was something much closer to home. It seemed my journalist nemesis Jim Neale had been a very busy boy of late with some investigative work out in Spain. He had uncovered the real reason Keith had swiftly left the hypnotism circuit on the Costa del Sol and returned to Essex. While it did have something to do with housewives, he hadn't been helping them to quit smoking.

PRICE'S PAL SHAGGED MY WIFE

Prem ace 'counsellor' is stage hypnotist who slept with married women

LONDON City United star Richie Price's performance counsellor fled Spain in terror after sleeping with the stunning teen wife of a local Mafia boss, The Sunday Citizen can reveal.

The 19-year-old - wed to gangster Juan Garcia, 50 - was one of at least seven married women Keith Sykes had sex with

while working as a show hypnotist at hotels across the Costa
del Sol.

One jilted husband, who asked
not to be named, said: 'One minute my wife was on stage
pretending to be an angry
chicken and half an hour later
she was shagging the hypnotist
on a sun lounger by the pool.
The bloke's a wrong 'un.'

**Full Story - Pages Four
and Five**

Inside the paper was another two-page spread with all the sordid details of Keith's Spanish adventures along with pictures of two of the women he'd slept with posing in bikinis while pressed up against one another. They hardly looked like innocent victims. There was a separate story that covered the relationship between Keith and me. It said we were old school buddies (not strictly true), that he had helped me overcome my fear of playing football (not true at all, but I'll let them have that rather than the truth) and that I know all about his lothario past (again, not true). It even said at the end my representatives had not responded to their request for comment. I didn't have a representative.

The main thrust of the article was about how Keith had seduced the young wife of this Mafia boss, who seemingly found out about the tryst and put very certain threats upon Keith's life. He'd scarpered off stage when a couple of hoods turned up at one of the hotels and left five audience participants in a trance.

He laid very low for a couple of days before getting a boat across to Morocco and then a flight back to Blighty where he hoped to keep hold of his head.

I was fucking livid. Not so much with the story, but with Keith. I knew the bloke was a twat, but he hadn't let on about any of this.

Even when I or Neil had made a joke about his return to Essex, he insisted he'd grown tired of the old life and just wanted to help people here. Alright, so we weren't the best of pals and I certainly didn't want to share any details of my personal life with him, but this was kind of important considering we were putting ourselves in the spotlight. I was also startled by the fact he'd managed to get one woman to sleep with him, let alone seven. I'd seen his pulling technique up close and often and it wasn't pretty. I mean, he hadn't done anything untoward like hypnotising the women into getting naked. In fact, the two women in the picture were even quoted as saying they fell for his swagger and charm *before* they got up on stage and only did that to be near him. That sounded less convincing than me becoming a professional footballer, if truth be told.

I tried to ring Keith, but it went through to answerphone and he didn't reply to my texts. I got messages from some of the players, Harley and Julie, but nothing from my co-conspirator. Then my phone vibrated and the name Sean Clark came up on the display. Shit. This wasn't going to be an enjoyable call.

'Richie. I've been in conversation with the owner and some of the board members and we've decided that it's in everyone's best interests if your friend Mr Sykes stays away from the club and the training ground indefinitely. OK?'

'OK.'

'Thanks. Good luck. Ciao.'

Twat. I wanted to throw the phone across the room, but it was a new handset. The art of slamming the phone down on someone is pretty much dead now.

I slumped down on the sofa as the realisation of what Clark had just said washed over me. Keith could no longer come to games or to training. That's Keith, the hypnotist. The Amazing Syko, who puts me in a trance that transforms me into a world-class footballer. Without him, I'm just a 42-year-old fat bloke with bad knees. I'll last less time than Ali Dia did at Southampton (he managed 53 minutes in a match against Leeds in 1996 before they realised he was an imposter and hauled him off).

What the fuck was I going to do? For all his many, many faults, hangover or no hangover, Keith had been there at the training ground every day and went to all the matches home and away to ensure that if I was playing I was in the right frame of mind. He was getting paid handsomely, of course, but he kept up his side of the bargain.

I tried to call again, but still nothing. If I had any hair I would've pulled it out.

It was another hour before he got in touch. 'All getting a bit hairy here geez. Ain't my fault if I'm irresistible ;-) Laying low for a few days, can't say where. Call ya later.'

Going away for a few days? Fuck, fuck, fuckety fuck. No. How could he do that? This was going from bad to worse. I'd come too far just to jack this all in, plus there would be consequences if I came clean now. I might have to tear a hamstring or develop a heart defect and retire. A heart attack didn't seem too much of a stretch at this point. Going out onto the pitch as myself was not an option. I can just about kick a ball, but not at the sort of level they were expecting. I would humiliate myself. And I wasn't fit enough to last even 20 minutes of a football match. Everything was coming crashing down around my ears and I had a good idea of who was to blame. It had Adam Bush's prints all over it. Because I knew his 'secret'. Maybe Sean Clark was involved too. I wouldn't be surprised if the pair of them were up to their eyes in this together to get me out of their club. It seemed to be working.

When things went tits up in years gone by, there was one person I could talk to and get advice. Fortunately, he was the only other person who knew about our scam. I grabbed my phone and flicked through my recent calls – shit, had it really been that long – until I found my best friend Neil Jason.

Members of the paparazzi were camped out the front of my apartment block. That wasn't too unusual as I wasn't the only famous face who lived here. They would always hang around outside at all hours hoping to get a snap or two that the tabloids would pay a couple of hundred for. But there were more than usual today, plus some reporters, so I didn't fancy going out anywhere. Luckily, Neil agreed to come to see me.

'Be nice to see where you're living these days,' he said on the phone. I must admit, I hadn't kept in touch in the last few weeks. He didn't like what Keith and I had been doing, plus I had been pretty busy with all that was going on. It was nice to see him though. We had a man hug (that differs from a bro hug in that it's a full embrace with back-slapping) and I showed him in.

'This is the living room,' I said as we entered the living room.

'Really?' replied Neil as he looked around a room furnished with a couple of sofas, coffee table, bookshelf and a big fuck-off TV hanging on the wall. 'You surprise me. Next you'll be telling me that room with the sink, shower and bog is the bathroom.'

Point taken. The truth was that I was a little bit nervous. I didn't know what Neil's mood would be like and I needed his help and support now that Keith had gone into hiding. I didn't know the right way to ask for his advice or if it would be forthcoming. I got my answer in four words.

'Jack it all in,' he said, bluntly.

'What? No. I need your advice on how to keep going.'

'Nah, Rich mate. You need to jack it in, come clean, tell them it was all a trick. Lie if you want; say it was research or something, but tell the truth and we can go back to how things used to be before.'

'How things were? What me living above a pub on my todd while my wife and son live with the male model she's banging in the house I paid for? That sounds like fun. Cheers pal.'

'She's still banging the male model in your house even though you've become a "superstar", so I don't see your point.'

'I'm working on it, mate. It takes time.'

'Didn't take him much time, did it?'

This wasn't going how I'd hoped. I wanted my friend to come on board and give me some great advice, but we were just bickering. We never bickered. We both took a few moments of time out to cool off in case we said something we really regretted. Then I tried again in a softer voice. 'Listen, Neil. Keith's been compromised. He's out the picture. He's been banging married women, you've seen it in the papers, and now he's been banned from the club. I can't just walk away from this, I'm too invested in it now, but I need your help.'

But Neil wasn't in the mood to offer any help. There were other things in play that I hadn't known at that point.

Neil was a good guy. He was married with a couple of kids – two cute little girls – and he loved his family dearly and worked hard to support them. But there was another love in his life – Southend United. It was his escape from the pressures of day-to-day life. We had been going to games together for years, decades even. While I was now too busy on Saturdays and midweek to go and watch games with him, he was still there, rain or shine. He had the club's badge tattooed on his shoulder. He wore club T-shirts, replica kits and scarf and hat whenever he got the chance. He carried a Southend United pen around with him and had an 'I follow the Blues' sticker on his car. And even though he hadn't followed my example by naming either of his children after a Southend player, he did have a dog called Freddie after the striker Freddie Eastwood. Neil was a true Blue through and through. And what came next was a further indicator that he wasn't going to help me continue my escapades.

'Have you seen the news this morning?' he asked. I hadn't and he picked up the TV remote from the coffee table and turned it on. Blokes may, stereotypically, forget their loved ones' birthdays and anniversaries, but they never forget the channel number for Sky Sports News. Unless Sky changes it, of course. It's seared into the memory. Neil pressed the three buttons and it flicked across. Luckily, the presenters were not talking about me or the 'exclusive' in the Sunday Citizen. Instead, they were reporting on the golf, but down the side of the screen in a bright gold panel was a list of football fixtures. It was the draw for the fifth round of the FA Cup. I'd missed it what with everything else I had on my mind. We – London City United that is – had a Premier League game coming up against Everton on Wednesday and the cup tie was on the Saturday.

Neil was now stood next to the telly pointing at one fixture in particular with an extremely stern look on his face. LCU were going to Roots Hall to play Southend United in the cup. Those goddesses of fate must have been laughing their tits off at that one.

'You can't play in that game. It's time to stop it and own up.'

'It might not be so bad if I did,' I laughed. Neil didn't. 'Mate, I don't even know if I can play like I have been. I've got no Keith and he was pretty vital to this. But I've signed contracts and things. I can't just walk out, you can see that, yeah? The chief executive fucking hates me as it is and he'll completely fuck me over if he can. I'll be in a worse place than when I started.'

'You made your bed Rich...' Neil didn't finish the sentence. He put a hand on my shoulder for a moment, but then left me alone in the apartment.

Fuck is a peculiar word. It has its obvious base meaning as a crude way of saying 'having sex'. But it can also mean to cheat someone, as in 'You fucked me over'.

You can also use it in the following different ways:

- ⊗   Don't fuck with me.
- ⊗   You dumb fuck.
- ⊗   To fuck about.
- ⊗   To fuck up.
- ⊗   I've drunk so much I'm completely fucked.
- ⊗   Fuck off.

⊗   I'm going to just fuck around for a bit or do fuck all.

⊗   That's as funny as fuck.

⊗   Fuck it, who cares?

⊗   Well, fuck me!

⊗   WTF?!

⊗   Go fuck yourself.

⊗   Why the fuck did you do that?

⊗   That is so fucking cool.

There are many other ways to use it, but right now I just needed that one word to summarise my situation. Fuck. Or maybe with a few extra letters – ffuuuuuuuuuuucccccccckkkkkk! I could describe to you the knot in my stomach at that time or the nausea or the guilt or the loss at which I found myself. I could tell you how I paced around the living room, felt thirsty but was unable to drink, and that anger and dismay rippled through my brain in equal measure. But I'll save time by just using that one word. Fuck.

Then my phone pinged. I withdrew it from my pocket and flipped it over, expecting to see another barrage of shit from someone to add to my worries. But it wasn't. It was from Mollie, the girl I had met at the party. I don't remember giving her my number, to be honest, but then a lot of that night involved drinking. And she sent the message along with a selfie of the two of us gurning like idiots, so I guess I must've done. The message was short, simple and just what I needed. 'Oi Dick. Fancy a coffee?'

I took the lift down to the underground car park and walked up the ramp to get out. Rather than following it all the way up and into the path of the waiting throng of paparazzi – what is the collective noun for a group of photographers? A flash? A snap? An intrusion? Who knows? – I climbed the wall and dropped down onto the footpath that runs alongside the Thames. From there I was able to walk around to Tower Bridge, hail and cab and make the relatively short journey across the river to Borough Market. Mollie had suggested we meet at a little street food place nearby. My appetite was still absent, but she tucked into a generous pot of Bombay noodles as we chatted. I made do with a cup of tea.

We spoke about Keith and the article, as well as how important he was to me in performing on the pitch. I didn't tell her the truth, of course. I played the part and explained Keith's role as my performance counsellor. White lies. Ish.

'There are a lot of people in acting who could do with something like that,' she said. 'To get over the nerves of being on stage or even just going for auditions. If he gets bored of helping sportsmen, send him my way and I'll get him some new clients.' That seemed unlikely now. The acting profession as a whole was wary of anyone acting improperly. A hypnotist with a fondness for married women didn't seem like a good fit. I don't think Keith could ever make it in the world of theatre now, even with his own stage show.

Mollie had read the article in the paper and thought I may need someone to talk to. I did, but not about the Keith stuff. I needed to escape from all that. Julie used to be brilliant in man-managing me. If she saw I was down, she'd arrange for a day out somewhere or a boozy night at the pub just to get away from it all. I couldn't call on her now, but Mollie was proving to be an able substitute. We had a canny knack of talking inconsequential bollocks. We made silly observations, talked about films, and then a bit about family and aspirations without getting too deep. We then invented a game called 'punched or punching'. This involved looking at couples as they milled around Borough Market and judging whether or not the female was better looking than the male. If she was better looking, the male was punching above his weight. But if she was uglier than him, then he was getting punched. We played that for over an hour.

'So who's punching in your relationship then?' she asked.

'My relationship?'

'Yeah, with Julie.'

'Well, it's not really a relationship at the moment. But I am, definitely. She's a stunner. And really fun to be around and a great mum to our boy Tilson. But she can be a bit of a twat sometimes, you know?'

'Aye, but everyone can be a bit of a twat sometimes,' Mollie said with a smile. 'Especially you.'

I feigned being hurt by her words and we both laughed.

'Anyway, she's with this Matt guy now so I think that's died a death,' I said, sadly.

'What's he like, this Matt?'

'Ugly. Like really fucking ugly. Face like a dropped pie. And no personality at all. And he's got a tiny penis.'

'Oh really, how do you know?'

'I stood next to him in the gents once...'

'And you looked?'

'No. But he had to stand right up close to the urinal whereas I was a foot or so away.'

'A foot or so? Get you. How did Julie ever let you go?'

We laughed again, but the reminder that Julie had let me go stung a little.

'Nah, really he's a fitness guy. Trainer and model type. Much younger. Abs, big arms with veins all popping out. And you can actually see his jawline rather than all this chub...' I said jiggling my chins. 'And he's got long floppy hair that gets millions of likes on Instagram. Not that I've been looking or posting abusive messages of course.'

'Oh, of course. He sounds like Turbo Curbo.'

Not another one. 'Yeah, that's the over-inflated prick. Do you know him?'

'Wow. Well, er, yeah, I follow him online. He's getting kind of a big deal. He'll have a book or DVD out soon, I'm sure. Cos he's cute and, you know, very well put together, you know,' she realised that wasn't helping. 'And he's your competition? Sheesh.'

'He's a homewrecker, Mollie.'

'I thought you and Julie split up first before they got together?'

'Yeah, well, he knocked a chunk of plaster off the wall in the living room with one of his weights so, technically, he wrecked my house.'

Mollie smiled and placed a hand on my arm. 'Well, it's her loss. I like hanging out with you. You make me laugh and you haven't tried it on with me, so that's a bonus. You know what; I have a thing to go to in a couple of weeks that might be dull. Do you want to come with me to make it fun?'

'Er, maybe. What is it?'

'There's this production company that I've done some work with, they do theatre and TV and films, and they're having a big party to show off and schmooze people they want to schmooze. I've been invited and it would be great for me to show my face and meet some people who may or may not offer me work in the future. It's black tie and all that so you'll have to dress smart, but we can take the piss out of people. We might even be able to find you a new lady friend.'

'Or you a new fella.'

'What made you think I was straight?'

After a second or two of flapping, I realised she was teasing. 'So will you come?'

'Yeah, alright. Why not?'

17. BACK TO TRAINING

THE afternoon spent with Mollie had been great fun and really did take my mind off things. But the reality of my situation came crashing back down as soon as I got home and remembered I had to go into football training with a Premier League club the next morning but without the brain magician that made me a Premier League footballer. I would have to do this by myself, as myself. Shit.

I did text Keith again to see if there was something he, we or I could do, but the little fucker never replied. I tried to think of ways of doing it myself because I knew the trigger words he used. But once I was in the trance, I wouldn't have a way of getting myself back out of it. It's all well and good being able to kick and flick a football like Cristiano Ronaldo, but I didn't want to go home and spend the evening rubbing creams and lotions over my body while looking at myself in the mirror. I assume that's what he does.

So, I did what any self-respecting worker would do and I called in sick. Yeah, it seems a pretty obvious thing to do after the newspaper exposé, but there was no way I could train. I figured that I could say I was ill for a couple of days to buy some time so I could stay at home and work out what my next move would be away from the football pitch. But that's not how sick days work when you're a Premier League footballer. You don't get to sit at home under your duvet watching Jeremy Kyle or complete boxsets of American dramas. By being a footballer, you become a product. You are someone people pay money to see and when that money goes into the coffers of a greedy football club chief executive, they are extremely keen to keep you fully functioning at all times. So at 8am on that Monday morning, rather than being in my Avengers PJ bottoms and comedy hamburger slippers, I was picked up by a driver and taken to the training ground just off the M25 for a full inspection by the club's doctors.

'How do you feel?' one asked as a sample of blood was taken from my arm.

'Er, just run down, you know? Tired. Low on energy.'

'Is this to do with your counsellor?'

'Partly,' I lied. It was totally to do with him.

'Well, we have another performance counsellor coming in today to meet with you. Hopefully, she can get you operating like Mr Sykes did.'

I very much doubted she could. Less than 30 minutes later, I was in a room with Dr Shari Butler as she tried to reinvigorate the footballer in me. To be fair, she was amazing. We spoke about my anxieties and where they stemmed from. I had to lie a little because I wasn't actually anxious about playing football; it was just playing football at that level without Keith. We then did some visualisation and reassurance work and I was made to feel like a million dollars. I actually felt extremely positive and confident. Well, I did until she looked at her phone and said, 'Great, well, we'd like to get you out there for a bit of training now. The manager wants you changed and on the training pitch ASAP. Chop chop.'

As a man in his early 40s, I know how to get dressed. I've done it loads of times. What's 365 times 42? That'll give us a rough guide. Shit tons, right? Over 15,000. I've got dressed more than 15,000 times. I'm an expert at it. Well, apart from those skinny jeans, but that was more about undressing. And I can guarantee you that I had never got dressed as slowly as I did in the changing room that day. I'd put a bit of a sock on and then wait for a few minutes before pulling it up any further. For a good chunk of it, I just sat there in my pants frozen by the fear of what was going to happen when I went out on the training pitch as myself. Although, it had just turned February and was pretty icy out, so I was frozen out of coldness too. My nipples stuck out enough to pick up Essex FM.

'Hey, hey. There he is. Come on Rich, let's get moving bruv.' Harley Wells always seemed to be in a positive mood – except when I got him arrested, of course – and usually it was infectious, but not today. 'Listen, I know Keith ain't here, but this is the perfect chance for you to show him how far you've come with his help.'

No, it really wasn't.

Slowly and begrudgingly, I pulled on my kit, my boots and a training bib and trotted out of the changing rooms towards the pitches. The rest of the players were already playing a two-touch practice match and didn't respond too much as I came over to join in. Harry Jacobs was pretty much the only player to still be wearing shorts and a short-sleeved top in the chilly weather and he was the only one who acknowledged my arrival. He fixed me a steely stare and through gritted teeth said: 'So, did yoos bung 'er, eh, tha blondie?' I didn't really know what he meant, so I just nodded.

When Julie and I still lived together, there was a man who lived next door to us who was really old. Well into his 80s. He was very frail, but always liked to go out into his garden to feed the birds or pull a few weeds or whatever. Whenever he did, Julie would watch him from our patio window to make sure he got there and back to his house OK. She was paranoid that we'd find him collapsed in the garden one day. We would call out to him, 'You alright Jeff?', but often get no reply because his hearing was shot to pieces. To get his attention, you had to shout at the top of your voice. You had to holler as if he'd just stepped out in front of a bus and you were trying to get him out the way. 'JEFF! JEFF! ARE YOU ALRIGHT JEFF?' 'Oh yes, thank you, Julie,' he would reply meekly and mildly surprised. He'd always add an 'Up the Blues' if it were me calling to him. I had offered to take him to Roots Hall to watch Southend, he could've had Grandad's seat, but he said it was too much for him at his age. I timed Jeff once as he walked the 15 yards from his back door to the bird table with a few crumbs and back. It took him nearly eight minutes. If he dropped something, you weren't really sure he would survive the bending down to pick it up. Old, slow and frail. You get the picture.

Now imagine the dance troupe Diversity. You remember them off Britain's Got Talent, right? All flips and moves and jiggles all over the place. About 15 of them flying across the stage left, right and centre. Athletes and acrobats in perfect harmony with each other and the music while showcasing their individual skills and brilliance. Energy, youth and athleticism.

Well, the training match that I was now taking part in was akin to putting Old Jeff Next Door in with Diversity and expecting him to keep up with their dance routines, back-flips and all. I tried my best just to hang about on the far side of the pitch, far away from the manager and coaching staff, but the bastard ball just kept coming my way. One time it rolled straight under my foot and out for a throw, another time it hit my shin and bounced to an opposition player. Often I was tackled before I could even think to do anything and when I did get the ball under control, I fluffed the pass or shot. And I barely ran at all.

Even Horatio Emmett, my supposed best friend on the team, lost his rag with me. Players at this level take everything to do with football very seriously. When I used to play for Leigh Ramblers veterans over the park, my teammates would take the piss if I slipped over or scuffed a shot. Actually, I didn't have to do anything for them to take the piss. They often called me '50p head' or 'Toblerone feet' because you never really knew which direction the ball would bounce off once I made contact with it. There were several times I had to buy a jug of lager in the bar after the game because a shot or two had gone out for a throw.

But in the Premier League, players got annoyed by mistakes. You were meant to be brilliant, that's why you were there. You had to be at least as good as them and if you underperformed then your teammates would let you know in no uncertain terms. Out of all the players at LCU, Horatio had shown me the most support right from day one. But today he snapped: 'Is this a forking joke? Forking, sort yourself out. You meat-headed shit sack.' That last bit was actually from Gangs of New York, which showed he'd expanded the film collection from which he gathered his insults, but it wasn't the time to point that out. The truth was that I was trying my best. Except that my best at that point wasn't the same as it was when Keith was able to tinker with my brain.

'Alright ladies, that'll do for today. Go and get showered and fuck off in your Lamborghinis,' said Mike Cusick. He had been the coach in charge of the trial game. His footballing career hadn't been an illustrious one, but he knew his stuff when it came to coaching and he was one of the only English coaches at LCU. 'See the fitness team if you need to. Any tweaks or strains, get them seen to please. Horatio, Danny and Paolo, are you sticking around for some freekick work? Oh, fat boy. Price. Manager's office. Chop, chop. And I don't mean pork chops.'

This was not going to be good. Summoned to the boss's office. I'd had plenty of chats and briefings with him over the past few weeks but a one-on-one in his cave was a rare thing. I started getting changed and did my best to make it last as long as it did earlier in the hope the gaffer would forget and go home. Fat chance. Then Harry took a hold of my right arm with a vice-like grip that both scared the shit out of me and hurt like hell, but he had a smile on his face so I knew I wasn't in trouble. 'So waz she worth it? She looks a wee cracker.'

I shook my arm free and asked him what the hell he was talking about. I really had no clue, but he had a look in his eyes that told me he wanted answers and was possibly prepared to use a blowtorch, pliers and other industrial tools to get them from me. Hard to imagine that he spent his spare time oil painting. Harry called to one of the other players to pass over the paper, which he passed on to me. And these footballers claim they don't read papers! But there on the folded page was a picture of me and a 'mystery blonde'. The 'mystery blonde', of course, was Mollie.

RICH PICKINGS

PREMIER League ace Richie Price needed no extra time before he transferred to a new woman in his life.

The London City United sensation, 42, was spotted having lunch with a mystery blonde in trendy Borough Market yesterday afternoon.

The couple were then seen walking along the banks of the Thames. An onlooker said: 'They seemed to really enjoy each other's company and were close. The girl, who looked half his age, held onto his arm.'

With his estranged wife Julie now dating fitness hunk Matt Curbishley, it seems both the Prices have traded in their partners for a younger model.

Sneaky bastards. 'She's just a mate, Harry. I met her at Bush's party. She's a laugh.'

'Jis a mate? Aye, sure she is pal.'

I wasn't in the mood to argue the point any further. But how did they the paper know about Julie and Matt? I unfolded the rest of the paper and the horrific truth was laid bare. Across the rest of the two pages was Matt's punchable face and half-naked body staring back at me. He had sold his story to the Daily Citizen. He'd done a kiss and tell. *'Prem star's wife is a firecracker in bed says her fitness hunk lover,'* read the headline. I scanned the page quickly and another name leapt out at me. Tilson. He'd spoken to them about my son. The motherfucker. Wait till I...

'Oi, fat boy,' shouted Coach Cusick. 'Manager's office. Come on. He's got shit to do. Hurry the fuck up. Pretend there's a Curly Wurly on his desk with your name on it. Move.'

Franco Capece was sat in a comfy armchair tucking into a bowl of pasta and watching a football match on the big screen TV in his office when I entered. It was a smaller room than I thought he'd have as the boss and there was a lot packed into it. The back wall was all glass and looked out onto the training pitches. There was a small balcony that, I assume, allowed him to step out and bellow instructions or motivation if needed. In front of that was a modern, dark wood table with a flashy-looking computer on it and a row of phones. Along one wall were shelves filled with hundreds of DVDs of matches and players' highlights. On the other side of the room were stacks of books and manuals and several filing cabinets. It created a tunnel to the chair he now sat on next to a sofa under the great big telly. He ushered me in to sit down and said 'one moment' without taking his eyes off the screen now above me. I tried to crane my neck around to see, but it was too far to sit comfortably. Instead, I sat facing Franco but tried not to look at him eating his lunch and watching the box.

Finally, the manager pressed a button on the remote to pause the game, placed his bowl to one side and picked up a pad and pen from the table between us to make some notes. We sat in silence. As you would expect for an Italian ex-athlete, Franco was in very good shape. He was in his late 40s now and his hair was going grey, but he still had a healthy, tanned glow to his face and his sea-blue eyes were piercing and alert.

'Now,' he said, putting his pad to one side and fixing his gaze on me. 'Today, that was total shit.'

I went to speak, but he raised his hand to indicate he didn't want to hear it and that he wasn't done yet.

'First off, you don't call in sick like this is some sort of office job. OK?' I nodded. 'Second, that football out there was no good. No good at all. Mistakes? OK, you can make them, sometimes. Sometimes a lot. But there was no desire in you today. The mistakes did not upset you. There was no desire in your eyes, in your heart, to do these things better. You did not care. That is very disappointing. Mistakes I can take. Not caring, I cannot. You will not be in the squad for the game against Everton on Wednesday. You're dropped.'

'Yes gaffer, I understand.' Wow. What a relief. Being dropped was music to my ears. I wouldn't have to play in a proper match as myself. All I wanted was to get out of the Everton game and it worked, in a roundabout way. Now I would have some breathing space to find a long-term solution. However, I was so caught up in my own relief that I failed to see the face of the Italian opposite me turn an angry shade of red. This was a man who, in his playing days, had a bit of a reputation for losing his shit. He was once sent off during a Champions League semi-final after he picked up a ball boy and threw him into the crowd because the lad didn't return the ball quick enough. His team went out and he got an eight-match ban and missed their entire run in Europe the following season. He had calmed considerably since he hung up his boots, but that fire was still in him. And right now, it was focussed at me.

'NO!' he yelled, slamming his hand down on the arm of the chair and sending the bowl of leftover pasta crashing to the floor. 'You should not understand Price. You should be...' he paused, seemingly looking for the right word in English. '...outraged, angry, begging me "No gaffer, you keep me in the team, I will do better", not this wimpy, whiny "Oh, I understand Franco". What the fuck are you?'

My initial thought was of how well he spoke in his second language when he was angry, especially when you consider English was Harry Jacobs' first language and I needed subtitles to understand him most of the time.

'I'm sorry Franco, but my head just isn't right. I just need a bit of time to adjust...'

'Fuck you. Fuck off. I don't want you here. I don't want you near the team now. Go. Go now. Return Monday. You are fined a weeks' wages. No two. Get out my office.'

He picked up the remote and put the game back on without looking at me again. His teeth were gritted, but he was done with me now. I got up and left.

It was good news really. I would miss the Everton game on Wednesday, training for the rest of the week, and I would miss the cup game against Southend so Neil couldn't be pissed off with me about that. But I couldn't help feeling I had let the team down – LCU that is – and Franco Capece, who had put a lot of trust in me before now. Despite all the money, the flash cars, the designer clothes, the mansions, the plastic girlfriends and all that stuff, these guys were professional people trying to do a professional job that they cared very much about at the highest level. Among my many mistakes, I had underestimated that. But there was not a lot I could do to redeem myself right now. In any case, I had someone I needed to go and lose my temper with. Matt fucking Curbishley.

18. REVENGE

I'M not a man prone to aggression or violence. During those torrid years at school when I was bullied over my appearance, I learned that it was best just to take it and move on rather than retaliate. They were only words after all. Hurtful, spiteful words that once I got home and behind the safety barrier of my bedroom door made me sob relentlessly into my pillow until it was soaked, but only words nonetheless.

Some would say that if I gave some back to the bullies then they would leave me alone and respect me more. But I didn't want their respect and I didn't want to act like them either.

I could count on the fingers of one hand the number of times I had truly lost my temper and let the anger take over.

I remember playing football one Saturday and my team was winning (I wouldn't have been on the pitch otherwise). We had a nippy forward – a clever young lad called Mark – who was attracting the rage of one of the opposition players for no real reason. He hadn't been lippy or anything, but this guy just kept going into tackles trying to hurt him, and failing. The other team caught us on the counter-attack but, being quick, Mark was the one who got back and managed to nudge the ball out of play before his nemesis could get his shot away. Instead, the guy swung his kick at Mark and clattered both his legs away with a huge thump. But he wasn't done. He continued to kick him in the head and body as he rolled on the floor, curling into a ball to try and shield himself from the onslaught. I happened to be the nearest player – other than our goalkeeper who just ran to get the ball – and I surged in, furious. I shoved the guy away with a massive push and then connected with my forehead across his nose and mouth. It wasn't a full head-butt, but was enough to leave him clutching his face. It was the angriest I'd ever been on a football pitch. It was the cowardliness of the attack and the fact Mark wasn't able to hit back. The opposition player was sent off and lucky not to be reported for assault, but the ref – either through moral support or lack of eyesight (probably the latter) – let me stay on for the last few minutes.

Another time I lost my shit was at a nightclub. I'd had a few beers and alcopops and fancied myself as a dancer so I hopped up on to a podium by the edge of the dancefloor. Julie was with a couple of her friends having a boogie when two blokes sauntered over and tried their luck. I can't begrudge them that; it's what lads do on a night out. And I could see that Julie and the girls had made it clear that they weren't interested. But the two chaps persisted. Their Ralph Lauren knock-off shirts and overpowering wafts of Joop! aftershave had made them think they were irresistible. But they were met by more rejection. Even through the dry ice and coloured lasers flashing in my eyes, I could see from my lofty position on the podium that Julie was shaking her head and telling the pair to go away, before turning back to her pals. For a second, they did go away. But then one of the lads turned back, lifted my girlfriend's dress up from behind and grabbed her chest. Even back then I wasn't a particularly aerodynamic fellow, but I leapt from that podium as if I was Superman about to fly around the world a bazillion times at high speed to turn back the clock. It only took me a second or two to realise the distance between the podium and these guys was too great for me to make. Everything seemed to slow down and I saw revellers' stunned faces looking at this testosterone-fuelled drunken idiot as he belly-flopped onto the hard, wooden dancefloor with a horrible thwack. I'm pretty sure the thud made the record the DJ was playing skip.

The dancefloor in McCluckie's nightclub had always been sticky from night after night of booze being spilt by errant dancers. Now I saw it up close and could feel its grip tightening on my white shirt (well, it had been white) as if an octopus clinging to the side of a huge aquarium. Even if I wanted to get up, I'm not sure I could've at that moment without assistance. I was like a beached whale with a captive audience. Everyone in the club had stopped and turned to look at me – even Julie, despite her bottom half being exposed for all to see. My beautiful Julie. I had taken attention away from what had happened to her, but I still hadn't taken my anger out on the little shit that'd done it. Fortunately, when I dived I had done so with one hand out in front – I told you it was like Superman – and that hand was now gripped around the ankle of the chav who'd pulled my girlfriend's dress up and groped her. It took him a moment to register and when he did I yanked as hard as I could. His foot slid towards me, but the other was stuck fast to the dance-floor by congealed Apricot Bacardi Breezer and chewing gum. The slow-motion returned and as mouths gasped and hands went up to cover them, the twatty chav was midway to performing an unlikely splits. As his legs inched apart, the stitching around the crutch of his trousers began to give way under the strain and expose some frankly hideous green underpants.

The crowd – now including an assembled throng of bouncers, keen to have an input into any punch-up – followed the path of the lad's splits and realised the direct route between his Y-front-encased testicles and the sticky dancefloor was blocked by way of a broken bottle stump.

The music in McCluckie's was still blaring away as this whole episode took place, but Baby D's Let Me Be Your Fantasy was no match in volume for the sound that came out that lad's mouth as he hit the ground with a thump, a rip and a spurt of blood from his ballbag. Most people looked away, a few heaved and one or two dashed to his aid. Me? Well, I couldn't do much at all as I was being dragged away by my arms, shirt and hair by the bouncers who didn't much like the shedding of blood in their nightclub unless it was their doing. Before that kid had the chance to clasp both hands around his torn nutsack, I was being tossed through the double doors and straight into the road. Still, at least I didn't have to queue for a taxi.

The other time I lost my temper was in December 1993 when Barry Fry quit as manager of Southend United to join Birmingham City. Fry had arrived at Southend at the end of the previous season and kept us in the old Second Division (now the Championship). He had overhauled the squad and we were looking good. This was a golden period for the Blues and the prospect of a place in the top-flight of English football was not as ludicrous as it had seemed before (or now for that matter). We had a great squad of players like Ricky Otto, Chris Powell, Brett Angell, Andy Ansah, Paul Sansome in goal and Jason Lee. We could have won promotion. We could've been the new Wimbledon back when being Wimbledon was something to be admired.

But then Fry got his head turned and left. He said that he wouldn't leave, but then changed his mind. He fucked off and fucked it up for everyone. Birmingham got relegated that season, but Southend never really recovered from his exodus and within a few seasons went down, down, down to the bottom of the Football League. I was so angry when he left that I tore down the squad poster from my bedroom wall because it had his smug face on it. The blue tack on the poster stuck to the wallpaper and ripped two great, long strips off. Grandad wasn't too happy about that.

We did get one bit of revenge though. Only a few weeks after Fry and his management team left for Birmingham, they were back at Roots Hall for a league match in the away dugout. New Year's Day it was. The match was a sell-out and Bazza took absolute pelters from the home support. I can't even repeat some of the things that were said. Truly disgusting. Not by me, of course, nor by Grandad. He was always a gentleman, even at the football. A little shake of the head was as far as he went, but that was as much towards the bad language used by the Shrimpers' fans to their former manager than to the former manager himself.

Southend won 3-1. Keith Jones scored the first before Jonathan Hunt – a player who followed Fry to Brum the next season – curled in a beauty from the edge of the box for the second and Jason Lee notched the third. We were ecstatic at the result. Grown men cried and strangers were hugged. But I suspect if you asked Fry now he'd say he had the last laugh.

So, there was the retaliation for my mate getting booted at football, the disco dancefloor debacle and Barry Fry leaving Southend. But now added to the list of things that have caused my blood to boil and prompted a desire to inflict horrible things on other people was Matt 'Turbo Curbo' Curbishley selling his story to the Daily Citizen. I say 'story' in the loosest sense of the word.

I didn't care that he was in the paper or that he mentioned me. What really pissed me off was the fact he revealed intimate things about my wife and that he repeatedly spoke about my son Tilson and how he was acting as a stand-in dad while I was off enjoying the high-life as a Premier League footballer. What a wanker.

In the films, I would be seen haring down the motorway, weaving in and out of cars at 100mph as I raced to confront my foe. But, being an ex-driving instructor, I had a respect for the rules of the road. Plus I knew there were loads of average speed cameras along the A13 from London to Essex and I didn't fancy losing my licence. Also, a Ben Howard CD was playing in the car and it really chilled me out, which was exactly how I didn't want to be when I confronted the arrogant prick. I'd gone in cold before and come out second best, this time I needed to fuel the rage.

About five minutes from the house, I pulled over and grabbed my phone. I fired up Spotify and found a playlist of Tilson's that I had downloaded. I pressed shuffle a couple of times until I heard the perfect tune. It was very noisy heavy metal; very shouty and lots of guitars. I would have to speak to Tilson about the music he was listening to, because some of the language used in this song I would hope my teenage son didn't know. But it was perfect for me at that moment. I turned it up loud enough to make the windows vibrate on the car and it put me back in the right frame of mind. When I turned into our road, the anger had risen in me again. At that moment I could've walked through a brick wall.

Julie had either seen me pull up or heard the music blaring from down the road because she was waiting for me at the front door as I approached. 'Where is he?' I growled in a manner not too dissimilar to Batman. To be honest, I had practised that in the car on the way down. I wanted to sound menacing, but it does actually hurt your throat after the first few dozen times. Anyway, Julie stood to one side and ushered me into the house with a flick of her head. I was so angry that I didn't even take my shoes off before walking on the cream carpet in the living room. When I lived at the house that was a crime punishable by death or, more likely, a really hard stare and a tut. But, on this occasion, I was wearing a new pair of Converse and it was unlikely they would have got dirty between my apartment and the car and the car and here.

The room was empty. No Matt.

'So where is he?' I asked again, although this time in a tone less Christian Bale and more Christian choirboy.

'He's not here love,' said Julie. 'I just didn't want you making a scene out in the street. There's probably photographers out there.'

She looked at my face and could see the mixture of anger, frustration and helplessness. 'It was a shitty thing he did,' she added.

'Shitty? Did you see what he said about you? He referred to you as a milf. In the paper!'

'Well, I don't think that's particularly derogatory,' my wife said with a smile that could melt the heart of a South American warlord.

'No, no. But it's demeaning…' Julie didn't look so sure that it was. 'Well, it's objectifying you. And he spoke about Tilson. There was no need for it, at all. He's using me – using us – to boost his modelling career or whatever and I want to punch him in his pretty little face.'

'And what good would that do, eh? Break your hand and give him another story to sell to the papers – one that would look even worse on you and you as a father. I know Matt has been stupid and I've told him so in no uncertain terms. Leave him to me.'

'Have you dumped him?'

'I'm not 12. No, I haven't dumped him. I don't even know if there's dumping to be done. I haven't decided what this thing is anyway…' Zing! A glimmer of hope for me '…but he's not here right now, OK? He's at work and I've told him not to do anything like this again.'

'Too right. He's pathetic and shameless. Using other people like that to get publicity.'

'Well, he's not the only one, is he? Your new girlfriend isn't backwards in coming forwards in that department either. And while we're talking about Tilson and family and so on, don't you think you should've told us about her before we read it in the paper?'

'She's not my girlfriend. She's a friend. A nice person. Someone fun to hang around with, like you used to be.'

'Someone who happens to be an aspiring actress and who happened to be followed by a photographer when she met Premier League sensation Richie Price for a coffee and a stroll. Was that her idea or yours?'

'Hers, but...'

'And did she choose the location?'

'Yes, but...'

'Oh, what a surprise.'

'Oh, fuck off, will you. It's not like that at all. Stop trying to take the attention away from your muscle-bound drip of a boyfriend selling his soul. He's the one posing in the paper with his top off.'

I left shortly after. I had called Matt a roid-popping, talentless cockwomble and Julie said Mollie was a parasitic jailbait slut. I think her insult was more cutting, but mine was more creative, not that I took any great comfort from that small victory.

I did drive to the gym Matt worked at, but thought better of going in. I just let two of the tyres down on his car and headed for home. My phone went during the drive. It was Mollie. What Julie had said niggled in the back of my mind as I answered.

'Hiya pet, you alright?' she asked. I lied and said I was. 'I just seen the paper. Awkward! Didn't cause you any trouble did it?'

'No, not really.' Lie.

'Cool, in that case, do you want to meet up later?'

My spidey-sense was going ten to the dozen. Was Julie right? Was this a set-up? As a test, I asked Mollie when and where we could meet, but she said it was up to me.

'Look, I, er, I've had a bit of a crappy day at training and just had a row with Julie...' shit, shouldn't have let that slip '...well, not a big one, but I just want to go home now, you know?'

'I could come over if you like. You know I'm shit hot at Fifa, so I could kick your arse on that again.'

'No, no. I'm good thanks. Bath and an early night. Maybe another time.'

'Oh, OK, yeah, no bother,' said Mollie, dejected. 'You're still cool for Saturday though?'

'Saturday?'

'The gala – the party thing I told you about the other day. You promised you'd come.'

'Ah, yeah. I'm not playing Saturday now, so should be fine for the evening. Text me the details.'

Luckily, she didn't ask why I wasn't playing Saturday. I'd still not heard any more from Keith and I'm not sure spending more time alone in the flat would do my mental health any good. But I was starting to feel very lonely in my new life.

19. FATHER AND SON

FOOTBALL is a funny old game and footballers, in general, are funny people. When the managers and players say in interviews that they're just focusing on the next game, they really mean it. Everything else goes out the window. Being banished from the training ground for the week pretty much made me dead to my teammates. It's like when Patrick Swayze's busy trying to get Demi Moore's attention in the first part of Ghost, before the pottery shagging bit. No response. The players just got on with their jobs. No one called or texted to see if I was OK or why I wasn't training. Weird.

To fend off the isolation, I persuaded Julie to let Tilson come and stay with me for a few nights, which was cool. I took him for dinner at a proper swanky restaurant in the West End. It was delicious, but the portions were so small that we ended up getting a pizza delivered to the apartment when we got back. We ate it in the hot tub on the balcony.

On the Wednesday night, we watched London City United's game against Everton on the telly. Tilson kept asking what this player or that was really like, who earned the most money, what cars people drove, and so on.

'That's Dave Andrews,' I told him, pointing to the full-back. 'We call him the Professor.'

'Is he actually a professor? Is he really clever?'

'No, he just got seen reading a broadsheet newspaper one day at the training ground. It's the most intelligent thing most of them have seen. And that's Danny Diegbe. He's a fun lad. He has about five or six girlfriends at a time and sometimes he mixes up their names by accident or invites more than one of them to meet him after games and they start fighting and so on. Go on Danny son...great cross....oooooh!' The ball drifted over all their players in the box and out for a throw on the other side of the pitch. The game was still 0-0. If we won, we would move into the top four for the first time this season.

'Had that cross come in from Richie Price, with the sort of form he's been in, then Everton would've been caught square there, but it's a waste from the boy Diegbe,' said the pundit.

'Price, of course, left out the squad tonight, not even on the bench,' added the commentator. 'Not exactly sure why, the club says he's dealing with some personal issues, but we wish him a speedy return because he's been a revelation for LCU since the turn of the year.'

I didn't really like being spoken about in my absence or the reason the club had given for me not playing. What's wrong with them saying I had a minor knock or pulled a muscle? Everyone understands that and accepts 'minor knock' without question. But 'personal issues' makes it sound like a major trauma, which it was really considering I still hadn't been able to speak to Keith directly. He had sent me a text to say he'd be back in the country on Saturday and we could speak then, but I still couldn't get any calls to connect. At least I knew he wasn't being held to ransom by the Spanish mafia for shagging their wives. We could still salvage something from this. Maybe.

I looked over at Tilson and saw concern in his eyes – concern for me. 'Shall we turn this off dad and do something else? Football's pretty boring when you're not playing. Maybe we could play Monopoly or Game of Life. Have you got any of them here?'

We loved a good board game. Monopoly was the favourite, even though Julie would always steal money out of the bank when she thought no one was looking.

I didn't have Monopoly though, but I nipped down and borrowed chess from Colin the security guard and played that with the football still on in the background. I really missed spending this much time around my boy.

LCU lost the match 2-0. Had we won, we would've moved into the Champions League places. The crisis club that had flirted with the lower reaches of the division earlier in the season and had been caught up in the dodgy agent scandal that left a huge chunk of the squad suspended was now aiming for the top four. A title shot was not completely out of reach, although getting above Manchester City, Manchester United and Tottenham would be a tall order. Especially if we turned in results like that against Everton when the main architect of the club's revival – aka humble old me – wasn't available for selection.

I was gutted at missing that game, more than I thought I would. Me in the zone, as it were, could've made the difference out there. Those lost three points could be huge at the end of the season. I was less disappointed about missing the cup game against Southend United on Saturday, although playing at Roots Hall would be a childhood dream come true. LCU should win the game with the talent in the squad, but I didn't want to be the person who put the Blues – my real team – out of the cup. I don't think I'd ever be able to look Neil in the eye again if that happened. And it would feel like I'd betrayed Grandad.

A journalist from the local paper knew I was a Southend fan and got in touch asking if I would do an interview ahead of the game, but other than that I wouldn't have any involvement at all and that suited me just fine.

Keith was going to be back on the scene at the weekend too – although I wouldn't know whether to hug him or throttle him – and we could work out some way of hypnotising me remotely so I didn't have to play as me again and embarrass myself. Things were going to be OK.

20. THE REPORTER

AS a lad, Jim Neale also had aspirations of becoming a professional footballer. He played in the youth set-ups at Charlton, Crystal Palace and Millwall, but they all felt he was too small to make it. That seemed a harsh thing to decide about a young teen still going through the ignominy of puberty and body growth, but he wasn't quite good enough for them to take a chance. To be fair to them, they were right. He never grew past 5ft 5ins tall and his body seemed to grow outwards instead of upwards. He looked like a bowling ball with feet.

He toured around non-league with such clubs as Carshalton, Tooting & Mitcham and Sutton United for a bit. But as the booze and late-night kebabs took over, so did the size of his stomach, and his fitness and reliability plummeted. By the age of 22, Jim's playing days were numbered. Instead, he started earning some money by selling knock-off goods. His dad worked in an Argos warehouse and often accidentally dropped a pallet of this or that (sometimes both) out of the back door and into a mate's van in the dead of night. Jim also sold a few stories about the football world to a few journalists on the national newspapers. Football has always been a pretty incestuous business, so the people Jim played with or was coached by knew someone who knew something that was going on at some of the bigger clubs. Transfer gossip, rifts, and so on.

He was drinking in the Red Lion in Catford, South London, just a short walk from the house he was born in and still lived with his parents, when he got talking about football to a chap at the bar. The guy turned out to be the editor of the local newspaper and, impressed with Jim's knowledge of the game and his contacts, offered him a job then and there as a non-league football reporter. Being able to combine three of his great loves – football, gossip and drinking – meant he excelled and even stopped shifting so much hooky gear. Three years later he moved to the Daily Citizen as their South London football reporter and the seeds of his eventual reign as the king of the sleazy side of the Beautiful Game were sown.

In the old days, he'd slip players or a coach or the kit man a ten-ner here or there, or buy them a few drinks in return for quality gossip about transfers and footballing matters. He got a ping of pride whenever he saw his byline, especially when it appeared on the back page. But that was nothing compared to his first front page recognition. He'd been having tea and biscuits and whisky with a groundsman at Millwall who had a mate who worked at Chelsea who had seen the club's athletic young left-back Howard Jeremy – a hopeful for England's 1986 World Cup squad – having a bunk-up with a woman who was not his pregnant wife in the back of a Ford Capri in a quiet corner of the training ground site. Over the next few days, Jim paid a few people a few quid, hid in a few bushes and parked outside a few houses for a few hours on end until he caught sight of Jeremy and the girl in the act. In flagrante delicto. But rather than going in all guns blazing, Jim waited and confronted the young woman alone. He told her that her side of the story would be portrayed sympathetically, that Jeremy was the love-rat, and there was also a chance she could be signed up to be a topless model for the paper too.

It was a straight up-and-down kiss and tell story, but Jim Neale was hooked. He loved the thrill of the chase and – even more so – seeing his name in lights on the front page and the acclaim that brought him.

The game itself would now play second fiddle as Jim spent the next 30 years trying to dig up dirt, entrap and frame England's elite footballers into becoming the sacrificial lambs at the altar of his tabloid infamy. He wasn't much liked among the football fraternity any longer, but some saw him as a necessary evil. It helped some get rivals or teammates into trouble, or unsettle players or to push a transfer along. But there were some who saw major benefits in keeping Jim Neale onside. Sean Clark, the tidy-bearded and perma-tanned chief executive of London City United, was one such person. A smart cookie. He fed Jim stories from the changing room that were newsworthy and embarrassing to the player involved – someone who had rocked the boat or threatened to – but not damaging to the individual or the club in the long term. In return, Jim kept any major scandals Clark wanted to remain secret off the back pages. He also took home an extra bit of wedge that the taxman never knew existed. Everyone was a winner.

Jim's latest focus – one that Clark had put him on to and, unusually, given him free reign over despite him being an LCU player – was Richie Price.

Football is full of stories about later developers. Stuart Pearce was working as an electrician and playing non-league for Wealdstone when he got snapped up by then-top flight Coventry City in 1983. But he was still only 21. Ian Wright was a plasterer when he joined Crystal Palace, but was also in his early 20s. Jamie Vardy was a little older. He was 24 when he moved out of non-league to sign for Leicester City, whom he would spearhead to an unlikely Premier League title in 2016.

But Price was something else. Something different. Not only was he into his 40s, but he had no footballing history at all. He hadn't been doing the business in non-league or played for an established team as a youth or anything. And speaking to his former teammates at his park team Leigh Ramblers, which Jim had done several times in recent weeks, he barely played for them either because he was so woeful. 'Saying he had two left feet would be praising him too highly,' one had said. 'He barely even had one left foot. He was shit…well, apart from that last game he played for us when he came on as a late sub and scored five goals to win us the game single-handedly, but that was just weird.'

But despite having no footballing pedigree, this overweight train wreck was now turning in performances at the highest level of English football that would put him in the same bracket as Messi, Ronaldo, Maradona, Pele, Zidane and the like.

Something was most definitely up – not just his cholesterol – and it most definitely had something to do with Keith Sykes aka The Amazing Syko. Price had not trained or played since Sykes was banished from the club following Jim's expose about his Don Juan antics on the Costa del Sol. Another great scoop for Mr Neale. He was pleased with that one and earned a nice little kick-back from his friend in the chief exec's office at London City United.

But Sykes didn't seem to be too bothered about his banishment right now. Because right now he was poolside at the five-star Sandale Bay Beach Resort Hotel in Miami, Florida, in a pair of very tight yellow budgie-smugglers, knocking back his third pint of the day. It was 11.15am. He only seemed to move to tip his Ray Bans down to allow him to leer and wink at any passing woman in a bikini and pass on a complimentary and complementary 'Nice rack, darlin'.' He had done the same thing for the past two days.

But one thing that was niggling Jim was the cost of this place. From what he'd learned, Sykes didn't have a job other than his 'counselling' of Richie Price and he certainly didn't have much cash in the bank. But the suite he was staying in with a sea view would set him back the best part of a grand a night. Was Price picking up the tab for this? If so, why? Why did he want Sykes out of the country? Or maybe Sykes had blackmailed him into paying it? What dirt did he have on Price? What were these two up to?

Jim Neale decided to let Sykes knock back a couple more pints before he went over and introduced himself as another Brit travelling alone in the US and suggest they have a couple more beers together. It was all on expenses anyway. Loose lips sink ships and all that.

21. BLACK AND BLUES

T HE build-up to London City United's FA Cup clash with Southend United actually turned out to be quite fun and exciting. I'd had a call on the Thursday before the game from the media team at LCU saying they'd had a request from the BBC for me to be a studio guest for Match of the Day's coverage alongside Gary Lineker and Alan Shearer.

I was a massive fan of Lineker as a kid to the point where in the summer of 1986 I never went anywhere without a length of Tubigrip on my wrist after the England striker hurt his arm. Grandad even bought me an England shirt so I looked like the real deal. I wasn't religious, but I actually prayed by my bed at night on several occasions and asked the big man in the clouds to make Gary sign for Southend United because I knew he would score the goals to fire us into the First Division. But, alas, he opted for Barcelona and Spurs instead.

I accepted the BBC's invitation and the media team made the arrangements on my behalf. They inserted their own stipulations such as me not being allowed to comment on my fitness, why I wasn't in the team or any other first-team matters. I invited Julie and Tilson to come along to watch too from the directors' box at

Southend. I also had to ask Julie to go up in the loft and dig out my Gary Lineker scrapbook so I could get him to sign it. She asked what was in it for her and I said she might get the chance to meet Alan Shearer and that sealed the deal.

Because I wasn't so great with the ball as a kid, I was forever making scrapbooks to fuel my passion for the game. It was another side-effect of being an only child and orphan, and rarely going out. Grandad would get a copy of The Sun or Mirror every day, as well as the local papers, and I'd cut out the football pictures when he was done and stick them in my books. I had a Southend United scrapbook and another one for my favourite pictures of players from other teams. After his Golden Boot heroics in Mexico, Gary Lineker got his own one too.

The only other player to get his own book was Steve Tilson, my favourite ever Southend player and inspiration for my son's name. He wasn't a particularly spectacular or free-scoring player, but he always worked hard. An industrious midfielder. And I had a fascination with his hair. He always seemed to have exactly the same style season after season after season. Paul Pogba would be driven insane by such hirsutal consistency. Steve's was a sort of a short back and sides with the front spiked up a little and it never moved, even in hurricane-force winds. It was like it was made of Lego and he just clipped it onto his head every morning. But I loved him as a player. Whenever he got the ball, I would stand up excitedly, expecting something good to happen. Grandad would shake his head and pull at the bottom of my coat to let me know I needed to sit down.

I even went to watch Tilly play after he left Southend in the late 90s and moved down the road to Canvey Island where he was an all-action, free-scoring midfielder. He even played for Canvey against Southend a couple of years later. That was in the FA Cup too. The Blues won 2-1. And Tilson was, weirdly, employed by Southend at the time of that game as a youth coach. He eventually became Southend's manager in 2003 and led the club to the Championship with two successive promotions, two appearances in the League Trophy final and knocked a Manchester United team including Cristiano Ronaldo and Wayne Rooney out of the League Cup in 2006.

But I'm not just fanboying for my own benefit, all these memories about the Blues and Tilson and watching games with Grandad came up during an interview for the local paper with their Southend United correspondent Bernie Phillips. The Blues let us do the interview and a photoshoot at Roots Hall, which was great fun. We sat where my season ticket was for a bit and also went on the pitch. My first time doing so. I tingled all over, it was magic. Grandad never let me go on the pitch, even when others were pouring out from the stands onto the green grass after a big win or at the end of a season. I almost went over the wall when we beat Barry Fry's Birmingham on his return to Roots Hall, but resisted. Being on it now felt special, but there was also a pang of disappointment that I wouldn't be out there for the match and experience the stadium packed to the rafters.

But an added bonus was that Bernie told me Steve Tilson would be at the game too as an expert summariser on BBC Radio Essex. I would get the chance to meet two of my footballing heroes in one day. I really needed Julie to get those scrapbooks out the loft now.

Jimmy Greaves could not have been more right when he said that football was a funny old game. For a nearby fixture like the cup tie with Southend, London City United would normally spend the night before in the luxurious, scientifically-constructed accommodation at the club's training ground. The rooms were soundproof, with special wallpaper and aromas pumped in that helped ensure the optimum sleep and then perfect rousing in the morning. Fully refreshed, the players would then head for a very light session first thing in the morning, followed by a rub down and expertly-prepared food well in advance to allow for it to be digested ahead of the coach ride to the ground and so on.

But either Franco Capece had a bizarre brainwave or someone with significant influence convinced him and his team to take the players on a team-building jaunt to Southend seafront on the day before the match and stay overnight at a hotel in the town. On paper, it may not seem like too much of a bad idea. But like football, a bunch of lads on a day out is not played on paper. The LCU players – left to their own devices during the day so long as they were back at the hotel for a team meeting at 7pm – were not exactly inconspicuous and the Southend United fans out and about in the town seemed to do their best to nobble their Premier League opponents at any opportunity.

Horatio Emmett was the first victim. He had never been to a theme park before and was awestruck by Big Rollers Pleasure Palace (which many had joked sounded more like the name of a brothel). Insanity was their big rollercoaster and it was the first Horatio had ever been on. Once round, he was hooked. He spent the whole of the day running from ride to ride with a smile as wide as Southend's Golden Mile.

He raced up to The Spider ride and his mouth dropped open with excitement. He loved spiders. There were eight huge arms coming from the central body of the spider and each had a set of two seats. Once the ride was going, it would spin around and around while moving up and down and getting faster and faster. It was a short ride, only a couple of minutes, but the power was intense. He'd seen others wobbling with dizziness as they came off and he wanted that feeling too. The delightful butterflies in his belly.

'We're closing this ride now, sorry sir,' the young lad operating The Spider said politely. 'The others are still going, though.'

'No, no, no,' said the Brazilian footballer. 'I need to ride this motherfucker now. I've not been on it. One go, one go. Come on man. Close after me. Please.' With a mischievous grin, the lad unclipped the chain barrier and let the £80million striker stroll through delighted. 'Fucking love you Gumbo,' Horatio added.

Just then, a man and his teenage son approached the entrance to The Spider but were turned away. 'Sorry, this ride is closed just for Horatio Emmett, the footballer. He said he didn't want to share it with, er, local scum, I think he said.'

'Fackin' wankah!' the man shouted and made the hand gesture.

Horatio couldn't work out what the man down by the entrance of the ride was saying due to the thumping music, but he seemed to be waving so he waved back. This was great fun. He'd never had a day like this. He loved this feeling with the straps holding him tightly in place. It meant something really fast and powerful was going to happen. Once the season was over and the World Cup was out the way, he would spend his holiday travelling to the best theme parks in the world. If this was just a little theme park in a little town like this then who knows what else was out there.

The lad operating the ride came over and double-checked the footballer was strapped in correctly and then went back to his little booth, pressed the start button and picked up a copy of the paper to see what that fat bastard Richie Price had to say about Southend United. Almost 45 minutes had passed when one of the LCU coaches wandered past and saw the club's star striker being hurled around and around at 100mph and looking decidedly green around the gills. Within five minutes, two chubby lads in their St John's Ambulance uniforms were carrying him on a stretcher towards their first aid room while Coach Cusick caught his sick in a bucket. Horatio's world was still completely in a spin. He would not recover in time for the game.

It was a similar fate that met LCU's 6ft 6in Swedish centre-back Christian Halberg. He had been having a fun little jaunt around on the bumper cars, laughing and joking with a bunch of kids he'd posed for selfies with in the queue. But in one corner of the rink sat in a blue bumper car, naturally, was Tony Forsyth. Tony had once tried to set up the Southend United Extremists. He wanted an Ultras-style group to bring an aggressive, macho, violent and hostile section of the support to Roots Hall. He hadn't realised he had named his group SUE. It sounded like the nice lady on the check-out at Morrisons. Tony wanted flares being set off, threats to the opposition and huge flags to be passed among the home fans. There was some support for his plan, but things went wrong. He misread the measurements at the printing firm and his 30ft by 20ft 'Blues Extremists' banner flag came back at 30cm by 20cm. And he had entrusted the purchase of the flares to his mate Wes, but the idiot had rung the club to ask what was allowed. Having been told flares and fireworks were strictly not permitted and would be confiscated, he had turned up with 460 glow sticks he got for a bargain at the 98p Shop.

But now was the time for Tony to really make his mark. Now was the time where actions would speak louder than words. He counted in his head the number of seconds it took for Christian Halberg to steer his floppy blond body around the bumper car rink and then calculated his own acceleration speed and trajectory. As the Swede passed with a pleasant nod of the head to say hello, Tony slammed his foot on the pedal and pushed it to the floor. As he accelerated, he saw a child in front of him out to the left in trouble. The boy tried to correct his steering but he spun out, going coun-ter-clockwise instead of clockwise, and thumped into the side of Halberg's car, bringing it to a standstill. Halberg had, in fact, bashed his shins and it really stung, but he didn't want to look too pissed off in front of the locals. These were the sorts of people who bought the tracksuits he was paid so handsomely to model. Instead, he grimaced and tried to steer around the boy's stricken car. As he did, he looked up and saw the face of the Devil. Tony Forsyth had a twisted smirk across his face and every muscle in his body appeared to be clenched as he drove his blue bumper car like an arrow into the front of Halberg's.

The thud from the collision was immense. Heads turned to look from all around. Halberg's body was thrown back in his bumper car, his head clattering against the pole at the back that rose up to the electrical net at the top and then his neck snapped forward as it rebounded. The fire of pain from the whiplash tore through Halberg's neck, but the footballer then realised there was worse to come. Tony Forsyth had not bothered to put the loop of black material across his shoulder and so there was nothing to hold him in place. The collision sent the rear of his car into the air and catapulted his generous frame out of the seat and towards Halberg. Forsyth had the wherewithal to hold his arms by his sides as he transformed himself into a flabby torpedo and yelled 'Up the Blues' as he steered his shaven and tattooed head into the pretty nose of the Swedish international footballer and male model opposite him. Both were knocked unconscious and would miss the game due to their admissions to hospital. Halberg's nose would forever more contain less bone than a jellyfish. At least Tony knew he'd done his bit for the cause. SUE had stuck it to the soulless Man destroying the game he loved. But by fuck did his head hurt.

Franco Capece was livid when he found out two of his starting XI for the following day's FA Cup match were now incapacitated and unavailable. He ordered all the players back to the hotel that instant. Club staff were sent out to find those who didn't return within half an hour of his summons. Our imperious club captain Adam Bush was furious at being dragged out of the cinema mid-film and launched into the manager as soon as he saw him.

'I am the captain of the club and my country and I will not be treated like a fucking child,' he raged without mentioning he had been watching a kids' club singalong showing of Moana.

But the most distraught of all the players was Andrey Kozlov. He was one of the best full-backs in the world, with amazing pace and power and was equally good going forward as defending. London City United had outbid Real Madrid to land his services the summer before last for £48million. But while he had been blessed by the footballing gods, he was cursed by those who dished out looks. His facial features all seemed to congregate in the middle of a moon-ish head, as if they were pinched together. And his large nose zig-zagged more than a school crossing zone and jutted out to an angry point. His bushy monobrow was the least of his worries. He had cauliflower ears and teeth that didn't seem to want to stand next to one another. All of this had led to him picking up the nickname Curdle, because whenever he tried to chat up a woman, they would look at him and pull a face as if they'd just smelled curdled milk.

But, somehow, in the few short hours Kozlov had been given to roam freely in the grey-slab town centre of Southend high street, he had found love. She was a fellow Russian and, according to later reports from some of our teammates, was an absolute stunner. And not blind. Svetlana was a fan of Kozlov already and was overjoyed at serving him in Starbucks. Not only did she spell his name correctly on his cup, but she also left her name and phone number. They grabbed five minutes together in which they spoke hurriedly and excitedly about their homeland and how they found living in England and things they missed. They agreed to meet when Svetlana finished work at 5pm so that they could talk more for a few hours before Andrey was due back at the hotel. But then came the text that ordered him back to the hotel straight away and as much as he wanted to spend time with the beautiful brunette who knew his name and wasn't repulsed by his looks, he was also a stickler for the rules and would not disobey a direct instruction from his manager, however unfair.

Later in the evening though, two of the younger players in the squad had hatched themselves a little plan. They were very keen on sampling a Friday night on the town in Southend and seeing what the local ladies had to offer. And they knew that if they roped a more senior player into coming along, they would not bear the brunt of any recriminations and disciplinary measures should they be caught. It took some doing, but they managed to convince Andrey that it was his destiny to leave the sanctuary of the hotel that night to go and meet the new love of his life Svetlana at McCluckie's nightclub.

'We don't have to drink,' Danny Diegbe told him. 'We'll just have a dance for a bit, a couple of Diet Cokes, and get back here around midnight.'

'The gaffer ain't actually said we can't go out bruv,' added Hamilton Lee, an 18-year-old graduate from the youth team with more confidence than is safe for any one human. 'And you get to see your future baby mumma.'

'Maybe,' muttered Andrey, his heart torn between his morals and potential love. But by 11.30pm he was sat face-locked with Svetlana next to a table full of empty glasses that had once contained double vodkas. Danny and Hamilton, meanwhile, had made their way through a couple of bottles of champagne and shots and were now dancing nearby with pretty much every woman in the entire club making a beeline for them in the hope of hooking themselves a footballer. However, this pissed off the local lads considerably. They'd done themselves up to the nines, splashed on their best aftershave and were now spending their hard-earned on a big night out that would only be deemed a success if they managed to get a young lady home with them. Scrub that. A handjob out by the bins would be a success (a phone number would be like marriage) but they would take rubbing their semi against some twerking chick on the dancefloor as a right result.

But there was no chance of any of that with those Premier League twats who earn more in a week than these lads did in a year or two flashing their cash and perfect smiles. Wankers.

'Even that ugly Russian cunt has pulled a stunner,' one moaned. 'He's gotta face like a bag full of chisels.'

'All abaht the fackin money for these slaaags,' said another.

'Here, watch this,' announced a third before launching a half-empty bottle of Budweiser – or half-full depending on what level of optimism you have – towards the booth containing the three footballers and Svetlana.

Hamilton and Danny stopped dancing as the bottle exploded by their feet and sent a jet of beer across his designer trainers. They looked up to see another wave of bottles headed their way. Without thinking, Hamilton picked up an empty champagne bottle from the table and slung it back, but it was heavier than he expected and he didn't get the lift he had hoped for. The bottle flew straight into the face of one of the harem of women around them. As the blood pumped out relentlessly from the cut on her nose and down onto her previously-pristine white lace dress, the local lads had seen enough. 'Did you see what that cunt did?' shouted one, and they all stormed in. Fists flew, shirts got ripped, kicks made contact with delicate places and yet Andrey and Svetlana remained clasped together by the lips, snogging like their lives depended on it. That was, until another thrown bottle clipped Svetlana's head, shattered against the wall next to them and showered her in broken glass. Andrey flipped. He went from Bruce Banner to full Hulk in less than a second. Setting his new love to one side, he then began knocking out Essex boy after Essex boy one punch at a time. It was like a WWE hero storming into a Royal Rumble and clearing house. No one stood a chance. Even Hamilton and Danny took a step back and then tried to make a hasty exit. But they were grabbed by the bouncers and held in the foyer area until the police arrived. Even with all the badly-beaten locals in full retreat, Andrey was still raging. The dancefloor had become a battlefield and he was now pacing it like a demon looking for his next victim. Even the bouncers refused to go near him having seen how easily he had dispatched with the local riff-raff. They thought about storming him five on one, but decided it was not worth the risk. Svetlana tried to calm him, calling out in Russian, but her hero could not be tamed.

Andrey thought he finally had a bit more action when the police arrived en masse and began to circle him. But he was soon on the floor trembling as the twin spikes from the Taser pierced his chest and sent 50,000 volts into his system.

It had been a night of firsts for Kozlov. He'd directly disobeyed an order from his manager. He had climbed out of a hotel window. He had found love. It wasn't the first time he'd necked a litre of vodka and beaten up 20 men. Nor was it the first time he had been arrested. But it was the first time he had missed a football match in disgrace because he was being held in a police cell.

22. GAME ON

BEING away from the squad, I had no idea about all the shenanigans that had gone on in my delightful home town. I had intended to drive down on the morning of the game after an early night so I was fresh-faced and raring to go for Gary Lineker and the gang on Match of the Day. But then Neil texted to invite me for dinner and to stay at his place. It seemed rude to say no. With me not playing against Southend and possibly never again, he was thawing towards me again and I was keen to get things back to how they used to be. He was, after all, my oldest friend and the only person other than Julie who really knew me. I hadn't meant to drop him for my new football buddies, but he hadn't been keen to see me over the last few weeks and I didn't do anything about it.

My plans for an early night went out the window. His missus cooked us a lovely Mexican dinner and we cracked open a few cans of beer as we talked about the old times and the Blues in the FA Cup. I had gone with Grandad to Hillsborough in 1993 when we played Sheffield Wednesday in the fifth round. I vividly remember the ecstasy on his face when Stan Collymore tucked the ball away for Southend after five minutes and then how it turned to pained dismay as the referee disallowed it for offside. Turned out he had a cheeky tenner on Collymore to score the first goal at 8/1. Southend went on to lose 2-0 with Paul Warhurst scoring both for the home side despite being a defender playing as a makeshift striker.

The scoreline was the same a couple of years later when Neil went down to The Dell to see the Blues take on Southampton. He and a few other youngsters had gone down to the front of the stand to take the piss out of the size of Matt Le Tissier's nose during the warm-up. Le Tiss was so laid back that he just smiled and waved politely, but then got his revenge on the pitch by putting the Saints in front within a couple of minutes of the kick-off. Southend never looked like getting back into the game and Neil and his chums were put firmly in their place. Still, they got to watch Demolition Man on the coach on the way back.

As a peace offering, I offered to pay for a private box at Roots Hall for Neil and whoever he wanted to watch the game against London City United. He declined though as he wanted to sit in his usual seat near the usual faces, minus me of course. My seat would remain empty next to Grandad's.

Despite a groggy head the next morning, I was up with the larks. Kick-off was at 12.30pm, but I arrived at the ground in my best new suit and with my scrapbooks under my arm ready for signing at 9am. There were production meetings to sit in, I figured, and make-up and stuff to go through. Plus I wanted to have a proper chat with Gary and Alan Shearer rather than just punditing before, during and after the game. But I was still very, very early.

Franco Capece had always been an early riser. He was able to get by more than adequately on five or six hours sleep a night, so would always sit up until midnight analysing football videos of opposition teams, potential transfer targets or just generally excellent play and tactics he could use in his team. He would then be up by 6am to go for a run and be back in time to have breakfast with his wife – his kids were grown up and still lived back home in Italy – before heading to the training ground.

On this day, he was up a little later at 7am and also oblivious to last night's nightclub fracas. He still donned his tracksuit and began jogging out of the front of the hotel, down the cliffs, past the rough sleepers and off along Southend seafront. It was quiet and slightly foggy, which Franco found quite alluring. He saw a beauty in the greyness that others would dismiss. The water was still and silver and a cold breeze had made him bright and alert. Southend was nowhere near as pretty as his home town of Sorrento in south-western Italy, near Naples. But it had a certain charm to it that he liked. And being near the water did remind him of home and his childhood, even if this was a murky brown rather than clear blue.

He jogged past the small cafes that didn't seem to have enough customers to keep them all in business, past the entrance to the world-famous pier, past amusement arcade after amusement arcade after pub after amusement arcade after pub and out of the kiss-me-quick zone towards the B&Bs and residential properties. He nodded 'hello' to the other joggers and dog walkers, skipping over their mutts' shit on the way too. He stopped for a while against the sea wall and looked out across the Thames Estuary as a large container ship slowly drifted along on its way to Tilbury. *'That thing probably turns quicker than Richie Price,'* he smiled to himself. *'But I bet it can't score a last-minute screamer right into the top corner of the net from 30 yards.'* Franco knew he had to get Price back on that pitch in the right frame of mind. He could do with him today now Horatio Emmett and Christian Halberg were out, but it would be too soon. He needed to learn his lesson. Monday, he decided. He would speak to Price on Monday when he returned to training. He knew exactly what to say to get the big lad back to his best.

The Italian cleared his mind and began jogging back along the seafront and up the cliffs (well, they're more like big hills. Certainly not 'cliffs' in the White Cliffs of Dover sense) towards the hotel. As he climbed the steps, he saw his friend and assistant Alexis Colombo stood at the entrance with a concerned look on his face. The two spoke hurriedly in their native tongue with Colombo telling the manager that in addition to losing Emmett and Halberg to injury, he also now had three players who were due to start that day's match locked up in the police slammer.

Capece's gestures and exclamations grew louder and more exaggerated the more Colombo spoke. I wasn't there and I don't speak Italian, but I'll try to translate and provide subtitles.

'Boss, we have lost three more players for today.'

'What?'

'There was an incident at a nightclub last night. Three of the lads snuck out.'

'Nightclub? Motherfuckers. Who?'

'Kozlov, Lee and Diegbe. They got arrested.'

'My mother! Kozlov? Are you sure? The other two, yes. But Kozlov?'

'I'm afraid so boss. They were drinking and got into a fight.'

'Sons of whores. Drinking before a game? At a nightclub? Cock-sucking slobs of a donkey's tail.'

'Kozlov went crazy. The police had to Taser him.'

'Bitches. He's as crazy as he is ugly. The dumb Russian. They say the midwife tried to push him back up his mother's vagina when he was born because she thought the Devil had been born. I will gut him like a fish and let the scabies-ridden tramps of damnation feed on his intestines.'

'You can't boss; the police won't let him go. They may charge him with assault. The other two will be out at 10am. They could still play.'

'NO! They must have their testicles sandpapered by their grandmothers weekly.'

'But we only brought 20 players and we're down by five. We'll be putting kids in.'

'Stop bringing me problems you brown-nosing chickenshit. Fuck you and fuck them. And fuck this town and its greyness. They are all bad sportsmen. No respect. No honour. Go fuck yourself. I must try to sculpt the body of an Adonis from the shit of man.'

Well, it went something like that anyway. Alexis walked back into the hotel sheepishly as Franco Capece paced around out front in a rage. He then took a step back and launched a fierce kick at the surrounding wall. Any other man would have collapsed on the floor in absolute agony as every bone in their foot shattered like a pack of dropped Digestives. But Capece, whose nicknames from his playing days included The Legbreaker, knocked five bricks clean from their cemented home and left a hole in their wake, then strode purposefully into the lobby. He knew what he had to do.

The executive boxes at Roots Hall didn't suit the needs of the Match of the Day production team and so they had spent the past couple of days constructing a makeshift studio in the corner of the ground between the East and North stands that could still overlook the pitch. By 11am, I had met with the several MOTD people and been briefed about how and when to speak. They also showed me where I would shortly have to go to have my make-up done, but I had yet to even catch a glimpse of Gary Lineker. It was like the time I visited Lineker's Bar in Tenerife as a kid during the peak of my adoration for the prolific goalscorer. I met his brother Wayne and had my picture taken with him, but had apparently missed Gary being there by only a few days. I was gutted. Now, as I climbed the scaffolding steps up to the studio, a tingle of nerves shot through my belly as I realised I was going to meet one of my heroes (or it could've been the after-effects of last night's beers). Goodness knows what I'd be like if I actually did get to chat to Steve Tilson too.

I stood by the door and peeked into the studio. There were more cameras than I expected for a small room and there were several operatives and technicians busily setting things up. There were other people with clipboards and walkie-talkies to communicate with the dozens more in the huge production truck in the car park. I was a tad concerned about whether this makeshift structure could take the weight, especially with me added to it. Everything was clad in the Match of the Day branding, of course, and there, sat by a round table in the corner making notes, was Mr Gary Winston Lineker in all his glory. His ears weren't that big, and he looked healthy and friendly. My heart rate sped up as I lifted my hand to push the door open further and make my entrance. But just as I made contact, a voice yelled out from behind me.

'PRICE! RICHIE PRICE! I need you. I need your help. Please.'

I turned. In the centre of the Roots Hall car park – which doubled as a market on a Thursday – was Franco Capece on his knees with his hands clasped in prayer.

It had only been a week since I had last been in a changing room getting ready for a match with these lads, but this time something felt different. I was confident. I felt like I belonged there. Worthy. Yeah, you heard me right. I felt like I deserved to be pulling on the London City United kit as much as every multi-million-pound player in that room.

People often look at football managers and think it's a pretty easy job. It's why they come in for so much criticism, especially at the bigger clubs. The chairman gives them a bazillion quid to buy players and they just pick the best ones in the formation they think is best and let the footballers do their job. Simple right? Nah. It's all the stuff in between where they earn their money and kudos.

Franco Capece, as hard as nails as he had been on the pitch, was an exceptional man-manager and motivator off it. He knew how to handle even the most delicate of flowers in this squad of highly-paid prima donnas.

After his plea for my help, he pulled me into a side room in the bowels of Roots Hall's East Stand with a coffee in a Styrofoam cup and told me what had happened to the other players. Emmett, Halberg, Kozlov, Lee and Diegbe, all out of today's game. Then he told me how important I was as a player and a person to the squad, and what qualities I brought out in those around me. I had only been at the club a short time, he said, but my impact had been immense. And he extolled about my ability on the pitch.

'That goal you scored against Carlisle in the third round of the cup – wow! So much skill and power and you saved my skin. You did that. I understand you and your grandfather are Southend United supporters. He would be a man who wanted the best for you, yes?' I nodded. 'And he would be beaming with pride seeing you out there playing so brilliantly, yes?' I actually thought Grandad would be perplexed by it all, but I nodded. Franco put his arm round my shoulder and squeezed. 'It is you going out on the pitch Richie and doing these wonderful things. You. Not your mind friend. Yes, he may have helped you, but you are the person who delivers. You can do it. You alone can do it.'

By this point, I was nearly in tears. And my brain was buzzing. Keith Sykes had implanted all this stuff into my brain, but it was my brain and I was the one who physically performed those actions. If I concentrated and focused enough on the football, I was sure I could replicate it all. I could visualise it all in my mind. Franco was right, I could do this. Alone.

As I got into my kit, I exchanged reassuring nods with my teammates and they seemed to be feeding off my confidence. 'Good to have you back Rich,' one said. Even Adam Bush returned a nod.

The warm-up added even more assurance that I was meant to be there. I didn't feel out of breath, my passes went straight and I was on the pitch at Roots Hall as a player. Finally. Grandad *would* have been so proud. Completely fucking bemused that his tubby grandson was somehow playing for the former Premier League champions against Southend United, but proud all the same.

Neil was less proud. A quick look at my mobile before we went out for kick-off showed he'd sent a text of just five words. 'Two-faced lying Judas prick.' Not one to sit on the fence was Neil.

As we walked out of the tunnel and emerged onto the pitch, there was a huge roar from the capacity crowd, the LCU fans behind the goal in the North Stand and all other areas in the Blue of Southend. Drums banging, singing, electric. The circle of hairs around my nipples stood on end. As the referee did the coin toss and the captains exchanged banners, I slowly jogged over to the far side of the pitch, adding in a few stretches along the way. It was clear that the Southend fans in the West Stand were singing a warm and friendly greeting towards me. 'You. Fat. Bastad. You. Fat. Bastad. You. Fat. Bastad.' Even kids were joining in.

I looked up to where my, Neil and Grandad's seats were and made eye contact with Neil. His face was contorted with anger and he was jabbing his index finger in my direction. 'You. Fat. Bastad,' he chanted, despite knowing my sensitivities to my weight and lack of parents. 'You. Fat. Bastad.'

I mouthed the word 'sorry' but it had no effect on him or the thousands of others. Thank goodness Grandad wasn't there. Then the whistle blew for kick-off and we were away. I tried to block out all the calls and songs from the crowd. London City United dominated possession in the early stages of the game, but the ball stayed over on the left-hand side of the pitch away from me for much of it. The first couple of touches I got just needed a simple pass to carry on the move and I did that just fine, although to a chorus of boos from the home support. It wasn't until about 10 minutes in that I got my first real taste of possession. Southend broke down their right, but the cross into the box was too close to our keeper Paolo Antoine and he plucked it from the air with ease and quickly bowled the ball out to me near the half-way line out on our right.

All of a sudden, as the ball approached, I was surrounded by ghosts and apparitions.

'I am proud of you son,' Grandad told me. 'Don't let those bullies and naysayers get you down. Me and your nan love you very much. We know you can do whatever you want when you put your mind to it...your mind to it...your mind to it.'

'You are the master of your own destiny,' said Franco Capece. 'Take control and show the world what you can do...what you can do...what you can do.'

'You're alright for an old bloke, y'know,' Mollie said with a sweet smile.

'She's a slut and she's using you...using you...using you,' said Julie. Shit. It was going wrong.

'Give it up mate,' said Neil. The ghostly one, not the real one in the stands. 'You're a lying Judas prick...Judas prick...Judas prick.'

'Dad? Why did you lie to everyone? People at school are taking the mick out of me.' Ah man! That was Tilson. He looked heart-broken.

The ball bounced on the wet grass and zipped up towards me. Dazed, I lifted my foot to try to control it, but the ball hit my shin and spun off awkwardly.

'WAHEY!' laughed the home supporters to a man, woman and child.

'You couldn't control a telly,' yelled one wag, possibly Neil.

I chased after the ball to try and stop it going out of play for a throw, but I tripped and slid to a shuddering halt on my belly in front of the baying Southend United fans. They wanted blood and they were getting it.

'I bet he wished he'd stayed in the Match of the Day studio now,' quipped Steve Tilson on his radio commentary. And he was bang right. The first half went downhill from there and fast. I couldn't get near the ball for 10 minutes at a time and if I did I ballsed it up royally. Southend took the lead just after the half-hour mark from the penalty spot. I'd lost possession and Adam Bush stopped the breakaway with an abrupt challenge just inside the box.

He got away with only a yellow for the foul but I got a death stare from the captain. Then, as half-time neared, I scored. But for Southend. A corner kick was swung in towards the near post and I tried to head clear, but I closed my eyes and lost the flight of the ball. Instead of connecting with the centre of my forehead, the ball spun off my crown and up over Antoine's reach, looping into the net at the far post. 50p Head strikes again. Since I was a boy I had dreamed of scoring for the Blues at Roots Hall and now I had achieved it, albeit an own goal. Still, at least I brought some joy to Neil and the Southend faithful that afternoon.

Franco Capece was chewing through his own fingers – not the nails, the actual fingers – in despair at his team's shocking performance and one player in particular. Me. As soon as the second goal went in, he stormed off down the tunnel to prepare for a half-time ravaging, swearing indiscriminately all the way. Hot on his heels was my fitness coach, Harley Wells.

Seconds later, the ref blew his whistle to bring the first 45 minutes to an end and we trudged off towards the changing rooms. Despite my slapdash performance and scoring a goal for them, large elements of the Southend support were chucking pelters my way. You'd think they'd be happy I was seemingly sabotaging LCU from the inside, but no.

'You're fucking shit mate.' Yeah, I know. Always have been.

'Eighty grand a week? You should be ashamed.' I don't think it's quite that much, but I am a little embarrassed, yes.

'Your mum's a slag.' No she's not. But then, I never really got to meet her since she died when I was six, so your guess is as good as mine. You may be right.

'Judas!' Whatever.

'Nice job fatty.' Seriously? Even with only one brain cell, that's the best you could come up with?

'I love you Dad.' What does that even mean, you moron? Oh my god, it's Tilson. He was stood there in the directors' box above the tunnel with a sorry little smile on his face and waving from in front of his belly. There were two perfectly manicured hands on his shoulders. I looked up and saw my wife, Julie. She looked tearful. I mouthed 'sorry' for the second time today, but she just shook her head. It was the first time I really thought about how all this impacted on my family and I felt sick.

I approached the changing room with severe apprehension. I didn't really care what a lot of players thought about me, especially Adam Bush, as they weren't putting in much of a shift today either. But Franco Capece had put his trust in me and I had let him down massively. And he's not the sort of person you want to let down. In another life, he would've been a mafia enforcer. That Legbreaker nickname he acquired came when he was 29 and a referee was in the process of booking him for a foul. 'Foul? That was no foul,' he told the man in black. 'This is a foul.' He then launched himself two-footed and studs high into the legs of a passing opposition player, who was left crumpled on the ground in agony with – naturally – a broken leg. Capece didn't even wait for the red card, he just walked off the pitch and down the tunnel kicking water bottles and swearing indiscriminately as he went. I feared I may face a two-footed assault from the gaffer as soon as I entered the changing room. At least I would have an excuse for not playing again.

But instead of a boot to the face, I was greeted with a polite wave from the manager. I was puzzled.

He clapped his hands together to get everyone's attention and smiled warmly. 'Well lads. We've given the underdogs their two-goal head start, so now is the time for the big comeback, yes?' His jokey mood immediately lifted the players. They – I mean we – all knew the performance had been abysmal. We'd had our bollocking subconsciously and now was the time for the manager to lift his charges, not push them further down.

'Take on fluids. Any knocks?' he asked. 'And Richie…' here it comes. I was getting subbed off. It was all over. '…can you go and see Harley in the side room across the hall please.'

That was odd. Harley was my fitness coach and I wasn't injured; I was just shit. It was hard to see what he could do to affect things when we were 2-0 down mid-game.

'Quick, quick, close the door,' Harley said excitedly, closing the door himself. The room was small, cold and empty. I could hear the thumping of feet from the fans in the stand above us. 'OK mate, I've got good news but I need to blackmail you before you can have it.'

What the fuck was going on? That was the question I should've asked Harley, but he could tell by the look on my face what I was thinking.

'I know about you and Keith Sykes. Everything. I said you were up to something, but hypnotising? Man, that's just fucking mad. But I'll keep your secret and I will help you, OK? I got Keith right here on my phone on Skype. He can do his thing on that he says. He can get you back to the real you. Well, not the real you because the real you is clearly pretty shit at football, but the super you who bangs in all the goals and that. And then we can sort something out longer term via Skype or Keith teaches me or something, I dunno. But I ain't doing anything today, tomorrow, any other day unless you promise me something. And I mean proper promise because I've had to go out on a limb here for you, you know? Franco will have my guts too if this goes wrong.'

Harley spoke so fast that I didn't have time to get anything really clear in my head other than he had Keith waiting on Skype. I would've agreed to almost anything at that point.

'What is it?' I asked.

'Well…' There was a bang on the door and someone yelled for us to hurry up. 'ALRIGHT!' Harley yelled back at the door. 'Gimme a fucking sec, man. I'm working with a world class athlete in here. Give me a bit of privacy.' He fixed his gaze back on me and said:

'Well, a few of the players and coaches are pissed off with me and want me out of the club, er, because they think I'm shagging Adam Bush's girlfriend behind his back.'

'Ayesha? Why do they think that?'

'Because I am shagging Adam Bush's girlfriend behind his back.'

'Fucking hell, Harl. And what do you want me to do? Vouch for you and say they've got it wrong? Smooth it all over?'

'Nah. I want you to get Bushy to dump Ayesha so we can be together. She wants to be with me, but says she can't be the one to walk out. It has to be the other way. I don't know. Women, man.' He shrugged. 'So, what do you say?'

What could I say? I agreed and he handed me his phone. There smiling back at me was the tanned gormless face of Keith Sykes. I had never felt so happy to see him. 'Awight geez, whatya been upta? Ha. I know you're gonna forgive me for fucking off for a bit, because I can make ya. But I am sorry. Now then...' And he worked his magic.

23. TWO HALVES

'SO the second half is about to get underway here at Roots Hall,' said BBC Radio Essex commentator Geoff Sergeant. 'And I'm a little surprised to see Richie Price still out there for London City United after a dreadful first 45, Steve.'

'Yeah, you're right Geoff,' replied Steve Tilson next to him in the summariser's seat. 'He really was appalling in the first half. We expected a lot from him and there was a lot of excitement when we heard he'd been drafted into the starting line-up at the last minute this morning, but he really hasn't delivered at all. That said, he does look very focused out there now, no doubt after getting a rollicking from his manager Franco Capece.'

'And the referee blows the whistle to start the second half. Southend United leading Premier League giants London City United two goals to nil here, so a big upset on the cards. But the ball is played to Richie Price now on this far side of the pitch, shooting from left to right towards the away support, Price has switched sides this half, and he now has the ball under control...'

'That's more than he managed in the whole of the first half Geoff,' chipped in Tilson.

'Er, yes, quite Steve. But Price now on the move past one, two, three Southend players, they can't get near him. He's weaving, picking up pace as he goes past another and he shoots. GOAL! Richie Price scores an absolute beauty for City United. They're back in this. He cut through the Blues there like a hot knife through butter and finished with aplomb.'

'Yes Geoff. We were just saying how poor he'd been in the first half and really needed to step up his game and he really has there. They've let him get past them too easily there for me Geoff, but you can see the determination on his face there. No one was going to stop him. That goal, for me, was very reminiscent of the one Ryan Giggs scored against Arsenal in the FA Cup in '99.'

'Well, yes, indeed. I was going to compare it to one scored by another great Welshman, Nathan Jones, who ran half the length of the pitch to score the winner for Southend against Cheltenham Town in 2000.'

'Well, Price has his shirt off now and is twirling it round his head just like Giggs did, so I'll stick with my comparison. He's not quite got the same physique as Giggs and a lot less chest hair, but he'll get booked for that celebration. But all those are special goals and now London City United are right back in this cup tie.'

Yeah, about that. You know when players with a close connection to a club score against them and refuse to celebrate? They push their joyful teammates away with a stern shake of the head or hold their hands up dismissively as they're mobbed. Well, that wasn't me. I didn't really have full control over what I was doing though. A lot of it was programmed in.

So after I slotted the ball home for my first goal against Southend United, I pulled my shirt off over my head and waved it around as I sprinted past all the Blues fans, including my best friend Neil, in the West Stand.

I also celebrated my second goal that afternoon. And the third. And the fourth, fifth and sixth. Yep, I scored a double-hattrick against the team I had supported since childhood and celebrated each one like six-year-old dosed up on blue Smarties and Sunny D after being told he was getting a new bike and a PlayStation for his birthday.

I had humiliated the Shrimpers in their own back yard and then revelled in their defeat. Repeatedly.

The abuse from the home fans as I left the pitch at the end of the match was ten times more intense than at half-time, but Franco Capece was delighted with me. He hugged me and kissed my forehead over and over. As did many of my teammates.

'Richie, Richie, I love you,' the manager said. 'I was ready to tear off your head and piss down your throat at half-time. I was so angry I would've killed your family. But you turned it round. You owe young Harley there dinner or a nice wine. He convinced me to keep you in play. Thank him.'

I would've done so straight away, but there was one word Franco had said that got stuck in my mind. Family.

Tilson and Julie had been out there in the stands watching me play. I hadn't seen or spoken to them at the end of the game. Well, I couldn't, really. What an arsehole. I ran out the changing room, back up the tunnel onto the pitch to look for them, but they had already gone, along with the rest of the crowd. Shit.

No doubt Julie would've thought I'd snubbed them on purpose. Poor Tilson, what will he be thinking? The poor kid. He deserved so much better. I screwed my face up in disgust at myself and gripped the side of my hair.

'Tilson,' I wailed in despair and then chastised myself. 'You stupid, fucking, dumb twat.'

I opened my eyes to see Southend United legend Steve Tilson just two yards away. He looked horrified. 'No need to be like that, mate. I was only coming over to say well done. You can stick your scrapbook up your arse.'

Double shit.

Jim Neale sat up suddenly in his La-Z-Boy chair. It was his special football-watching chair that had a small moveable table rigged up to it on the left for when he needed to work. On the floor to the right was a mini-fridge. He was on his fourth beer of the afternoon when something clicked in his brain. His conversation with Keith Sykes at the hotel in Miami had been something of a dead-end. He hoped all the booze would loosen Sykes's lips, but he wished it hadn't. For three hours the obnoxious buffoon just rambled on about a load of old shit and just tried to boast about how much of a lad he was. And for the two hours after that, he was incoherent. Still, Jim had managed to put their bar tab on Sykes's room but kept a receipt to claim for them on his expenses. Winner.

The only thing that had stuck out at all during their lengthy chat was his response to a question about the similarities to stage hypnotism and helping sportsmen perform on the big stage.

'At the end of the day geez,' Sykes had told him. 'It's all abaht getting the person in the frame of mind to copy exactly what they're told to do, innit.'

Copy, Neale pondered.

He picked up the remote and rewound the telly to Price's first goal against Southend. But it wasn't the goal itself that had sparked Jim's brain into action. It was the celebration. He scored a goal just like Ryan Giggs and then copied Giggsy's celebration. And got booked. 'Wait a minute,' said the journalist as he put down his beer, pulled round his work table and fired his laptop into life. Within 30 seconds, he was on YouTube watching London City United's win a few weeks earlier against Newcastle.

'Price is moving forward now,' said the commentator on the clip. 'That's a neat one-two with Harry Jacobs. The Newcastle defenders are standing off him. Oh! I say! What a goal. Price chips it in from the edge of the box and City United are now firmly in control.'

Jim Neale carried on watching the footage and grinned in satisfaction as he watched me run with one arm aloft in front of the Newcastle fans just like Alan Shearer.

He's not scoring goals *like* the greats; he's scoring *the* goals of the greats. And Keith Sykes is the puppet master.

'I've got you,' he said and cracked open another can of beer in celebration.

'You're not drinking again are you James,' called a 40 fags a day, haggard voice from another room.

'Fuck off mum! It's my first fucking one.'

24. BACK IN THE GAME

WHAT worked a treat in the second half against South-end was now the way we worked for every game and training. With Harley Wells in on the conspiracy – ha! Listen to me. The Price Conspiracy! Sounds like I should be beating up spies, doing car chases and shagging lots of pretty women. But with him in the loop, he could whip out his phone pre-training or pre-match and Skype Keith to do the business. We just had to make sure Harley always had a decent wifi connection. There was the added bonus that I didn't have to see Keith so much; just a couple of minutes before and after each run-out.

And it meant the football was back on track for both me and London City United. We won our next six matches without conceding a goal. I scored another hattrick as we thrashed West Ham 5-0 in the Premier League in our first game after beating Southend. I got a Duncan Ferguson-style header at the far post and a Lineker-esque tap in. But I was most pleased with the third as it was one of my favourite goals from, you know, real life. Fit-again Horatio Emmett combined out on the left side of the pitch with Andrey Kozlov, who was now out on bail ahead of a court appearance the next month following his nightclub brawl and Tasering in Southend. They then spread the play into the centre where Adam Bush had stepped up from the back. He then played it wide to Danny Diegbe, who steered the ball into me on the edge of the box. In one deft movement, I controlled the ball and flicked it up with my right foot, rolled across the defender so close behind me that I could smell the Weetabix on his breath, and then volleyed the ball with my left foot into the top corner a la Justin Fashanu for Norwich against Liverpool in 1980. 'O-oh what a goal. Oh, that's a magnificent goal.'

We also beat Watford 2-0, Leicester 3-0 and Crystal Palace 5-0 in the Premier League, plus Horatio scored a last-minute winner against Arsenal in the FA Cup to put us through to the semi-final.

By this point, we were well in the top four and a convincing 3-0 victory at home to Manchester United in our next league game put us right in the mix to be challenging for the title. Harry Jacobs scored the first with a clever turn and shot from the edge of the box, our skipper Bush got the second with a thunder-buster header from a corner and then I got in on the act. United had a corner, but we cleared and launched a counter-attack. I picked up the ball inside my own half out on the left. My brain flicked through its Rolodex of options before settling on Ronaldinho for Barcelona against Sevilla in 2003. Surging forward, the first defender came in to try to halt my progress but I quickly sidestepped him. Then another came across at full speed, but I suddenly slowed down, dragged the ball across as he flew by and he too was out of the picture. Then I nudged the ball forward again and launched a 30-yard rocket that looped over the keeper's head before crashing satisfyingly against the underside of the bar, down into the turf beyond the goal line and back up into the roof of the net. Emphatic. Then I did a samba dance at the corner flag with a silly, toothy grin on my face.

With Spurs having fallen away in the title race, that win put us level on points with United but ahead on goal difference. We were second in the table. Who would've thought that for 'crisis club'

London City United at the turn of the year? It was an amazing effort from everyone at the club and there was a real buzz about the place. Plus, our next game was against the leaders Manchester City, who were only three points ahead. A win there and we'd be top.

But something else happened in the Manchester United game that I hadn't cottoned onto until I got a call from my friend in the LCU chief exec's office, Sean Clark. It was both a joyous and worrying call from the bearded twat. You see, I had now made more than 10 first-team appearances for London City United. In fact, I'd played 11 matches in all competitions and scored 21 goals in the process. So that thing I said earlier about just because I was really good it didn't mean we'd win every game and I'd score loads, well, I was wrong. But it was because the whole team lifted their game. But anyway, by passing the 10-match mark I had triggered both a pay rise from the club and a two-year extension to my contract. Ker-ching! I was now signed on to London City United till the age of 45!

'As much as I'm loathed to see you do well and have to approve this extension,' Clark told me on the phone after training on the Monday. '...I'm sure this whole charade isn't going to last much longer. From a few contacts I have in the Press, it seems something is brewing. They have some very juicy information, I'm led to believe, and are just addressing the finer points to the tale before they unleash it on the world. When they do, your world will come crashing down and I will be there pissing on your remains.'

'Sorry Sean,' I replied. 'The phone crackled then. Did you say that you're passing a Great Dane?'

'I said I'll piss on your remains.'

'Sorry, you're pulling on the reins?'

'PISS ON YOUR REMAINS!'

'I don't need you to clean my drains Sean, but thanks for the offer mate. And thanks for the contract. Bye.'

But I had heard him alright. The Press were on to me; I knew it. Two minutes till midnight. Who had sold me out?

25. PARTY TIME

YOU know what; I've missed out a big chunk of the story. What a knob. But I'd better go back because it's all very important and it feeds into that last question of who grassed me up. You'll remember that after the Southend cup game I'd raced out the changing rooms to see if I could see Julie and Tilson to apologise for not coming to see them at the final whistle. Then I inadvertently insulted my Blues hero Steve Tilson and ended up apologising to him profusely. He never did sign my scrapbook, but his hair was still immaculate. Anyway, I sent Julie a text to say sorry, but she replied saying they'd had to leave before the end of the game because she was going out that evening. But they had seen my goals. 'Tilson was so happy,' she said. 'He leapt up and cheered whenever you got the ball or scored. He got funny looks from all the Southend fans, but the people around us in the directors' bit were nice enough. When he said you were his dad, one man said you should play for the shromps, but we didn't know what that meant.'

He said Shrimpers love, I thought. It was one of Southend's nicknames. She often said the wrong word or got her phrases mixed up. It was a quirk I loved. 'Don't beat around the grass,' she'd say, or 'you look like the cat who got creamed'. I suppose that one still works if your mind is dirty enough.

But I was off the hook there and I was really chuffed that Tilson enjoyed seeing me play. I'd kept my match shirt from that game and planned to get it signed by all the lads and framed for him. It would be nice to see that up on his wall alongside his band posters.

And I had plans that evening as Mollie, my friend from Adam Bush's party, had invited me to this party thing, so I got myself home sharpish, had a doze to recover a little from my exertions on the pitch, scoff some dinner and get changed. I had more of a trendy wardrobe now with some real quality clothes in there. I'd picked out a suit I had made to measure from Charlie Allen of Savile Row no less. None of this mix-and-match jacket and trousers nonsense like the day I went in to sign my first contract with London City United a few weeks back. So much had changed in that short space of time. The suit was a beautiful, proper fitted affair and I had a crisp white shirt to go with it. I never liked ties because when I was at school the other kids loved to yank mine really hard and yell 'Peanut!' or tie it to the handles on the bus so tight that I'd miss my stop while trying to get loose. Houdini, I was not. And I never really wore them during my working life either and I wasn't going to start now. But a bow tie is a whole other story. I wasn't quite Bond, but it was perhaps the smartest I'd ever seen myself.

'You can't polish a turd, but you can roll it in glitter and make it sparkle,' I said to myself in the mirror as I posed with my fingers in a gun as if I'd just turned and fired.

'Well, fuck me. Look at you, you handsome bastard,' said Mollie as she came out from her house to meet the car. 'I think anyone looking now would say I was the one punching above my weight, don't you think?' She leaned in to give me a kiss on the cheek and then used her thumb to wipe off the lipstick mark before feeling the lapel of my suit jacket, giving a nod of approval. 'Nice. Very nice.'

She was talking bollocks of course. I may have been in a very nice and very expensive suit and had a few dashes of top-notch aftershave on, but I was still a balding fat bloke in his 40s. Mollie, on the other hand, was in her mid-20s and stunning. She had gleaming blonde hair in a collar-length bob and ruby-red lips that set off perfectly against the emerald cocktail dress she was wearing. 'There's a few people I want to meet and impress tonight and they're Irish, so I thought green would be a good idea,' she said. I told her she was right. But she would never be punching. Not that we were a couple, of course. I'm serious. That thought never crossed my mind, even if those looking on did. As pretty and as fun as Mollie was, Julie was my girl and I was doing all this football stuff to win her back (not that the re-wooing was going that well). I liked Mollie's personality, humour and friendly nature. I would've wanted to hang out with her if she'd been a 30-stone heifer with a face like a bucket of smashed crabs or a bloke (come to think of it, that would've been her side of the friendship looking at me). She just happened to be a looker and maybe she got her confidence from that, but we're not here to analyse her psychology so I'll carry on with the story.

The car was getting near the venue at around 8pm and Mollie asked if I'd prefer if we went in separately, given what happened when we went out for coffee before. There didn't seem to be many photographers outside, but there were a few people hovering so I said it may not be a bad idea. We parked up and I slid the door across. A doorman trotted over and held an umbrella above Mollie's head to shield her from the drizzle as she shuffled across the short red carpet and into the entrance area of the Old Billingsgate building just a short way along the Thames from the Tower of London. The driver then did a loop around as the rain grew heavier and he pulled up at the same entrance again about 10 minutes later. I thanked him, stepped out the car and looked up at the looming statue of Britannia on top of the building. For some reason, I gave her a little nod of acknowledgement. At least she had a hat on to shield her from the rain. The doorman hadn't bothered to come out to greet me with a brolly – must have been a West Ham fan – so I quickly trotted inside with my shoulders up to provide some shelter.

The function itself was in what they call the Vault; a vast room with exposed brickwork and vaulted ceilings, and it was packed. There were dozens of large tables filled with guests, plus many other seated and standing areas where party-goers swigged on their drinks and chatted enthusiastically to one another in groups. The music was very poppy and although it seemed early in the night to be doing so, there were 10 or so women already on the dancefloor. Because of the size and busyness of the place, and with all the pillars dropping down to block a complete view, I couldn't see Mollie. But there wasn't likely to be too many beautiful women in bright green dresses, so I figured she wouldn't be too hard to spot. Where's Mollie rather than Where's Wally. She'd laugh at that gag. I grabbed a glass of champagne and started to wander around.

There were several hundred people at the party and I could see a few pointing at me as they spoke to their friends and others recognising my face and offering a 'great game today' comment. But no one pestered me, which was nice. It was getting harder just to pop to the shop for milk or go for a walk around where I lived without a gazillion requests for selfies or for me to call their friend. I remember once seeing the actor Rupert Grint at a music festival at the height of his Harry Potter fame. He'd taken to wearing a horse's head mask when watching bands among the hoi polloi so they didn't recognise him and mob him. I only know it was him because I saw him putting it back on as he came out of one of the rancid, overflowing chemical bogs. The only type of mask you want to wear in one of those is a gas mask. We made eye contact as he stepped out and, in that moment, I saw the panic – the fear that the game was up and the dismay that he was just a kid who wanted to see some bands he liked in peace.

I mean, it might have been the vomit-inducing stench from the toilet that made him look that way. I went in there afterwards and it was not pretty (he certainly didn't use any magic cleaning spells). But I could see all that emotion in just one glance and I often now felt the very same way. I almost feel bad that I asked him for a selfie now. But, you know, it's Ron fucking Weasley.

I had been at the party for 20 minutes and was sipping my third glass of champers – the other two had gone straight to my head and given me the taste for it – but I still hadn't found Mollie. Then I clapped eyes on a familiar and perfectly-chiselled face.

Matt Curbishley had been working hard for the past three years at trying to become famous. Tens of thousands of people were now following Turbo Curbo on Instagram and watching his videos and liking his workout pictures. But he was still not 'famous'.

There was, of course, a time when his only followers on social media were people he went to school with and who would take the piss out of what he was doing. 'Put a shirt on, FFS mate,' someone would comment. 'You have your protein shake pal and I'll stick to Maccy Ds,' another would say. Back then he was working at a chain gym where he had to rent a space alongside other personal trainers who didn't really care about their clients. They might show newbies how to use the machines so no one got hurt, but other than that they just chatted and took the piss out of the fatties trying to lose weight by walking on a slight incline for 30 minutes. And this was their job. Brilliant.

To give him some credit, Matt wanted to open his own gym and run it the way he saw things. But you needed a lot of money to invest in the space and equipment to do that and so, instead, he started to use the internet and social media to build his profile and reach the clients he wanted to help virtually. About a year to 18 months down the road, with lots more followers and clients, he was offered the manager's job at a larger gym where he could be in control of how things were run. He took it with the assurance that he could carry on promoting himself and his fitness regimes on the side. It was at this new gym that he met Julie Price. She had split from her husband – he used to be a member too, but never ever worked out – and was feeling a bit low. Matt had a thing for the older lady and thought Julie was a proper milf. So, on the pretence of showing her some healthy recipes, he invited her to his flat for dinner and a couple of glasses of wine. Julie enjoyed it so much, she came back for seconds. But before he knew it, Matt was picking her son up from school and doing odd jobs around her house. It wasn't ever meant to be a thing. She was well fit and he liked the sex, but he just wanted the latter bit. He didn't need all the baggage that came with it like the son who kept going on and on about music and the mental husband who always made snidey comments and tried to fight him. Literally fight him. He was done with it. He wasn't ready to start settling down with anyone. Even if he did, he would probably go for someone more his age and without all the 'history' hanging around.

Matt had gone to her house to tell her it was all over when everything went crazy. Somehow, unbelievably, the husband had been signed up by London City United football club. The guy was pushing 50 and obese, yet there he was being thrust into the lime-light – fame and riches – and Matt, jealous, wanted a piece of it. There were coattails there to cling on to. So rather than dump Julie as planned, he moved in with her and over-played the role of surrogate dad while he waited for the right time to act. Then he saw the story in the Daily Citizen about this guy Richie's counsellor or something being a massive sleaze. He'd only shagged a few women and Matt couldn't see too much wrong with what he'd done, but it was all over the front page and a few more inside. To use a football analogy, he was being presented with an open goal and all he had to do was tap the ball home. So he emailed the address at the end of the story and soon got a call from a chap called Jim Neale, who was desperate to talk to him and feature him in the paper.

Next day, there was a massive spread across two pages, the chance to boast about his fitness work and recipes, as well as show off his physique and model looks to the masses. And the paper paid him a few grand to go on the record. The phone had not stopped ringing since with offers, let alone the DMs and emails from adoring fans. Some of the pictures sent to his inbox were outrageous. But the serious correspondence included offers of publishing deals and endorsements. One of the things he was mulling over was a possible live stage tour around the country. 'The fitness people will come for the fitness stuff and the housewives will come because they think they've gotta chance of pulling you,' his new agent told him. 'But they will ALL buy your books and merchandise there and then. This will be a huge earner.'

That was why he was here at this posh party in London, laughing at the terrible jokes of middle-aged gay men pawing at him and their fag-hag friends. His agent had said these were the people who knew about theatre tours and needed to be 'glad-handed'. Matt didn't like gays. 'Adam and Eve, not Adam and Steve,' his dad had drilled into him. (It was actually Adam and Ayesha and Alexis, but we'll get onto that later).

As one of the fat poofs threw his head back in exaggerated laughter again and put his hand on Matt's bulging bicep, Turbo Curbo spotted a familiar and unfriendly face across the room.

26. THE CHASE

LTHOUGH I hadn't seen Mollie at the party, it turned out she had seen me while she was talking to a director she was trying to impress. She had been torn over whether to break off the conversation to come and grab me but could see my attention was elsewhere. By then, my eyes were fixed firmly on my nemesis – Matt Curbishley. Mollie later said that my face had changed from a relaxed, puzzled expression of a little boy lost to one of grimaced hatred. 'Redder than Man United's kit,' she said of my face and I'm not surprised.

This guy had sold himself and, in the process, exposed my wife and son to all that filth. That act, that wanker at the football all those years ago booting my mate, that chav prick groping Julie at McCluckie's nightclub and Barry Fry leaving Southend United for Birmingham all swirled up from my belly in a vicious wave of anger and formed a sickening taste for vengeance in the back of my throat. I remember making a very conscious decision that I was going to grab the muscle-bound wanksock by the scruff of the neck, drag him upstairs by his cheap suit to the beautifully-lit outdoor area overlooking the Thames and Tower Bridge, and I was going to toss him over the seawall into the cold water below.

Our eyes made contact across the hubbub of the room and everything froze for a moment. Then I pounced. Mollie said I just dropped my champagne flute to the floor and charged, but I was sure I had the manners to place it on a table.

In any case, I began to march through the crowd of party-goers towards Curbishley and could see him making his excuses to the group he was chatting with and diverting sharply across the room. I changed direction to track him, but he went behind one of the vast brick pillars and double-backed.

To begin with, none of the other guests except a nervous Mollie had noticed what was going on. But as I got nearer and the chase intensified, people began pausing their conversations and stood aback as the game of cat and mouse spiralled up towards fever pitch. I went to go one way and Curbo moved in the other, but then it was my turn to double-back. I took a wide but speedy loop around the room in the opposite direction to which he was looking. I was actually running now and there were a few yelps of panic from other guests as I bumped a few or they leapt back out of the line of danger, being careful not to spill their bubbly or drop a vol-au-vent. As my trajectory straightened and I made a beeline for my enemy, he spotted me and darted upstairs and out onto the patio area under the watchful eye of The Shard. It was right where I wanted him. And then something happened that had never happened before. Without the aid of The Amazing Syko's hypnotic influence, my mind started going through its Rolodex of options and came up with the perfect play. Well, perfect for what I wanted in this situation.

With Turbo Curbo running out of space and me hot on his tail, I transformed (mentally only) into 21-year-old Eric Cantona playing for Auxerre in 1988 and he became Nantes' Michel Der Zakarian. You may think you know The King's kung fu kick on that fan years ago, but that was just a bad repeat. I was doing the original. As I neared my frantic prey, I leapt into the air, pulled both my knees up to my chest and then thrust my feet down into Curbishley's thighs, bringing him to a shuddering and sudden halt like a stick through the spokes of a bike, and he crashed into the foot of the seawall.

I tried with all my might to then heave his hulking frame off the floor, over the wall and drop him into the Thames below, but a voice stopped me in my tracks.

'Rich, what the fuck are you doing?' It was Julie. I knew it instantly. I untangled myself from Curbo's flattened corpse on the floor and stood to meet her puzzled and disappointed gaze. She looked amazing. She was wearing a fantastic black dress and as she walked towards me, the light from an outside lamp gave her a glorious halo. My angel spoke softly: 'Put him down you silly sod. You're making a scene.'

'He disrespected you,' I pleaded. 'And Tilson.' Others were now rallying to Curbishley's side, checking he was OK. Seriously, the guy was built like a brick shit house, but one kick from me and you'd think he'd been hit by a truck. He barely had a hair out of place. Me? I was a sweaty wreck.

With Julie now in front of me, I said: 'He's a scumbag love.' And with the next two words, all my anger melted away. 'I know,' she said. I was the Incredible Hulk calming and turning back into Dr Bruce Banner. *The sun's getting real low*. And just like him, I'd ripped my fucking trousers to shreds.

Julie reached forward, took my hand and led me down the side of the building and out onto the main road as onlookers gossiped about what they saw and Matt Curbishley limped sheepishly back inside. My wife held out an arm to flag down a passing black cab and as we climbed into the back and closed the door, she said the coolest thing ever: 'Just drive.' I thought people only did that in movies, but there we were being driven around the streets of London at night with no particular place to go. Outside it swapped between historic grey buildings, office blocks and the neon lights of a world altogether more exciting. Julie was sat to my right-hand side with a wry smile on her face. She was so beautiful. I looked down and realised that we were still holding hands, but didn't draw attention to it in case Julie pulled hers away.

After a while, probably a good 15 minutes, she broke the silence, shaking her head and saying: 'You daft wanker.' We laughed and sat in silence again.

'He deserved it. He's a cock,' I said. She squeezed my hand tighter for a few seconds and then released it to how we were before, still holding. Silence again for a few moments. 'What did you mean when I said the Steroid Kid was a scumbag? You said you knew.'

'Exactly that,' she replied. 'I ditched him after he did that story in the paper about me.'

'But you...'

'Yeah, yeah. I know. But I didn't want to give you the satisfaction either, especially with you having a young girlfriend on the go. I saw her there tonight, she looked pretty. The cow.'

'She's not my girlfriend, I told you that. Never was. What were you doing there anyway if you'd split up with knobcheeks?'

'He told me that Andrew Lloyd Webber might be there so I made him promise to take me to meet him otherwise I would turn the tables and go to the papers and tell them what he's really like in the bedroom and where he's lacking...'

'Alright, alright. You're still my wife, remember?'

'OK love. But I'll use that knowledge to make sure he doesn't go to the papers again about tonight's little episode.'

There was another pause in the conversation and I ducked my head down a bit to look out the window of the cab. The rain was still coming down heavy and it blurred the glow of the city. I reached down and felt my leg. My suit trousers were torn from just below the waistline and down the seam to my knee. There were a few other rips and I had a large graze on my thigh from where it had slid across the concrete during my flying tackle. I winced a little as I touched it. All the while, Julie was watching my every move, studying my expressions – she always said the lines on my face gave me character, but I was never sure whether to take it as a compliment – and feeling the pain of my sore leg along with me. Great empathy that woman.

As I turned back toward her she let go of my hand, shifted herself into the centre seat next to me, guided my face to hers with a soft touch of her hand and we kissed. They only usually have fireworks along the Embankment on New Year's Eve, but tonight they were going off in my head, my belly and my underpants. I'd have to be careful what the rips in my trousers exposed.

'Fackin' typicaw,' yelled the cabbie through his rear-view mirror, shattering the moment like a wet fart at a funeral. 'I get a Premier League footballer snogging a bird in the back of my cab and it's his own fackin' wife. Haha! Carry on!'

Julie laughed and looked all coy, before asking me a question to warm my heart right through. 'How about a coffee and a kebab at your place?'

'OK, but go easy on the onions, alright?'

Julie hadn't been to my apartment before. Very few people had really. In the lift on the way up, with Julie cuddling my arm and shoulder, I racked my brains trying to remember whether I had left the place in decent shape. No, I hadn't. Shit. My cleaner had been in the day before, but I had slept longer than intended after the football earlier and then rushed around getting ready to go out. There were dirty clothes and wet towels dumped on the floor for sure, and I had just left my dinner stuff on the side in the kitchen. At least the living room would be tidy.

'Wowzers trousers,' Julie said as I showed her in, quickly scanning the room for any dirty pants that might kill the mood stone dead. When I viewed the apartment before renting it, I just stood in one spot in the room, looked around, nodded and then moved on to the next. But Julie was studying everything like she was hunting for clues or evidence. Maybe she was. I half expected her to pull out a brush and start dusting for prints. She walked along touching the walls, feeling the fabric of the curtains, checking the softness of the sofa, checking out the sideboards and tables, room to room. Sherlock Holmes Under The Hammer.

'Well, judging from the state of your bedroom, you weren't expecting to bring anyone back tonight. I suppose she wasn't your girlfriend after all.'

'Nah, I've just sent her straight to my sex dungeon,' I replied and regretted it, but she smiled.

I watched as she unlocked the bi-fold doors and stepped out onto the balcony to take in the view. She poked her head back in and said: 'Hot tub? Really?'

What could I say? It was there when I rented the place.

Once she concluded her forensic examination, she gave me her verdict. 'Very nice indeed. It could do with a bit more input on the interior design front but, all in all, not bad at all Mr Price. But what I want to know is how you did it, or rather, do it. The football thing. You were always so…' she paused to think of the right word, '…shit. Like abysmal at it…football.'

I puffed my cheeks and with little hesitation, I told her the truth, the whole truth and nothing but the truth. Being at my wit's end living in that flat above the pub, the first meeting with Keith Sykes, testing it in the park, the trial with London City United, Buck Schulz, Sean Clark, Mario Gonzales, the deal and how it never happened but then did, Harley Wells, and how I had become one of the best footballers in the world all through The Amazing Syko's mind tricks.

'I've done it all for you and Tilson,' I said. 'To prove to you that I'm somebody and that I can make something of myself. Somebody, hopefully, that you'll respect and…' I paused '…fall in love with again.'

I would go into detail about what happened next, but a gentleman never tells. Let's just say that the hot tub needed to be drained for cleaning the next day (which is the pain in the arse in a penthouse apartment). It was electric. Being coupled with my wife again was everything I'd wished for. And I got such a thrill as she strode across the living room in nothing but a London City United shirt with my name on the back. Talk about a striker. I felt like a teenager all over again – the Frog Prince who got the beautiful princess and lived happily ever after.

But it was more like 'happily for five minutes' than 'ever after', because I managed to thump the size 9s that had so masterfully scored a double hattrick against the Blues earlier that afternoon squarely into my own mouth.

'I knew this would happen eventually,' I said as we lay naked, snuggled under a blanket on the living room floor, with half-drunk glasses of champagne by our sides. Sky Sports News had taken on a rather voyeuristic role this evening on the big telly, not that I remember turning it on.

'What? You knew we'd end up fucking in your jacuzzi and I'd knock my kebab over and get burger sauce on your lovely white carpet?' I had smelt onions, but didn't realise she'd knocked her kebab over. However, I didn't intend to spoil the moment by making an issue out of that, oh no. I had something else up my sleeve to spoil the moment.

'No, I mean I knew that once I was back up on my feet that you'd come back to me.' I said it proudly, giving my wife a squeeze. But she sat up, agitated.

'Riiiight, not sure what you mean, but go on.'

'Well, you know love, you were always attracted to me when I had the money before and less so when it all went away, and that's fine, I understand. So, I knew that I just had to get a bit of wedge back in the bank and my sweet, sweet love would come a-crawling back.' I said it smugly. I was smug. My dreams were coming true. My plan had worked. I even jiggled my eyebrows when I said the word 'a-crawling'. I couldn't have been any cockier had I dressed in an inflatable cock outfit and parachuted out of a cock-shaped aero-plane and landed on Cock Island, leaving a cock-shaped imprint on the sands of Wrong End Of The Stick Bay. I smiled and raised my hand to softly stroke Julie's face, but she pushed it away sharply and stood up, taking the blanket with her. I swiftly grabbed the discarded LCU shirt to cover my exhausted bits and bobs.

'What?' I squeaked, perplexed as only men can be when they do or say something wrong but are too stupid to know what at the time. Hindsight was yet to kick in. 'Julie? What is it?' She didn't reply. She just shook her head, tearful now, and started picking up her clothes.

'Julie, babe…' I cringed, remembering instantly how she hated being called 'babe' and any such pet name. 'I mean, what is it? What's up? What did I say? This is good, isn't it?'

My wife turned to me with huge tears streaming down her red-dened cheeks, off her chin and leaving darkened marks on the carpet below. She sniffed, wiped her nose on her hand and smiled briefly as she attempted to compose herself. 'So that's what you think, eh? That's what you think of me? A gold-digger? That I was only interested in fucking money? You fucking idiot. I wouldn't choose to spend my life with someone – to bring a child into the world with someone – just because he had a few quid in his pocket. How shallow do you think I am? You fucking, fucking moron.'

She began increasing the pace with which she picked up her clothes and started putting them back on. Shit, she was going to leave, badly. Part of me realised I had fucked up and needed to fix it quickly. I tried to control all the various thoughts racing through my head, but it was like herding cats with my brain dulled by tiredness, emotion and lots of booze. *'Apologise profusely,'* said the sensible side of my head. *'Beg. Get on your hands and knees and crawl. Don't let this goddess – your princess, your queen – slip from your grasp once more. Tell her it was a badly-judged joke. Tell her you didn't mean it. Say sorry a million times and then once more.'*

But I did a typically blokey thing and did the opposite of what seemed sensible. I started to feel offended that she felt offended and went on the defensive...by attacking her. Not physically, of course. I hit back: 'Well, you can't blame me for thinking that, can you? You never took a second look at me until the last year at school, no one did other than to bully me, and by then I had some money. When I was skint and ugly, no one wanted to be seen with me – including you. And when I lost all my money again, that's when you kicked me out and got in the golden lover boy, eh? Am I wrong? I'm not wrong.'

Julie was now tucking her tights into her handbag and trying to locate her other shoe. She didn't seem to be listening and didn't appear to be in the mood to carry on the conversation any more. But I continued baiting her and, by now, the tears were rolling down my face too. All those fears of rejection and of being alone resurfacing from my youth and laid bare for her to see. Raw. In the past, she would cuddle and console me. I was orphaned at six, lost my grandparents in my 20s and was bullied at school for years, so this wasn't the first time she'd seen me cry, not by a long shot. But, her being the target of my ranting now, there was no sympathy or understanding. Her stern silence pushed me on. 'Am I wrong?' I taunted again. 'You saying nothing would suggest I'm not.'

She bit. 'You want to know why I got with you, huh? It's because when you had the world stacked against you, you fought back. You didn't wallow in the shit and sulk and whine – you did something about it. While every other boy was just trying to get laid and drunk, you were building something bigger. It gave you a glint in your eye to be proving people wrong. You made something of yourself when people said you'd amount to nothing, but you never went back and rubbed it in their faces. You rose above. Bigger and better. I fell in love with your spirit and your character and your humour and the forgiveness you showed the world when it really didn't deserve it for what it had done to you. You were a fighter.'

'I…' no other words formed in my head or mouth.

'But then you gave up. That's why it went downhill. You sold your business, which is your right to do. But when things turned against us, you just gave in. You lost your fight. I tried to mimic what you had and got a full-time job with the charity…' To be honest, I thought she was volunteering. I never actually asked what she was bringing to the table because I was too busy being a bloke about everything, but I wasn't going to mention that now. 'Everything that…all that shit that happened and you just shrugged your shoulders and accepted it. I won't lie, you gave us a very comfortable life for a long while and I did – I do – enjoy it. I know I'm lucky. But I love the Richard Price who isn't afraid to call the world a cunt and kick it in the bollocks when it deserves it. And that's what I thought you were doing now, love. I knew you were up to something with the football because it's just so fucking…crazy. But you were up to something. The glint was back in your eye and the fire back in your belly. That's what was winning me back; the old you, not your money. But…you…you fucking idiot.'

She opened the door, sighed and left. The click from the latch reverberated around the apartment for hours as I sat in silence and absorbed it. All of it.

27. LOVE AND WAR

H ARLEY Wells' love life was, it's fair to say, as up-and-down as mine. After being reunited with his childhood friend Ayesha Khan – aka the sensational Shima – at Adam Bush's team-building party, the two of them kept in touch regularly to talk about old times. And the more they spoke about old times, the more they enjoyed each other's company. And the more they enjoyed each other's company, the bigger the rumours grew. Like me and Mollie, it seemed people couldn't handle two people of the opposite sex just being friends. But, to be honest, we already know those two grew to be more than friends.

But Ayesha was, of course, Bush's girlfriend and had been for quite a while. They were a glamour couple that the tabloids and magazines like Wowzer! loved featuring every time they opened their front door. The England captain and his knock-out girlfriend were up there with Posh and Becks. There were rumours in the papers of an engagement and possibly a child to come in the not-too-distant future, although nothing was confirmed officially.

However, there were also counter-rumours from gossips and critics that something was 'not quite right' about the relationship. One visitor to the house had told a showbiz news website that the couple slept in separate beds. 'To ensure he gets a full night's sleep ahead of matches, Mr Bush sometimes sleeps in a different room to his partner,' his spokesman had said.

Others had reported 'friends' fearing the couple were to split up because Bush preferred to spend his time 'with the lads' rather than her in his spare time. There was a no comment reply to that.

But it did seem that, aside from high-profile events, awards dos or film premieres, he did prefer to spend time with his mates playing golf, fishing or shopping than do stuff with his girlfriend Ayesha. And having shunned the fakeness of some of the other WAGS, she often found herself lonely and with little to do. So, having an old friend like Harley turn up out of the blue and be happy to shower her with attention was more than welcomed.

At the end of their first catch-up after the party over coffee, they gave each other an awkward hug and air kiss. The next time – after a longer and boozier than expected meal – it was more relaxed and Harley held onto Ayesha's hand and kissed her cheek as he told her what a wonderful time he'd had. On the third meeting, they fucked like rabbits in the changing rooms of one of the department stores at Westfield shopping centre. Her screams of ecstasy were so loud that security were told someone was being attacked (Harley seems to have a habit of that...the latter bit I mean) and four male guards raced to the scene. Hearing the kerfuffle outside, Ayesha opened the dressing room door and stepped out just in her lacy underwear. She told them she'd caught a glimpse of herself naked in the mirror and had been overcome by the urge for a bit of self-love. Harley, meanwhile, stood as still and as silent as he could behind the door despite the fact he had an erection like the Eiffel Tower. For the drooling guards who spent much of their time watching porn on their phones or trying to spot fit girls on the CCTV, Ayesha's story was one for the wank bank and their mates down the pub. They took it hook, line and sinker.

Despite the close call, Ayesha and Harley kept meeting up for a session of how's your father. Post-coitus on one occasion, she confided in him that she was trapped in the relationship with Adam Bush. When he asked why she didn't just leave, Ayesha said: 'It's complicated. Too complicated. I can't really explain.' Harley was disappointed, but he didn't want to put too much pressure on her and possibly scare her off. He was in love. But having seen what I had seen at the team-building party – namely our captain copping off with one of the assistant coaches in an upstairs bathroom away from the crowd – and looking at Ayesha's original background as an actress trying to establish herself, I think I could explain. And as Harley had blackmailed me to sort this problem out in return for him helping me to get back to being a Ballon d'Or contender, I had to confront the situation head-on.

I can't say the welcome from Adam Bush was a particularly friendly one as I arrived at his front door on that Sunday afternoon, but that wasn't unexpected. I can't say that I was in a good mood either after the previous night's calamities with Julie. But a promise is a promise and I'm a man of my word. Most of the time. Plus Harley had been good to me so I wanted to help if I could. The blackmailing aspect just speeded things up.

I still wasn't entirely sure how I was going to broach the subject of my visit as Bush led me through his large hallway, past the marble steps that led down to his party room – The Den – and into a kitchen the size of a small village.

'Tea? Coffee? Beer? Pie?' he asked. I could see and smell the coffee already percolating, so I opted for that and black to help clear my head and hangover. 'Good performance yesterday,' he added. It was the only compliment he'd given since I joined the club and even that didn't sound convincing. 'Well, the second half anyway. Found your shooting boots again, so to speak.'

'Yeah, thanks. It was good. Shame it came against Southend, being my team and all that. Got a few mates that aren't happy. Well, a mate. But, er, you know, you've got to be professional about these things, right?' I was babbling.

'Hmm. Has that Wells kid replaced the nonce as your counsellor?'

'Keith's not a non...no, ah, Harley's just helping me, you know, he has done since I got there. But he is what I wanted to talk to you about. Harley.' Bush looked at me, his face giving nothing away but I was pretty sure he knew what was coming. 'Well, him and Ayesha to be precise.'

'So it's true then, the rumours?'

From that, I decided it wasn't worth trying to sugar coat things. But I tried to explain that these were two people, Harley and Ayesha, who knew each other as kids. They had a history and got on. They' grown close and, yes, 'things' may have happened (I wasn't about to tell him the story about them in the changing rooms). But this wasn't just a naughty knee-trembler for thrills. These were two people who had fallen in love – perhaps they shouldn't in the way they had, but they had – and want to be together.

'But you have some sort of hold over Ayesha where she seems scared to talk to you about this. I haven't spoken to her, admittedly, but it seems, for me, that you have two people who want to be together but are being prevented from doing that out in the open. You, I mean, well, that should be something you understand, right?' I dropped that little bombshell of insinuation on the table and sipped on my coffee, eyes down. When I did look up, Adam was staring straight at me. He looked angry.

'Are you serious? Blackmail. You're going to blackmail me?'

'I'm not, honest, I'm really not. Emotionally, maybe, yes. But Harley's a good kid and he's desperate to be with Ayesha without sneaking around and he can't for whatever reason because she's with you despite the fact you're gay.'

'Bye.'

'Oh no, c'mon Adam, don't just dismiss this. I know we haven't seen eye-to-eye before, but you don't really know me. I'm a bit of a softie at heart and I know those two are in love. Ayesha seems like a lovely girl and you must know that otherwise you wouldn't still have her around. I'm guessing there's some kind of mutual benefit to it, something that ties you together, but give them a chance. Do it for them. And I totally understand you don't want the world to know you're gay.'

'Bye.'

'Alright, alright, I'm going. But please, please think about it Adam...why are you laughing? This is people's lives. What's so funny?'

'You fucking idiot,' he replied. I'd been hearing that a lot lately. 'I wasn't saying 'bye' as in 'bye-bye'. I was saying 'bi'. You kept saying I was gay, but I'm bisexual. I like men and women. And you're right, I do like Ayesha very much, but she's not my number one. Not for a long time. But I don't want the world to know I play for both teams, but I refuse to be blackmailed over it either.'

We took a moment each for pause and to reset ourselves. Adam refilled our coffee cups and then told me the story of him and Ayesha. He had met her after a show in the West End which was her first role out of drama school. They then dated for six months and got on like a house on fire. They loved each other's company and connected on a deep level very quickly. But the lure of intimate male company above that of Ayesha became too strong for Adam. She was at a crossroads in her life having spent years training to be an actress, only to get there and be completely unsure it was what she wanted after all. That's when Adam offered her the role of a lifetime – but an all-consuming one. She would move in with him and play the part of a loving, loved and fulfilled girlfriend in a bid to put an end to the rumours that were circulating around the football world and becoming songs on the terraces. I mean, why would the average football fan have reason to doubt Adam Bush's sexuality when he had Ayesha on his arm? As well as a 'performance' fee (not in that sort of way), Adam would use his contacts and high profile to help her achieve a career in showbiz, somehow. The sensational Shima persona that grew out of that was as much to protect Ayesha and give her an income of her own as it was to make her famous. They still had their moments from time to time because they loved one another, but certainly not in the last year or so since Adam hooked up with Alexis Colombo.

Despite their close friendship, Adam had made Ayesha sign a watertight non-disclosure agreement that meant if she told a soul about the truth then she would be ruined, financially at least. But she was happy to sign because she couldn't see how someone as caring as Adam would ever hurt her to the extent she would feel OK with releasing that information. She didn't even tell her best friend Mollie, who just assumed Ayesha had given up on her acting dream to pursue the reality fame route. She didn't judge. Ayesha was old enough and talented enough to make her own decisions. And Ayesha certainly hadn't told her new love Harley, because she knew that if the truth emerged in the club environment then she would never be able to trust him again and the whole thing would be for nothing. Why even put him in that position?

'We've been like that for four years now, but if an idiot like you worked it out then we're clearly not doing everything right,' he conceded. 'But I can't just let her go like that. I'll be exposed. Too many people have ideas of things. I need some insurance. I need to be in control.'

'Why don't you just come out?' I thought it was an appropriate question, but it came from a position of privilege. No one questioned me about anything really.

'Why should I? It's my life. I don't want the pressure or the abuse. I don't want to be anyone's poster boy. I just want to play football and then come home to my partner, and whether that be a man or a woman is no one's business. If you liked your missus to put on a strap-on and fuck you up the arse at the weekend, do you think the world has the right to know?'

'Chance would be a fine thing.' It raised a smile and eased the tension. I apologised.

'And what about you?' he asked after a moment. I wasn't sure if he was still talking about the strap-on or not. He could tell I was puzzled. 'Well, you know my big secret. How do I know you won't go and tell the papers even if I do sort something out with Ayesha?'

'Well, I haven't told anyone yet despite the fact you've been a complete prick to me. Doesn't that tell you all you need to know about the type of person I am?'

'Nice try, but no.'

With a deep breath and not enough thought, I told Adam all about Operation Hypnotise A Fat Bloke Into Being A Footballer too. Everything. Now he knew my big secret. And so did Julie after I told her the night before. And Harley, of course. He may have told Ayesha. Keith knew, obviously, and Neil, who may have told his wife. And – unbeknown to me – so did Jim Neale and Sean Clark. The whole point of a secret is that very few, if any, others are meant to know it. Our circle of knowledge was getting bigger and bigger and the time on my little adventure was ticking away.

On the positive side of things, Adam and I reached a compromise. He agreed that he and Ayesha would split up in a very stage-managed way that would not damage either of their reputations. She would then have to wait for three months before starting her new relationship with Harley Wells in public, but never rub it in. She'd be fine with that. The pair of them could, of course, see each other in the meantime, but do their absolute utmost to keep it under wraps. Adam would also get another stringent non-disclosure agreement for her to sign, and me. And Harley was never to know the truth.

'I can tell you one thing,' Adam said as we shook hands while he led me out towards his front door. 'If our secrets ever do get out then I'm definitely denying knowing anything about yours.'

28. THE CALL

AN unplanned bonus of my Sunday afternoon chat at Maison Bush was a massive release in the tension that had gripped the squad at London City United. Where before there were splits, cliques and backbiting with some teammates barely sharing a word, now there was unity and harmony. We were a team. It was lifted from the moment Adam came over to me in the changing room before training on the Monday morning and sat down next to me. Others in the room stopped what they were doing and watched attentively as if things were about to descend into an old school, Jerry Springer-style brawl. But we just exchanged pleasantries and Adam passed me a bag of the coffee we had the previous day at his house. It had been good.

Out on the training pitch, there was laughter. Nutmegs were now met with a joyful cheer of encouragement and gentle ribbing rather than threats of revenge, and there was a genuinely good atmosphere. It also loosened up the manager and coaching staff, who no longer felt they were seconds away from being referees in a fight where they didn't know who was on which side or why.

This massive upward shift in mood was, of course, a major factor in London City United's six-match winning streak I spoke about earlier. We were now in the FA Cup semi-final and just three points behind leaders Manchester City in our push for the Premier League titles. And they were our next opponents at the Grand Postal/MegaMobiles Arena. We had more than a week to prepare for the biggest match of the season and to get everyone fit and raring to go. Plus the cold and wet weather of the year so far was giving way to warmer and brighter days. Everything was brightening up for LCU. I had been getting fitter too with each match that passed and myself, Harley and Keith now had the system down to a T. We all felt like winners.

Unfortunately, the upturn in fortunes hadn't rolled over into my personal life. Julie was still pissed off with me about that night in the flat and what I'd said. I did buy a really nice watch and a massive bunch of flowers to take round there as a peace offering, but on the way I realised that it's probably not best to say sorry for branding someone emotionless and money obsessed by bringing them gifts that cost a lot of money. Admittedly, I did save the watch for another time, but there's not much you can do with flowers so I went down to the cemetery and divvied them out among mum, dad, nan and grandad's graves. It really was a huge bunch so I ended up putting some on about eight or nine others too. Took me ages.

Such was her disdain for me at the moment – probably the worst it had been, to be honest – Julie didn't even come to the door to say hello when I picked Tilson up on the Wednesday night to go for dinner and see the latest Marvel film. He got my mood up though by taking the mickey out of me for wearing a hoodie, cap and sunglasses in the cinema. I told him, quietly, that I needed to do that now because otherwise I get mobbed by selfie-seekers and autograph hunters. 'Dad it's dark in here and there's only three other people and they're watching the film,' he said. We had a late-night walk along the seafront afterwards, nipping into the arcades to play a few video games for a bit and then we got him a bag of freshly-cooked doughnuts. The smell was amazing and the temptation tremendous, but I resisted. Big game Saturday. Not risking it.

I also had to apologise to Mollie for a) not meeting her at the party, b) for causing a massive scene at the party and c) for running out and leaving her alone without a date for the rest of the night. 'Ah, well, if you got your end away with the missus then it was worth it,' she texted back. 'Does this mean Turbo Curbo is back on the market now and fair game? He's cute.' He was certainly something beginning with a c.

'Paolo Antoine in goal. Back four of Andrey Kozlov, Adam Bush captain, Christian Halberg, and Markos Michaelis. Billy Shivdasani holding in midfield with Harry Jacobs and Luca Tartaglia ahead of him. Front three of Danny Diegbe, Horatio Emmett and Richie Price. That's our starting team. Good.'

Franco Capece looked happy, relaxed and stress-free as he fronted the team meeting. It was hard to believe he was 30 minutes of football away from being sacked only a few weeks earlier. This was a task he often offloaded to his assistants – giving out the team, going through some opposition plays on the big screens and issuing detailed instruction dossiers to individual players. But having him in charge and leading from the front showed us all that this was a big match and that we all need to bring our A-game. And 24 hours later, I brought mine. Granted, a private tete-a-tete with Harley Wells in a room off the main changing room was needed. He pulled out his phone, Skyped Keith Sykes and he worked his magic from the comfort of his own home. Or it may have been the pub toilets. Anyway, as I've said before, just because I can pull out the tricks of football's greatest players, it didn't mean the result was a foregone conclusion – even if we had just won six on the bounce. Manchester City were a team packed with very, very expensive world-class international footballers. They were top of the Premier League and weren't looking to be knocked off any time soon.

They ended our run of consecutive clean sheets within the first five minutes and should've been 2-0 up on the half-hour mark when Halberg gave away a penalty for handball. Our goalie Paolo Antoine closed his eyes, mentally flicked through the instruction folder he'd studied on City's penalty takers the night before and found the history for Marvin Fifi. It really wasn't too much of a difference from what I was doing. Fourteen of Fifi's last 15 penalties had been placed into the bottom right-hand corner. Antoine watched his rival and French international teammate intently as he paced back to start his run-up. It was slightly different from the videos he'd watched, only a fraction different, but enough. As the striker strode forward and struck the ball powerfully with his right foot, Antoine had made his decision and was moving. Rather than low and right, he dived up and left – and guessed correctly. Fifi knew he'd been studied and tried to bluff his mate – at the last minute deciding not to double-bluff – but his penalty was saved. Less than three minutes later, London City United were level.

The visitors from Manchester were trying to hit us on the counter-attack, breaking down the left-hand side. Somehow, I found myself being the nearest defender as Fifi, still smarting from his penalty miss, raced forward at speed towards me. My brain flicks, chooses and executes the play. Bobby Moore, England versus Brazil, World Cup 1970. I shadowed Fifi as he moved towards the edge of the box but, as he tried to go past me, I stretched out my right leg and snatched back possession with a perfectly-timed swoop and then strode purposefully across the pitch with the ball towards the right-hand side. I could see Danny Diegbe breaking forward between the two opposition centre-backs. Brain flicks, chooses and executes the play. David Beckham for Real Madrid versus Zaragoza in the 2006 Copa Del Rey semi-final second leg. (I know! My brain was now filled with so much football it was ridiculous). I paused and let the ball roll to a stop just in front of me. Then, with my arms outstretched either side for balance, I swung my right foot at the ball and curled a physics-defying cross beyond the reach of the first defender and into the path of Danny to slide home.

We ended the half 1-1, but took the lead 10 minutes after the restart – and I had nothing to do with it. Luca Tartaglia floated a corner into the middle of the box, the Man City keeper flapped at the ball and after a mad goalmouth scramble, Horatio Emmett prodded the ball over the line. We were 2-1 up but then seemed to stop playing as a team, almost like we had been before the run of wins. City dominated us for the rest of the game and how they didn't score again was beyond me. Paolo pulled off some worldie saves, the defence stood firm mostly and when it did look like the away side had finally found a way to score, they were thwarted by my penis and testicles.

This was, perhaps, the only thing I ever did on the pitch plucked from my own memory banks and it was worth any goal or assist from the greats. City had a corner, Fifi controlled the ball and fired it goalwards through a crowd of players and, for the first time that afternoon, left Antoine rooted to the spot, helpless. I was on the line and, as the ball thundered towards me, I realised it was too high to get a foot up to kick away and too low for a header. The temptation was there to use my hands, but I didn't want to get sent off and then still leave them with a penalty. My hand moved out instinctively, but I balled it into a fist and pulled it towards my side with the same vigour that I then used to thrust my hips forward and smash my genitals into the pristine Nike Ordem match ball and steer it away to safety. Then I collapsed on the floor in agony. My crown jewels retreated so far up my body that I genuinely had a lump in my throat. Childbirth? Nah, you can keep that. The pain and nausea ripped through my body and I thought I was going to chunder. 'Don't rub them, count them,' one wag yelled as they always do when a player gets the ball in the nuts. The incident added four minutes of injury time to the end of the game that we could've done without, but it also gave rise to the beautifully constructed terrace chant of Great Balls of Price (sung, of course, to the Jerry Lee Lewis classic). If ever I wanted to leave a legacy in football then that was it.

But there was still a game to finish and I gingerly re-joined the play after the physio poured a bottle of ice-cold water down my shorts to freeze my balls and the referee waved me back on. As we entered the injury time caused by the Great Balls of Price, I brought the game to a grandstand finish. Adam Bush hoofed the ball forward in an attempt to just get the thing clear for a while and a Man City defender nodded it back into the midfield area. Brain flicks, chooses and executes the play. I controlled the ball on my chest and then nudged it forward with my knee. The first defender thought I was about to shoot and so jumped and turned his back on me to block it, but I cut inside with an extra touch and then let fly with an absolute rocket of a right-footer that rose up into the top corner of the net. I ran off towards the cheering home support while pumping both hands in the air. Tony Yeboah, Leeds versus Wimbledon, September 1995. What a beauty.

The win over Manchester City put us level on points with them but ahead on goal difference, which was a remarkable achievement for a club with a chunk of its first-team squad suspended over the dodgy contract shenanigans of Mario Gonzales and a ban on new signings in the January transfer window. And it had been an extraordinary turnaround when you consider the team's shabby performances in the first half of the season. Franco Capece was rightly getting a lot of credit for the change in London City United's fortune and was named Manager of the Month for March. I got Player of the Month. It seemed my performances were getting noticed in all the right places.

There were huge celebrations in the changing room after that game, a real party atmosphere. There was music playing and players posing for selfies to go up on Instagram and Snapchat. Franco was keen to ensure we didn't get carried away – we hadn't won anything yet – but even he requested some beers be brought down for the players and coaches so long as they didn't feature in those photos going on social media. Across the room, I saw my new friend Adam Bush taking a call on his mobile. He was smiling and nodding as he listened to the voice on the other end. He looked up and made eye contact with me for a moment, but then looked down again as he spoke to the caller. However, a second or two later he stood up, covered the mouthpiece of the diamond-encrusted, gold iPhone and walked over to me.

'Someone wants a word with you,' he said, flicking his head towards the treatment room in a manner that told me it would be a private call. I mouthed 'Who is it?' but he declined to tell me and instead made sure the door closed behind me. I looked at the display for a clue, but it just showed the initials RL. There was only one way to find out who the caller was.

'Er, hello, it's Richie here, who's this?' I said, putting the phone to my ear.

'Ello son, it's Ron Lewis,' boomed back a broad Lancashire accent. 'I've really been enjoying your performances of late lad and I want you to come to our get-t'gether for the next week or so and get to know you. Alright? Good. Well done.' The phone went dead without me saying another word.

Ron Lewis had been a journeyman midfielder in the late 1970s and 80s until his playing career was cut short by a road accident in the summer of 1986 while the attention of the footballing world – and me – was on the Mexico World Cup and Gary Lineker bagging his golden boot. Ron was offered a coaching job at his then-club Huddersfield Town in the old Second Division. He spent a year there before moving into management with Leyton Orient the next season. It's fair to say he has come a long way since then with spells managing in Spain and Italy, as well as in the top-flight here in England. He now found himself in charge of the national team.

Yep, that's right. That call from Ron was to notify me that I was being called up to the England squad.

Jim Neale nearly spat out the mouthful of his mum's homemade rhubarb crumble and custard he was chomping on when he saw the England squad being announced on the telly. Richie fucking Price? The fraud. What a disgrace. He hadn't felt so disgusted and delighted at the same time since he found out Adam Bush was gay. 'A bender in the changing room, backs to the wall lads, hahahaha!' he'd said to his editor. He thought those university types were supposed to be clever, but none of those stuck-up pricks in the office ever got his jokes. The boss didn't even raise a smile. 'Bushy, gay!' Jim said again. 'He's decent, but imagine how good a player he'd be if he wasn't staring at the oppositions' arses all the time, yeah? Ha! No wonder he likes to mark so tightly, Ha!' Still nothing.

In the end, he'd sat on the story. The editor wanted more concrete evidence than hearsay, and when he went to the club he was asked by the chief exec Sean Clark to keep it under his hat. He didn't want the details of the club captain's sexual orientation splashed all over the front and back pages at that time. Jim was loathed to hush the story up but Clarky, as he liked to call him, had dropped 5,000 reasons not to print it in his bank account, as well as giving him the exclusive on the sale of their then-top scorer Tony Gardner to Arsenal.

And as upset as he was about seeing that cheating scumbag Price in the England set-up for the last friendlies before the World Cup squad was announced, the news had come off the back of a phone call that filled him with joy. Someone – 'a source very close to the player' as the article would eventually say – had not only given Jim the missing pieces of the Price puzzle, but the instruction manual too. And this time he would have the blessing of Sean Clark to bring down an LCU star. Both of them wanted the useless fat imposter exposed and made an example of as much as the other.

29. THREE LIONS

I HAD planned to spend Sunday afternoon with Tilson at the zoo (possibly the only thing I was willing to go to Colchester for). The only time I let my boy swear in front of me without telling him off was to flick the Vs at Col U's stadium as we drove past it once on the A12 on our way to a caravan park up in Norfolk. The zoo, though, was a good day out and we hadn't been for a while so I thought I'd take Tilson and ask Julie along too. She gave me a 'maybe, we'll see', which was better than I expected. But now I had to let them both down. Again. I had lions of a different kind to go and see. The three of England.

And so instead of driving up the A12 to north Essex with my boy by my side listening to his loud, shouty music, I was now driving up the M1 towards Burton-on-Trent with Harley Wells at my side listening to his loud, sweary music. His tastes were very different to mine, so we agreed to an hour's choice each and then the radio. I know this is something those past a certain age say about younger people's music, but it all sounded the same. Rap, hip-hop, grime, RnB, swearing, repeated mentions of booties being shaken and parties, and lots of Harley bouncing from side to side while making hand signals with one hand and scrolling through his phone with the other. Now I don't mind a bit of old school rap like your Public Enemies or Will Smiths and so on, but this wasn't for me. And other than mumbling through the lyrics, Harley barely said a word to me for that whole hour. But when it was my turn to play my music, I couldn't shut the fucker up. It was all 'Me and Ayesha this' and 'Me and Ayesha that'. I kept subtly nudging up the volume with the button near the steering wheel, but he'd just turn the dial down on the radio after a bit and carry on jabbering about holidays planned, trips to the shopping mall, details of dates past and future, and all the funny and cute little things she said or did. It was sickening. And he turned down Toto's Africa just as it hit the chorus. No appreciation of the qualities of a power ballad that boy.

But I had to be grateful he was here really. After getting off the phone to Ron Lewis and the immediate exhilaration of my England call-up subsided, I realised I was stuck in that position again of not having the access to Keith to put me in the state to play proper football. My teammates mobbed me in the changing rooms when Franco Capece announced I had been called up. He'd spoken to Ron Lewis before the game, but asked to keep it quiet. But it was brilliant. I felt part of something amazing in that group of players. Then Adam pushed through the crowd and asked for his highly-valuable, custom iPhone back. Once that was safely in his pocket, he told me he'd 'sort it'. He said that with a knowing nod, but I couldn't be sure whether the knowing nod was because he knew what I was worried about or something else. Imagine if he just thought I didn't know how to get to the England training base in Burton and just 'sorted' a lift or if he thought I was enamoured with his diamond-encrusted iPhone and would speak to his contact at Apple to 'sort' me one.

But he came through for me, my former foe. He called Mr Lewis – they had a close relationship as manager and captain – and explained that not only was Harley key to getting me to perform to my very best, but he was also an exceptional fitness coach who could make a good addition to the England set-up. That was a nice touch. And so here we were, Harley and me, on our way up the motorway to meet my England teammates.

We arrived at St George's Park in the early evening and were greeted in the reception area by a bunch of Team England staff, including the kit man who took my football boots off me so they could be laid out in my place in the changing rooms for when we went training.

Because everyone's coming from all over the country, the players arrive at these things in dribs and drabs, but I had already seen the Johnson brothers, John and Jon. Their parents had, essentially, given them the same name. The story behind it was that there was a family tradition that went back forever to call the first-born son John so that John Johnson would always be John's son and keep the name 'pure'. But as unlikely as it may sound, no one in the family had ever had two sons. So, when Jane Johnson bore a second boy two years after John was born, she and her husband were left with a bit of a predicament. They considered Johan for a while or a derivative of John like Ian or Ewan. But after returning from the pub to wet the nameless baby's head, John Johnson Snr decided that 'Jon' would be the single and perfect solution for his second son. And so he was christened.

Both John and Jon seemed nice enough. We exchanged handshakes and a smile and both welcomed me to the squad and wished me the best. Gary Smith, who got there just as Harley and I were being given details of our accommodation, was far less friendly. 'Ah fuck, the freak show's in town.' It turned out that 'Freak' was a nickname I had with players from rival clubs who didn't like me. By that point, I really didn't care. I was regretting my choice of outfit though, as I stood out like a badly-dressed sore thumb. They'd said to come casual. Everyone else – the players, the staff and the coaches – were wearing some form of tracksuit or sportswear.

Those who had been in the squad before generally wore their England team tracksuit and the newbies wore their own, designer ones. Me? I was wearing a pair of faded blue jeans with a hole in one knee and a Coldplay Viva la Vida tour T-shirt from their show at Wembley Arena in 2008. These were my comfy clothes, you know. I'd just had to drive for the best part of three hours to get here. It wasn't meant to be a fashion show.

Smith looked me up and down and sneered, making a weird 'tssking' sound with his mouth. If I hadn't been facing him when he did it, I may have mistaken it for him blowing me a kiss. But there was menace and attitude in it. He still shook my hand, but mainly because a young lad from the FA was filming all the arrivals to be posted on its YouTube channel. But despite only knowing him in passing from the 5-0 drubbing we handed out to West Ham, Smith wasn't at all pleasant. Still, I'd been there and got that T-shirt too from my early days at LCU.

Fortunately, when I got to my room Sports Direct had been sick all over my bed. Shorts, tops, T-shirts, tracksuits, polo shirts, flip-flops, trainers and anything else sporty-clothing-wise you could think of was spread out in front of me and all of it had the iconic Three Lions badge. For the first time in the whole thing, this whole 'being a footballer', I felt overly emotional. And guilty. This wasn't taking a few thousand quid a week off a mega-rich corporate football club any more. This was England. My country. 1966 and all that, and I was an imposter.

Then the call came through for dinner and I snapped out of it. I was fucking starving.

Jim Neale pressed the red 'end call' button on his smartphone and then double-checked the voice recorder had worked properly. It had. He listened to those four words again and smiled triumphantly. Then he slumped back in his chair and let out the most satisfying fart, wafting the fumes up from his crotch to his nose with his hand to fully enjoy the aroma.

He had loved the Rubik's Cube when he was a kid. If he wasn't out on the estate kicking a football around or watching telly, he'd be in his room fiddling with his toy. He became brilliant at it. At Christmas, when all his aunts and uncles and cousins came over for a massive roast dinner, loads of booze, presents, charades and the Queen's Speech, he would pick one of them to mess up the cube as best they could and then wow them all an hour later by having solved it. Admittedly, in the early days, he sometimes went to his room and painstakingly peeled off all the little coloured stickers and then put them back in the right place. But, as he got older, he learned the proper techniques and could solve a reasonably jumbled cube in five minutes or less.

His favourite part was not the reveal though. It was that moment usually five, six, seven clicks earlier when he knew he had it solved. When he knew that the right twists and turns controlled by him would bring about the result he wanted and everyone would be amazed. 'I don't know how you do it Jimbo,' his mates or relatives or editor or rival in the press box would say, 'but you just keep delivering.' And even though his Rubik's Cube was safely locked away upstairs in his bedroom, Jim had that same feeling of excitement now. He was only a few moves away from his big reveal that would amaze the world and he was in control of all those turns.

The caller had been nervous and a little unsure about whether or not to spill the beans, because it meant exposing someone they love or used to love. But Jim had been there a million times before and he knew the drill. He reassured them that they were doing the right thing and he'd say that, actually, he knew most of the details already and just needed them confirming. This was also a handy technique he used to keep down the price he paid the informant. 'I can't pay you five grand for telling me something I already know,' he'd say. 'I tell you what, I could probably square away one-and-a-half from my

bosses as a goodwill gesture. Best I can do mate, best I can do.'
Then he'd go quiet and let the caller mull over £1,500 or nothing.
Once they'd chosen the money and were convinced they were clari-
fying details Jim already knew, they tended to be a lot more open.
'Just explain in your own words...' was his favourite lead-in and
then he'd listen carefully for those little occasions where he could
predict what the person is going to say and get in there first, making
the caller think he did already know it.

'So, the person behind the scam, doing all the hypnotism side of
things, is an old schoolmate of Richie called...' and Jim could jump
in to add 'Keith Sykes.' The caller confirmed he was right and Jim
told him they had enjoyed a few beers together recently in Miami,
making it seem as though they were on talking terms.

'You'll know it already then, how they're fixing it with Keith
banned from the club,' the caller said.

'Yeah, yeah, of course, but tell me everything in your own words.
It's a much more reliable story coming from you than me.'

A devious and sneaky tabloid hack using his dark arts to trick a
naive person into gossiping about a famous friend, or a clever and
professional newspaper journalist using his years of experience to
get the truth in a matter of public interest? It's a matter of opinion,
I suppose, or a very thin line. I'll let you decide because I'm by no
means the paragon of virtue here. But what got Jim celebrating
amid the rancid pong of his floating faecal gas were the words
'Goat', 'Asylum', 'Texture' and 'Lollygag'. Those four words were
the key to him breaking the biggest sports story of the year. No, *the*
biggest story of the year. He thought about the awards and the adulation from his peers, the slap on the back from the newspaper
owner for the rise in sales, possibly a few extra quid in his pocket at
the end of the month. He might be able to get himself a really decent brass. Maybe two. Although, on second thoughts, he could
barely satisfy one. One and a good curry it is, he thought. He felt a
ripple in his gut and knew another celebratory parp was on its way

down the tubes. He clenched at what he thought was the perfect moment to give it additional thrust, but something very brown and very sticky began to seep out. Shit (literally). He would have to get changed. Later.

Back at St George's Park, things were going far less crappy, although training with this England team was quite different from that at London City United. Franco Capece favoured a patient, possession-based build-up unless there was a speedy counter-attack to be had. Ron Lewis wanted a more direct approach for the Three Lions in both his tactics and language.

'Don't fanny about with it there, fucking whack it son...Big man, either flick it on, head it down or hold the fucking thing up. There should be someone there by you soon enough...Baldie, go in hard but fair...put your foot through it, princess...Long! Go Long!...Get stuck in there you big ugly bastard."

It also became abundantly clear very early on that Ron didn't have a clue what anyone's name was, despite the fact we had our initials on almost every piece of clothing. He relied on pet names, observations about the person's appearance or nicknames of players that weren't even there. So far I had been called 'fat boy', 'son', 'you', 'Giggsy' (who is actually Welsh, retired, and never played with or for Ron Lewis in his career), and 'yes' followed by a repeated nod of the head in my direction. But it was effective enough.

In general, the rest of the lads in the squad were excellent. In our downtime in the evenings, a few of them were keen to get to know about me, why I'd never played before, what it was like coming into the game so late, how I managed to accelerate so fast despite my body shape, was I shagging that fit blonde actress I was seen with in the paper and, if not, could they have her number. It was all very chilled. We had two friendly games coming up. The first was at Wembley on the Wednesday night against Brazil and then we would travel to Spain for the second on the Saturday. The manager had already told me that I would be on the bench for both matches, which he said would help to temper both the expectations from the fans and media, and the nerves I was feeling. Ron was blunt, as always, and told me 90 per cent of his World Cup squad was already chosen and the remaining 10 was pencilled in. He was mainly dithering over which back-up goalkeepers and defenders to include.

'But your recent performances can't be ignored Raymond lad...'

'It's Richie,' I corrected, but he didn't acknowledge it.

'...so I wanted to see how you train, how you mix with t'other boys in the squad, how you handle t'pressure and so on before I have to name my squad. Just enjoy yourself and, of course, my intention is to give you some minutes on t'field in either or both of t'friendlies.'

And I did enjoy all of it – until the coach taking us down from St George's Park pulled within view of Wembley, with its enormous arch towering over North London and all the history the national stadium carried with it. Other than seeing the Foo Fighters, I hadn't been there since Southend United's League Two play-off final against Wycombe Wanderers in 2015. That was a really good day. Neil and I got the train up in the morning, walked around the stadium, found a pub to get some beers and grub, and then sat in the stands as soon as the gates opened for the afternoon. The game was 0-0 at full-time and we were 1-0 down as it entered injury time in the second half of extra time. Some Southend fans had seen enough and were already on their toes heading for the exit to beat the rush for the train home. Despite having an incredibly numb bum and being desperate for a piss, Neil and I stayed in our seats to see onloan Joe Piggott score a 122nd-minute equaliser. Southend then went on to win the game 7-6 on penalties and were promoted to League One. What a game. What a day.

And those were the sorts of memories just one match had created for us Shrimpers. There had been thousands of matches played at that special ground throughout the decades, in the old stadium and the new – and that night I would be stepping out onto that hallowed Wembley turf as an England footballer and a fraud. Maybe it wasn't too late to back out of this. Maybe I could own up and put an end to it all. Maybe I could suddenly remember my dad was Irish and my mum was Welsh and I wasn't sure who I wanted to play for. Then Gary Smith, the West Ham winger who had given me such an unwelcome welcome and whose position in the first XI was under threat due to my arrival, said something that settled my resolve and made me determined to follow it through and succeed.

'Come on Ricketts, let's get this over with.'

'Ricketts?' said one of the Johnson brothers. 'What are you on about?'

'Michael Ricketts. One-cap wonder. Like Franny Jeffers and Gavin McCann. This bell-end will get 10 minutes at the end tonight and that'll be it for him while we go off to the World Cup.'

I actually knew a bit about Michael Ricketts. He'd had an unimpressive and very short spell at Southend United in 2006 – just four years but a long way from his solitary England cap in a friendly against the Netherlands.

For at least an hour, the guilt and nerves had put me extremely close to throwing the towel in. But Smith's twattishness had replaced those butterflies in my belly with fire. I would play against Brazil and I would play well. Then I would play well against Spain in the next match and for the rest of the season for London City United, and after becoming the oldest and fattest outfield player ever to win the Premier League I would snatch Smith's place in England's World Cup squad. There were plenty of other players who seemingly stole a living in football over the years or who only put in the effort when their contract was coming to an end and wanted another big pay day. I was giving more than them, so why shouldn't I enjoy the benefits? Why shouldn't I take this to the very top? To paraphrase Starship, nothing's gonna stop me now.

30. THEY THINK IT'S ALL OVER

JIM Neale shovelled a hot sausage roll into his mouth almost whole and allowed the crumbs to tumble from his full gob onto his jumper and floor. The food was hotter than he expected and more debris fell out as he wafted his hand in front of his mouth. Yet he made no effort to clear any of it up. He'd been to countless football stadiums around the world in his decades as a sports reporter, but the grub in the media lounge at Wembley was a cut above the rest. Although Chelsea did a pretty good spread too. But that's why he always got to England games extra early, to make sure he had first dibs at the buffet. With the sausage roll still swishing round his mouth like a meat-filled washing machine, he picked up a prawn mayo sandwich and tried to shove that into the mix too. He then winced in delight as he saw a young female member of the catering staff bend over to place a tray of clean cups next to the coffee and tea facilities.

'Cor, I wouldn't mind having a go on that at half-time,' he said to no one in particular. The nearest person to him was a journalist from The Times who was trying to work out which were the vegan options. Like most of the media pack, he knew all about Jim Neale as a reporter and as a person – and detested every aspect of him.

'Pathetic dinosaur,' he muttered as he lost his appetite and went to get himself a coffee.

'Yeah, mate. Shooting across there to get in there first are ya?' Jim knew what he was saying wasn't 'PC' and there was a one time when he forced himself to bite his tongue and pretend to be someone else rather than say what he thought. But he found that the more successful he became in delivering top-quality stories and front-page exclusives for the Daily Citizen, the more confident he was at putting his blunt opinions across and the more the bosses would tolerate it. He knew where the absolute boundary was and stayed just – and only just – the right side of it.

Once, there had been a complaint made to HR that he was a sex pest. Nonsense, he just liked looking at the women in the office and if he thought they were attractive then he would tell them so. Nothing wrong with that. It's not like he went up to the ugly ones and told them they were mingers, too. Well, not to their faces anyway. He was also 'traditional' in his view that a relationship should consist of a man and a woman – none of this modern stuff where it was all mixed up and 'fluid'. Each to their own if they kept themselves to themselves, he supposed, but he didn't want to see all that flashed around in public or on the telly.

There were accusations that he had racist leanings as well, but how could that be when he went to school and played football with people of different colours? No, they were all just jealous of how successful he had become in journalism – the untrained lad from South of the river showing up all the spoilt, middle-class graduates living off the Bank of Mum and Dad – and now they were trying to hold him back. But he was about to deliver the greatest exclusive of his career and he was going to make it very, very public.

The copy had already been written, checked by the paper's lawyers and was ready to go live on the website as soon as he set the wheels in motion. Of course, he would have liked to have seen his exclusive in print first, but there was just no way with what he had planned. Wait and you miss out. There were three other journalists from the Citizen at Wembley to file the match report and reaction pieces from what was about to happen. The legal team had also sent out a letter to their rivals saying that if they reported on the Citizen's investigation then they would have to credit both the paper and Jim Neale. He could feel a twinge in his yellowed underpants just at the thought of someone like The Sun or the Mail or the Guardian having to give him a byline. He turned his thoughts to the prozzie he had arranged to meet at a hotel down the road after the game. Maybe he'd offer that waitress a couple of hundred quid instead. If she was stocking up sandwiches in the media room on a Saturday afternoon then she must need the money, he figured. Nah, she'd probably be one of those feminists and complain to her bosses or be a lesbian.

As Jim Neale delved deeper into his sexual fantasies, I was sat in the changing rooms at Wembley listening to Ron Lewis go through his final preparations and dish out a few last-minute instructions. Then the bell rang and we began our walk out into the tunnel area. Adam Bush was captaining the team and stood, naturally, at the head of the line, each player holding hands with a young mascot to walk out onto the pitch with. Opposite us now were the Brazilian players in their classic golden shirts. More world class players I'd only ever seen on the TV before, plus the smiling face of my pal Horatio Emmett. As a substitute, I was much further back in the line, but could still see a strip of the lush green turf and hear the buzz of excited chatter from the crowd. That buzz turned to huge roars as the referee and his assistants led us out and into the cauldron of a packed Wembley. My heart was thumping against the Three Lions badge on my chest. I had on my white England socks, navy blue shorts and a white tracksuit top, underneath which was my debut shirt bearing the number 19 below my name. My name on an England shirt and it wasn't a replica. Insane. One of the kit men had asked if I had a preference for number as a lot of the lads do; although 1 to 11 still tend to go to the starting XI in friendlies like this. I wore the 28 for London City United, but there weren't that many in the England squad so I picked 19. I remember watching Italia 90 and being mesmerised by the skill and brilliance of Paul Gascoigne in the Three Lions shirt with the number 19 on his back, so that was my choice. Even without the hypnotic interventions of Keith Sykes, I could feel the power of Gazza's 19 surging through my body and giving me added confidence. This was going to be a night to remember.

I'd invited Julie and Tilson along to the game in among all the other players' families, but I wasn't sure if they would come. I knew Tilson would want to, but Julie less so after our last get-together. But as I looked up at the stand, I was able to see both of their faces straight away. Tilson had a smile as wide as Southend seafront, while Julie's face was a long as the pier. I smiled, waved and blew up a kiss to either or both of them as I took my place on the bench with the other subs. Despite everything – my age, my body shape, my personal situation, the 'con' of being a footballer, the wages I was earning, the England call-up, the pressure to deliver, the fear of my secret coming out and the responsibility that came with representing my country – I felt surprisingly calm. The referee blew his whistle and the game started.

Jim Neale normally watched England matches tucked behind a desk in the Press section up in the stand with a laptop in front of him and a monitor by his side for the replays. But that set-up did not suit what he had planned for this match. Instead, he had acquired a photographer's pass that would allow him to sit pitchside during the game. It wasn't anywhere near as comfortable – he'd not brought his own stool like the other snappers and so was squatting down behind an advertising hoarding – but it was worth it. This was the prime spot. The players were lining up for kick-off and he had already seen Richie Price take his place on the bench. The fact his family were in the crowd was sprinkles on top of the ice cream. Another sweet detail to add to the story. Time was almost up for the talentless fraudster.

Harley Wells looked around Wembley Stadium and really couldn't believe he was there nor what had gone on over the last few weeks. He had been a humble fitness coach at London City United, one of many. Yes, it was a Premier League club and nothing to be shrugged at, but now he had seen the level above at St George's Park and was sitting on the bench as a bona fide England coach. And he was taking part in a massive con. Fuck. Why on earth did he ever get involved in this? Ayesha. Yes, it was worth it. Besides, he wasn't really doing anything. His only part in the whole charade was to allow Richie Price to use his phone to call his mate Keith on matchdays and around training. Other than that, he'd done his job. Richie was by no means a toned athlete like the others in the squad, but he was in far better condition and shape than when he arrived at the club. Only yesterday Ron Lewis, the England manager, had called him over to congratulate him on a job well done, adding: 'Just do whatever you do to get that fat lad Roger shooting on all guns blazing.' He didn't correct Mr Lewis's use of the wrong name or mixed metaphors. The Brazil game did pose a few problems for Harley, though. Usually they would be in a quiet room away from everyone else when they'd call Keith and do what they did, but to-day they were sat on the bench in view of thousands of spectators. They had a plan though. When Richie was given the nod that he was about to go on, he would go and sit next to Harley while he sorted out his shinpads and all that, during which time he would put in headphones attached to Harley's phone and just listen to Keith. No one would notice and even if they did it could easily be explained away. Motivational music or some such. They just had to keep their fingers crossed that Keith would be on the other end of the line when they needed him.

Keith Sykes was panicking. It had been the sneeze's fault. For the last few months he had been there every single time Richie needed to be put in a trance to play. Training, practice matches, trials, Premier League games, England training, the lot. If he hadn't been there in person, he'd been on the end of a Skype call. And all he had to do today was be available between 7.15pm and 10pm. On a Saturday night. God this was ruining his social life. But the money? Well, you couldn't groan at that now, could you? Keith had been in the pub that afternoon and got chatting to the barmaid with the big tits as he slowly made his way through six pints of Kronenbourg and put 50-odd nicker in the fruit machine.

'What time do you get off darlin'?' he asked around 6pm.

'Arf seven. Why?'

'Because I wanna stick my cock up your arse.'

'Ah beg your pardun,' she said recoiling in mocked horror. He was a bit odd this bloke, she thought, but she hadn't been chatted up by anyone in donkeys' years.

'I said, is that clock up there fast?' They both cackled and she touched his arm to steady herself, as if that would actually do the trick. 'Haha, no darlin', just kiddin', I just wondered if you fancied coming back to mine for a Chinese and couple of tinnies. I really need to be back by 7.15, but I can wait till 7.30 for you, if you wanna come?' He left the double entendre hanging.

'Yeah. Yeah, why not. That'll be nice. Ta.'

It was weird. When Keith got to the pub he didn't really think she was all that. Just big knockers to take the attention away from a face caked in slap. But now – three hours and six pints later – he saw she was quite attractive. She had a bubbly character. Well, you needed one to work behind a bar in a pub like this, didn't you? And she had laughed at all his jokes and chat-up lines. So, as they say in France, why le fuck not?

She finished work at 7.30, but it took another 10 minutes for her to get her stuff together and it was another 15 before they got back to Keith's place. He was busting for a piss by the time they got through the door. Luckily, Richie was on the bench and so wouldn't need his hypnotic services just yet.

'There's a couple of menus on the fridge love. Av a look and see what you fancy while I take a slash,' Keith said as he went into the loo. He decided he'd have a gentleman's wash while he was there just in case he got hold of her prawn crackers.

He lifted the lid of the toilet, unzipped his flies and pointed his short, chubby prick at the skid-marked porcelain below. Oh, that felt good. There was a buzz in his pocket and he pulled out his phone to check. It was a message from Harley Wells. 'Richie's on the bench. Keep an eye on the match as we'll have to act quick if he's subbed on.'

Keith knew that already and the beer made him angry at the fact he was being given orders by the kid. But he saw the time on his phone and realised the game was 20-odd minutes in. He'd best finish up and switch the telly on before he ordered in his Singapore chow mein, egg fried rice, sweet and sour king prawn balls and chips with curry sauce.

Then came that irresistible and unreachable tingle. That shot behind the nose that also makes your lip quiver in anticipation. Keith was the type of person who pinched his nose when he sneezed to keep everything in. He'd heard horror stories about people's eyeballs popping out their sockets when they did this, but it had never happened to him in 40 or so years so he was happy to carry on. At that moment, he had his smartphone in his left hand, with his right holding on to his spraying penis. He couldn't risk letting go of that because it could shoot off anywhere. He was wearing light chinos, which were the worst for showing up errant piss. Needing to change your trousers because you've splashed your own fluids over them is not conducive to getting a romantic banging off the bird from behind the bar at the pub. Shit. He didn't know her name.

It was by instinct that, as the nose tingling reached its climax, Keith's left hand shot up towards his face, discarding the phone in the process, and his thumb and forefinger clamped around his nose as the sneeze erupted with a force that shot a bright orange stream of urine up the wall behind the toilet and then down the right leg of Keith's light chinos.

But that soon became inconsequential as he saw his ageing Samsung device spin through the air, clatter against the lifted seat like a basketball off a backboard and plunge into the pool of stinking piss in the toilet below.

Melanie Darwin heard one hell of a commotion coming from the bathroom of the bloke from the pub. She had been in two minds about coming here, but he seemed to have a bit of money and had offered to pay for the Chinese, which doesn't happen very often. She cautiously walked across the living room, out into the corridor and saw that the toilet door had been left ajar. Tip-toeing as best she could for a woman of her size, she peeked through the crack in the door and saw Keith frantically squeeze a dribble of piss from what was a very disappointing and sorry-looking cock and then plunge his hand into the bowl below. She gagged and put her hand to her mouth to keep it in.

Keith plucked his phone out from his urine, but it was dead. Nothing. No response, no display, nada. He had no way of getting hold of Harley or Richie and he could get called to go on the pitch at any moment. Shit, shit, shit. Unless! Yes, he was a genius. He could call them through Facebook. They were friends on there. He just needed to get online, find Harley and ping him a message. He looked up and saw Mel from the pub – yes, Mel, that was her name – stood looking in at the bathroom door. With his own piss dripping from his hand and his shrivelled willy still poking through the flies of his jeans, he asked to borrow her mobile.

'No fuckin' chance you weirdo perv,' and she left. It was the first time she'd turned down the offer of a free Chinese.

Friendly matches involving England aren't often anything to write home about, but this had actually been a good game. There were no goals yet, but there had been lots of chances and the football was flowing. The ball was played up near the edge of Brazil's box to Gary Smith, but his first touch was poor and the ball ran away from him. As he stretched after it, he was clattered from the side by a player in yellow. Mattundo, an old-fashioned defender with pace and power and little else, had gone in hard and two-footed. Smith crumpled to the ground holding his right ankle, rolling from side to side and screaming as if he were a six-year-old girl who'd just been told that Santa thinks she's a twat.

The physios rushed off the bench and onto the field to treat the injured and traumatised West Ham winger. After swearing and gesticulating towards the field of play and exchanging words with the Brazil manager – neither spoke each other's language, but the language of such industrial insults is universal – Ron Lewis pointed to me and said, 'Get warm lad.'

Tilson Price was perched on the edge of his seat trying to peer forward enough to catch a glimpse of his dad on the bench below. There were so many people down there on the bench, but he was pretty sure he had made him out by the baldy bits on the top on his head and slightly larger body than the rest. But wow! His dad was playing for England. Bonkers. All Tilson wanted, though, was for his mum to be as impressed as he was with his dad's new career.

Surely she should think him playing for England was amazing and then they would get back together and dad could move back into the house and they could be like before. Or maybe he and mum could move into Dad's flat near the Thames and Tower Bridge. That place was cool. But then he'd have to move schools and that, so maybe they should stay at the house and just go to the apartment at weekends.

Tilson leapt to his feet when he saw his dad stand up, squeeze down the row of seats and then jog out along the touchline to warm up, waving to the crowds as he went. Maybe he'll come on for that player that got hurt, he thought. He didn't really understand football. The teenager looked at his matchday programme, found the number 8 and looked across. Gary Smith was the one hurt. His dad, Richie Price, number 19, could come on any moment now. He craned his neck as he tried to look to see if the man with the board with the numbers on was doing anything, but not yet.

'Look Mum, it's Dad,' Tilson said cheerily.

'Yeah, it looks like he might play.'

Inside, part of Julie Price cried out in agony every time she saw Tilson idolising his dad. Well, his footballer dad that is. Because she knew the truth, knew the truth would come out eventually, and knew that it could shatter Tilson's trust in his father. *Richie, what are you doing? Did you ever think about us?* There had been a chance of reconciliation. That night at his apartment was wild and amazing and everything she wanted and had missed. Even after he had told her about his silly little escapade she had still been in his grasp. It seemed he was doing it all for her and their son. He had that fire back in his eyes. But he had thought she was only interested in his money and that hurt. Not treading on a bit of Lego hurt, this was a toe-punt to the privates hurt that rises from deep and leaves nothing but nausea and pain in its wake until it feels like your skull is going to burst open. Christ, how she would love to kick Richie fucking Price in the bollocks right at that moment.

Jim Neale's back was aching, his calves were starting to cramp and he feared his haemorrhoids were beginning to prolapse. He had a new-found respect for photographers who did this game after game, week after week. A respect that would last only until he got feeling back in his legs. They were proper fucking moaners these photographers, but Jim's night had just taken a turn for the better. Pretty boy Gary Smith had just been clattered by that Brazilian lump on the edge of the box and was now flapping around on the floor like a carrier bag in a wind tunnel. He probably wasn't hurt one bit, but these poncey modern footballers want constant attention and sympathy. It was all me, me, me. Smith was just trying to cover up that dog-awful touch that had given the ball away.

But it now meant that fat imposter had been sent to warm up. This could be the moment he'd been waiting for. Jim watched as Richie Price stepped out from the bench and began jogging down the touchline towards him and the corner flag beyond. Jim had planned it perfectly. This was just the spot. A smug grin spread across his face and knocked the last crumbs of pastry from his sausage roll from his chin.

'Look,' he said, giving the Citizen photographer next to him a hefty shove. 'You can feel the ground trembling as that fat cunt runs towards us. Ha!'

'Fucking hell Jim, you've just lost me a great shot of Smith on the floor. And talk about pot and kettle.'

'Miserable prick. Right, now, let's get this right. We've only got one go at it.'

Harley Wells's heart was pounding in his chest and the panic was beginning to set in. He'd tried four times already to call Keith Sykes to get him on the line ready to help Richie, but the number had been unobtainable. He checked his wifi and phone signal and both had the full four bars, but he still wasn't able to connect via phone or Skype. Shit. What was he going to do when Richie came back from the warm-up ready to go on? He thought he could remember the first of the trigger words they used, but not all of them. Maybe Richie could style it out till half-time, it was only 20 minutes or so. No, shit. He remembered what happened last time in the Southend game. He needed Keith – that was the only option. He dialled again, but still no response.

Keith Sykes watched as the cameras followed Richie Price down the touchline to warm up and heard the commentators say he would be England's oldest debutant by a long way if he were to come on, which they said looked likely. They eulogised over his London City United performances this year and said he would likely be a wild-card entrant to England's World Cup squad. He could be the player that made the difference. He could bring football home. Keith reached down the side of his armchair to find the bottle of vodka, but his fingertips could only locate the shattered remains of his piss-soaked Samsung. It took him a drunken moment to realise the vodka bottle was nestled between his legs all along. He'd cleverly left it there in case he wanted more after downing the other half of its contents. This would be the calamitous ending to their epic football adventure and the end of the tens of thousands of pounds going into his bank account each month. Unless Richie Price could pull something special out of the bag. But that soft lad couldn't pull a pair of curtains. Drink!

Jim Neale felt the surge of adrenaline as he got to his feet, but it could've just been pins and needles from having squatted in such a shitty position for so long.

'Richie!' he yelled as the ageing LCU revelation lumbered towards him. *Warm-up my arse, he'd be better off just putting his coat on.*

'Jim Neale from the Citizen. Just wanted to get your thoughts and feelings as you prepare to make your England debut.'

The dumb fuck looked totally bemused.

'Er, yeah, good, ah, er, are you meant to be asking me stuff here?' Richie indicated with his thumb that he needed to carry on warming up. Jim had to act quickly to keep his prey within reach. 'I spoke to your close friend Keith Sykes in Miami the other week.' That stopped him dead in his tracks. 'How does it feel having conned an entire nation, no, the entire footballing world about who you really are?'

The photographer next to Jim had turned to fire off pictures of England's brightest (and most unlikely) footballing hope facing off against England's most despised (and unlikeable) football journalists.

'I, er, don't know what, um, you, er, I need to warm up, er, I can't....'

'Can't what Richie? Can't play football without the aid of a hypnotist? Can't believe you got away with this fraud for so long? Can't believe you've conned your family, friends and the fans?'

Richie Price just stood there, dumbfounded. How did this guy get all this information? Keith? Really? No chance. Why would he sell him out when he was earning just as much? It didn't make sense. He quickly had to decide what to do next because Ron Lewis was frantically waving him back towards the bench to send him on for his England debut against Brazil. Fuck. That's 'fuck' in all its forms, especially 'ffuuuuuuuuuuuucccccckkkkkk!'.

'You seem a little lost for words Richie. How about I help you? I've got four words in particular you might like – goat, asylum, texture, lollygag.'

Darkness, peace and silence.

31. IT IS NOW

I T'S funny, really, how it all ended and in a much more spectacular fashion than Jim Neale could ever have hoped or
imagined. He had thought that with those four words he had
been given the master control; the keys to operate the world's most
unlikely football star. But that's not how we worked. As I said
before, as we developed our system, Keith was able to refine and
tweak the hypnotics to allow me to be as conscious as possible
while being unconscious. We realised that I needed to be able to
retain an element of control over my actions, emotions and memories. What would be the point of being one of the best footballers in
the world if you couldn't remember any of it? So each time we
refined and updated the technique, The Amazing Syko would come
up with a new set of four random trigger words so that my brain
knew which gear to click into. The four that Jim Neale blurted out
– goat, asylum, texture, lollygag – were the very first.

Let me take you back to that infamous night at Wembley from a
spectator's point of view.

It's England nil, Brazil nil. Just over half an hour gone and it's
not a bad game. West Ham's Gary Smith tries to control the ball,
but it runs away from him further than most people can kick it.

However, he gets saved from the boo boys in the crowd by being hacked down on the edge of the box. He seems genuinely hurt and the physio comes on, but the ref is already preparing for the free-kick. He plonks the ball down about 25 yards out, pretty much centre of goal, sprays a line of his foam next to it and then paces out the 10 yards where the players in the defensive wall must stand and sprays out another line. There seems to be a bit of a commotion on the side of the pitch between a photographer and me while I'm warming up to come on to replace the injured Smith. Then, for seemingly no reason, I turn from the photographer (actually Jim Neale), trot out onto the Wembley pitch without having been subbed on and stand around 10 yards back from the ball. People are asking those around me what I'm doing, but no one knows. Neither do the bemused players or Ron Lewis, who's going ballistic in his technical area. I let my arms hang by my sides, puff out a breath of air and then start a run-up, arcing round slightly towards the ball, planting my left foot at its side and striking through with my right. While this is happening, the opposition players are shouting and waving at the referee, who is stood over the injured Smith and only communicating through harsh toots of his whistle. Some of my England teammates have also joined in the shouting, but with a more bemused look on their faces. I am too far under to know any of what is going on.

The ball, meanwhile, is curling beautifully over the rag-tag wall towards the top corner of the net. Despite the fact the ball isn't actually in play, the Brazilian keeper Lanneros is desperate not to let it go in and scrambles across goal to try and save it. No chance. Just like Beckham for England in their vital World Cup qualifier against Greece in 2001 – and just like me in the park behind our old school a few months back – it flew straight into the onion bag. There was nothing Lanneros and his makeshift wall or Neil and the pub stools could do. The ball is in the back of the net and the flummoxed crowd at Wembley Stadium let out a massive roar of approval.

I then copied Beckham's celebration, running off to the cheering crowd with my arms outstretched, jumping and swinging an arm. But instead of Emile Heskey being the first to hug me in joyous celebration, it was two stewards in orange hi-viz bringing me crashing to the ground with a rugby tackle and two coppers ready to arrest me.

As well as racking up millions and millions of views all across the internet, the footage of that incident was played in court several times over and from several angles. Jim Neale, who had received great acclaim in the media industry for his investigation and expose of fraudulent footballer Richie Price, was also more than happy to recount his version of events and how he had spent many months doggedly digging out the truth in his desire to 'keep football pure'. What a crock of shit. He did it for money, adulation and because the chief executive at London City United told him to. He got lucky really, especially with the mole who sold me out.

Neale had tried to imply that had been Keith. But despite him being a massive twat, it wasn't. He may have spoken to the guy in Miami, but he didn't reveal anything about our plot and he had too much to gain from carrying on with it. I later found out that Keith didn't know much about the goings on at Wembley that night because he'd got himself blind drunk in a panic after dropping his phone down the loo and being unable to dial in to fulfil his duties.

It wasn't Mollie either. I hadn't confided in her about what we were doing, but she was a smart cookie and could, possibly, have worked it out. But she wasn't the fame-hungry wannabe starlet that Julie thought she was and I trusted her. And my old nemesis Turbo Curbo didn't know anything either, so he couldn't be the mole. And as much as Julie hated what I was doing and the impact it might have on Tilson – plus the fact I still was off her Christmas card list after stupidly calling her a money-grabber – she still loved me too much to drop me in it like that.

It wasn't any of them, nor Harley, nor Adam Bush, nor any of my teammates or the coaches at London City United. It was my best friend Neil. He hadn't liked what Keith and I were doing from the start. Going ahead with it was like stepping into the ring with him. My double-hattrick to knock his beloved – our beloved – Southend United out of the FA Cup was the devastating body blow that put him on the ropes. And the thought of me taking the field to represent our country was the knockout punch that he was desperate to dodge – at all costs. So he called the Daily Citizen and spoke to a smug prick called Jim Neale and told him everything he knew about Richie Price, Keith Sykes and our plan to infiltrate the Premier League with football genius by hypnosis, including the four trigger words he'd heard Keith use on me that time over the park to perfectly replicate the Beckham free-kick.

Neil was also called to give evidence at the hearing, along with many of those named above. Luckily for Keith and I, the police had decided against any sort of criminal prosecution. We managed to keep Harley out of things completely, other than him being my fitness coach. Instead, this was a civil case brought by London City United's chief exec Sean Clark as he sought to reclaim the money they had paid me and compensation for damage to the club's reputation and any potential punishments brought by the Premier League, the Football Association, and any or all of the teams I played against. This was going to be very expensive. Still, I'd been broke before and the house was in Julie's name so there was no danger of them losing that. She didn't come to court.

'Ladies and gentlemen of the jury,' said Laura Long, the lawyer representing London City United. 'You have heard over the past few days from those taken in by Richard Price's heinous and un-derhand acts carried out with his accomplice Keith Sykes. You have heard how their behaviour could cost teammates the trophies and awards they have been striving towards their entire lives and may never get the chance again. You have heard from the brilliant journalist who travelled the globe to dig out the very roots of this fraud and then pulled them clean from the earth to show to the world in the most dramatic fashion. You have heard from the close friend of both defendants whose heart was broken when Mr Price scored goal after goal against the team they had supported, side-by-side, for many years, knocking them out of the FA Cup in an act of complete betrayal of that loyalty and that friendship. These are moving accounts indeed of those directly affected by the dishonest actions of these two men. But central to this claim is the effect the defendants had on London City United. This great and proud football club has suffered this year for various reasons and the defendants, led by Mr Price, took advantage of that desperate situation to extract from the club a contract worth millions of pounds under false pretences. Their actions could also land the football club with enormous financial penalties from the footballing authorities and competitors in the Premier League that could set them back decades in their development. The defendants were knowingly dishonest in their actions and should be held liable for their deceit and chicanery. My client is seeking £350million in damages. We are also asking for court costs.'

There was a squeal of terror as the lawyer read out that figure. It came from Keith sat to my left. 'Jeez. Fackin' hell geez, is it too late to tell them it was all your idea?'

I looked around the room and caught the eye of a grinning face. The gentleman was wearing a white jacket, blue shirt and red tie. I couldn't see his trousers from where I was sitting, but on his head was perched a large white Stetson. Buck Schulz, the American billionaire owner of London City United, sent me over a wink. I nodded gently in acknowledgement, but wasn't quite sure if his wink was a polite one or one that said 'I'm gonna cut your balls off and feed them to the cattle.' Sitting next to him was Sean Clark and there was no ambiguity over his face. It looked like a cat's arse trying to hold in a spurt of diarrhoea. I started to wave as we made eye contact but then morphed it into the classic wanker shake. Childish, I know. It was a move perfected on school coach trips when we passed another school coach on the motorway, but it felt appropriate.

Then Helen Winter, our lawyer, stood to make her closing statement. 'Ladies and gentlemen, my learned colleague is correct. It is sad that the actions of my clients had a negative impact on some of those close to them. And it is sad that some may have felt misled. But my clients did not lie to them and nor to the officials at London City United. Despite the fact that Richard Price is in his early 40s and, at the time of signing the contract the club offered, was obese and had never played football to any decent standard before, they did not once question why. And why didn't they question anything? It was because he delivered. London City United signed a player they thought was of a certain high standard and what they got on the pitch, mostly, was a player of that certain high standard. It is not as if they opened the box and found a decrepit wreck. They wanted a top-class footballer and they got one. In fact, he was even better than they expected – 22 goals in just 12 games that propelled an under-performing club from mid-table to the top of the Premier League and into the semi-finals of the FA Cup. Not once during that period did anyone at the club – from the very top executives to the kitman – openly question how Richard Price did it.

'You have heard that the defendants' actions breached no Premier League or Football Association rules – there was nothing in any of their laws to say that a player cannot play while hypnotised. The police and CPS also saw no criminal case to answer. This case has been brought simply out of the claimant trying to save face and renege on a legally-agreed contract with Mr Price. Ladies and gentlemen, even if you do find in favour of London City United, you must consider the level of damages they are entitled to and £350million is an outrageous claim. I would suggest they are entitled to no more than £350, if anything at all. London City United wanted a Premier League-standard footballer and they got a

Premier League-standard footballer. There simply was no fraud and there should be no damages.'

The judge gave the jury some direction and then sent them away for deliberations. We waited outside for more than an hour before being told to come back the next day.

I stayed at my apartment alone that night and got drunk. It's not like I would've been able to sleep had I tried to go to bed after my lawyer advised us that the verdict was a 50-50, perhaps even 70-30 likely to go against us. I'd already paid six months' rent up front for the place so I wanted to make the most of the hot tub while I still could. It didn't seem right getting in there on my own without a few cans to keep me company. I ended up drinking all 12 in the pack and, having not drunk that much booze for a while, I regretted it the next morning when my lawyer called and told me I had to get my arse to court.

'Order in the court,' the clerk yelled as everyone readied themselves.

'Sshh,' I muttered with a finger to my lips. My headache thumped as the coffee and paracetamol had yet to kick in.

The judge asked the clerk if the jury had reached a decision. This all seemed pretty pointless if they hadn't. Couldn't they have had this conversation earlier and saved us all a bit of time? I could've had an extra 10 minutes in bed. The clerk told the judge that they had and was then asked to call the jury back. Again, they could've done this while I was asleep. Now the judge asked the foreman of the jury if they had reached a verdict. It was like he didn't believe what the clerk had told him. Imagine it being your job to pass on a message and each time you do the person you pass the message to thinks you're a big fat liar and asks someone else. Again, all this could've been done earlier. I was so tired the bags under my eyes were bigger than Santa's sack on Christmas Eve.

It turned out that the clerk had been telling the truth all along and the jury had indeed reached a verdict. The foreman – a wiry young chap with a hipster beard and soulless eyes – was asked to read out the verdict to the court. My home, my car, my possessions and any hope of winning back my beautiful wife felt like they were being slowly pulled from my grasp. This was it.

'We find the defendants, Richard Price and Keith Sykes…' The pause was endless. This dude thought he was reading out the winner of The X Factor on live television, but without the charm and charisma of Dermot O'Leary. I swear that at one point he went to speak, but then paused again to draw it out longer. By God, did he milk his moment for all it was worth, the prick. '...not liable for any losses or damages incurred by London City United.' You skinny, hipster beauty! I hugged Keith excitedly and started shaking hands with my lawyer, but she shushed us and nodded towards the judge. There was more to be said. I gulped, hoping I hadn't celebrated a disallowed goal.

'The claim brought by London City United is hereby dismissed. This means the contract agreed between London City United and Richard Price remains valid in law and the remaining basic weekly wages stipulated for the term of the contract must be paid in full either on a monthly basis as per the terms of the contract or as a lump sum. The complainant shall also pay the defendants' costs in full.'

Party time.

32. THE FINAL WHISTLE

S O that's what happened. Pretty exciting huh? On the way out of court, I was pulled to one side by Buck Schulz, who had in fact winked at me in a polite manner in the courtroom. He told me he found the whole thing hilarious and the proceedings had been the most fun he'd had in ages. At least someone enjoyed it. 'When I watched that footage of you running on that pitch at Wembley and shooting the ball and getting jumped by security, that was some funny shit. I had tears. Real tears. Sean may not like you very much, but you made my day.'

Buck told me he'd pay up the contract in full and also asked to buy the rights to my story as he had a few friends in the film biz that may be interested. I told him I wanted to lie low for a while, but he would be my first port of call if I changed my mind. In the next few days, I was inundated with calls from TV shows, newspapers, magazines and event organisers, along with offers from companies keen to use me and my face to promote their wares. Some of the figures being bandied around were eye-watering. Maybe it was something I would take up in a few months or so once the madness had died down. Keith took a deal. He got a book and DVD contract for his hypnotism that more than matched the

£3million he got as his half of the London City United money. But my share was enough for me for now. I had plenty. Despite my fears, I had kept my car, my home and my possessions. I even started to patch things up with Neil. All he wanted was things back to how they were and his old friend back. We figured we'd both betrayed each other and decided to call it even. We'd laugh about it in a few weeks. I needed a friend now that I was toxic to all my footballing buddies. None of them wanted to be seen with me and I didn't even get an invite to Harley and Ayesha's wedding because so many of my ex-teammates would be there.

Tilson got part of his wish. He got to stay at the house during the week and at the apartment at weekends, but only because me and his mum were still separated. I'd like to have told you that Julie and I managed to patch things up, I'd whisked her away on a paradise break to the Maldives to rekindle our romance and that we are now living a contented life of luxury once more.

But she hasn't forgiven me for those things I said and for putting Tilson in the firing line with my fun and games. And she's been dating a bloke called John for a while now and, annoyingly, he doesn't actually seem to be a complete wanker. It's going well between them, he's good to Tilson and anyone looking on from the outside would think they were just a nice family living in a nice house in a nice town.

But Julie is still my wife, Tilson is my son and that is my house. I'm not entirely sure what I'll have to do to win them back, but I have something of an idea.

THE END

ABOUT THE AUTHOR

GREG FIDGEON is an author, editor and journalist from Leigh-on-Sea in Essex.

He spent 15 years working in local newspapers, including many covering Southend United and the various non-league teams in the area. He now works as a sub-editor on a national newspaper.

Greg also had an unremarkable playing career in Saturday and Sunday league park football, mostly with Leigh Ramblers football club. As a kid, he once scored eight own goals in one season.

Ball Or Nothing is his first novel, following the 2017 release of a collection of short stories. The Long And The Short Short Of It is available on Amazon.

ACKNOWLEDGEMENTS

WRITING this book has been a labour of love and hate for a long time. I came up with the daft idea of hypnotising someone to become a footballer around 2010 (I tweeted Derren Brown about making it into a show, but he never replied).

It sat and developed in my brain, but the writing process was a nightmare. I built it up so much that at times I was struck by anxiety that crippled my ability and desire to write. So my first thank you must go to the person who lifted the lid, tinkered with my brain and got it back into working order. Leah Butler-Smith, thank you, always.

My wife Helen has been so supportive and encouraging from day dot. Thank you, my love, and to our two wonderful boys.

My dad Graham was the person who not only got me into football, but took me and my brother Harley along to watch Southend United when we were kids and fostered a bond with the club that lasts to this day. Cheers pops. And thank you to all the players who graced the hallowed turf of Roots Hall. Come on you Blues.

Thanks too to all the players I shared a pitch with from a young lad to a grown man. It wasn't always pleasant to watch, but I had fun and there are great stories to tell (some in this book). Some of those friendships will last my lifetime.

I must also thank book whizz Colette Mason for her continuing help, and Adam Shaw and Jonny Greer for giving my book the once over before it hit the wider world.

Finally, thanks to you, dear reader, for taking a punt on my story. I hope it raised a smile or two.